I0627729

THE HIDDEN FACE

by

S. C. FLYNN

Book 1 of the Fifth Unmasking series

THE HIVE

The Hive
ISBN: 978-1-9997249-0-0

Cover art by John di Giovanni
Design by Shawn King
Map by Paul Weimer based on projections by Paul Walsh
Copyediting by Richard Shealy
Formatting by Tim Marquitz

PRAISE FOR *THE HIDDEN FACE*

"A fun and fast-paced fantasy adventure" - Dyrk Ashton, author of Paternus

"Tugs at emotional strings really quickly, in an incredibly effective way" - Revolution SF

"A thrilling little fantasy novel" - Superstardrifter.com

"The Da Vinci Code meets Indiana Jones in a fantasy setting" - Tome and Tankard

"I really had fun reading this book" - Purple Owl Reviews

"A great fantasy romp" - Youtube reviewer James Chatham

"I don't think I've ever read a fantasy quite like The Hidden Face" - Cover to Cover

"A strong, fast and gripping fantasy novel" - The Irresponsible Reader

A face without a face. An unmasking that leaves the mask.

To Claudia

ALSO BY S. C. FLYNN

CHILDREN OF THE DIFFERENT

Permian Sea

Seanor

Merech's Tomb

Axo

Liga

Trevi

Metos

Faustia

Apollinia

Magia

Nostro Sea

Theodorica

Magia

Karna

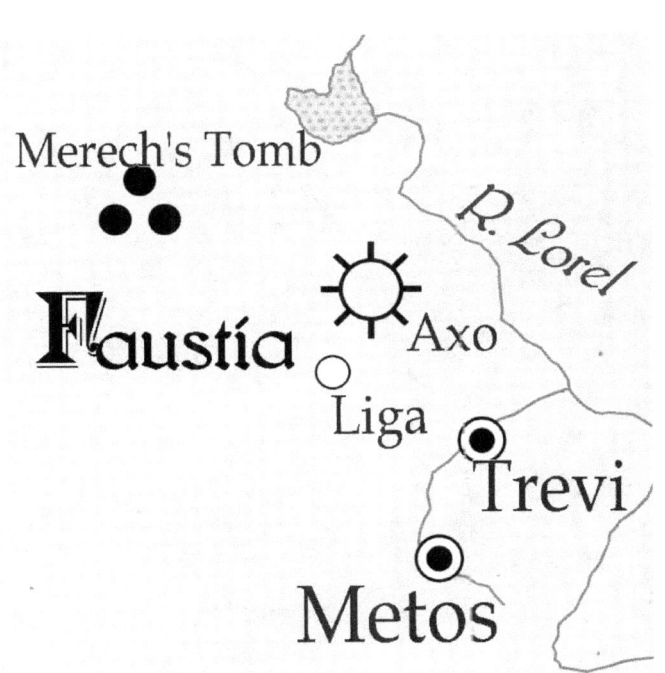

This time, the Face was born in a small Faustian town and lived in obscurity until the age of thirty. Then he declared that he was the Face of the Akhen, in the world for just the fourth time in history. At first no one believed him – there were impostors every year all over the world. Then the Face showed his powers and no one doubted anymore.

The Face presented himself to the king of Faustia and promised to make him the head of the greatest empire in the world. In just three years, the Face had made it happen and the Faustian Era had begun. Enemies were made into allies or followers, or destroyed if they refused. New wealth was discovered, new technology invented, new plans made. Old faiths and gods tried to resist but eventually fell away and vanished. How could they compete against the Akhen and its Face, who offered certain worldly power and wealth?

Then the Face disappeared, as in every previous Unmasking. No one knew why he had arrived or why he had gone, not even the Jaelite mystics.

From the Book of the Fourth Unmasking

PROLOGUE

575 FE (the year 575 of the Faustian Era)
The Octagonal Temple in Axo, capital of the Faustian
Empire. Before dawn.

The ring of metal on stone sounded like a death knell to Halakh.

He walked around the altar until he saw what had made the sound. It was lying in a pool of light thrown by a tall candle. He bent his tired old limbs to pick up the tiny thing.

Halakh's heart jumped as he saw what it was: a golden bee with fine stones inlaid in the wings. He whirled around, but the flickering shadows in the corners gave no answer. He saw the shadow of his own cap and long robe thrown on the wall. It was a strange place for him to die, Halakh thought, but he was calm now. Everything was ready. *The truth must survive.*

'I'm over here,' said a voice. 'I've been right behind you for days.'

Halakh spun around again. A shape slid out of the darkness. Halakh squinted his eyes to make out who it was and saw a short young man dressed in a black cloak. The face that peeped out from under the hood was handsome and the skin and eyes were clear.

Halakh felt a spasm of shock and looked again at the golden bee. 'But you're supposed to be dead – and you can't be one of Them, can you?'

The stranger unclasped his cloak and let it drop to the floor; underneath, he was wearing a white tunic covered in golden bees. Halakh saw the mound of a hunchback between the man's shoulders. The contrast with his face was shocking, and Halakh felt a shiver run down his back.

'You know what I want,' the hunchback said. 'The scroll you went to get from its hiding place today.'

Halakh stood still. He could feel the copper scroll inside his robe; his life was nearly over anyway. He saw the hunchback's eyes dance in the candlelight. Halakh said a silent last prayer.

The hunchback whipped out a small throwing axe and launched it with a flick of the wrist. Halakh saw it flash through the air like a gleaming bird. Everything seemed to happen so slowly that he had time to think of the sunshine flashing on the copper domes of the city of Theodorica, and of his favourite student he had taught so much. Now it was all over.

Halakh felt a dull thud in his chest and fell backwards. The stone floor was cold. He looked straight up past the twin layers of arches at the mosaic ceiling far above. In the centre glowed the symbol of the sun god, the Akhen, eight shining points sprouting from a central disc, and all around it were scenes from the Fourth Unmasking. Halakh stared at the huge golden lion in the scene showing the Face taming nature. The Face had a human body, as usual, but where the head would be, there was only a glowing circle. As Halakh watched, the lion stretched and then leapt down to carry his soul away. There was no pain. He would soon be dead, but the secret would live on.

The hunchback came over. Now Halakh felt his warm blood washing his robes. He watched as his killer reached down and took out the scroll.

The swarm of golden bees on the hunchback's tunic buzzed in front of Halakh's misty eyes. And then they were gone.

2

PART ONE

The Royal Palace, Axo, Faustia.

Dayraven woke with a start. A slim young soldier in helmet and mail coat was bending over him.

'You must come to the baths now,' the soldier said in a soft, husky voice.

Dayraven struggled to get his mind working. 'Baths? Now?'

'Yes. You're Dayraven, the son of Urland, aren't you? Emperor Calvo has asked for you.'

'In the bath.'

'Yes.'

'I think you've got the wrong man.'

The soldier stood his ground. 'Hurry. The emperor is waiting.'

Dayraven pushed his hair back from his face. 'It's after midnight, isn't it?'

'More than three hours past.'

Dayraven thought quickly. He had to obey the emperor's summons, but Halakh wanted to meet him in the Octagonal Temple just before dawn. As long as his meeting with Emperor Calvo was brief, he could still meet Halakh. Meeting his old friend and teacher again would be like getting part of his old life back; Dayraven had not expected to see him again so soon. It was as if Halakh's hand were reaching out from the world Dayraven had lived in for the past fifteen years. Dayraven's father had died when he was just six years old; for half his life, Halakh had been a second father to him. Halakh had often said, "When you turn thirty, I will have great secrets to tell you. Then you'll be ready," and smiled his mysterious smile. *Well,*

3

I've just turned thirty. Whatever Halakh has to tell me or give me, it must be important to bring him after me all the way to Faustia. Or he must be in danger – why else would he want to meet in a temple in the middle of the night?

Dayraven raised himself off the bench and looked around. Even under the high, pointed ceiling, the air was close with sweat and with smoke from the smouldering long fire running down the centre of the room.

He coughed and felt the cold of Faustia hug him like a damp shroud. It had been a hot, bright spring when he'd left Theodorica, and now it was a cool autumn in the great forests around the Lorel River. The journey had passed in a long series of bumpy wagon rides broken by short sleeps in inns and sessions of weapons practice, while the world turned colder and wetter. The fog and rain of his homeland were going to take some getting used to after fifteen years in the Magian Empire. *Fifteen years as a hostage of the duke of Theodorica, and now I'm a hostage to the Faustian weather.*

Dayraven pushed aside the rug that covered him and swung his legs off the bench. He had slept in his clothes so as to be ready for the meeting with Halakh. He draped his cloak around his shoulders and clasped it, his fingers fumbling a little in the clammy air. Dayraven stood up, his back aching from the hard bench. All the way down the long, thin room, off-duty soldiers slept covered by their painted wooden shields, keeping a hand on the hilts of their swords. Some of the men were looking around at the noise.

The soldier turned towards the door and Dayraven followed. He still felt a little self-conscious in these tight trousers and tunic after wearing looser Magian clothes for so many years. Dayraven had bought these clothes from a merchant in Theodorica before leaving, but they were not

4

identical to those currently in fashion in Faustia, as far as Dayraven could see. *And so uncomfortable!*

'Why is the emperor taking a bath now?' Dayraven asked as they walked.

'Oh, these days, he bathes whenever he feels like it and talks business with his advisers at the same time. Says he can't sleep at night and doesn't like to be alone.'

Dayraven remembered going as a child to the old royal palace well to the west in the traditional territory of the Faustians. It was strange to think that now Emperor Calvo hid himself away in the forest while his empire expanded to the east. Dayraven had followed all the news through letters from home and from what he'd heard from visitors and merchants who came to Theodorica. He had wanted to be here in Faustia, but instead, he'd been forced to listen to all those events as if he were standing at the back of a huge temple during a ceremony. *And now it seems the emperor has conquered much of the world while sitting in the bath.*

They turned down a long corridor hung with tapestries, and the thick stone walls told Dayraven that they must be approaching the centre of the palace. The air there was pleasantly warm, and Dayraven loosened his cloak a little; he had heard that there were tubes inside the walls that piped water from the hot springs of Axo to warm the palace.

Dayraven thought he'd take the chance to find out something about the place where he had to meet Halakh. They said that Urland's sword and hunting horn were kept there, to remember the great hero Dayraven's father had been.

'Where's the Octagonal Temple?'

5

The soldier looked surprised for a moment. 'Farther down the hill but connected with the palace. It's mostly kept closed – the emperor only uses it for special occasions.'

The soldier led the way through an open gallery lined with marble columns with huge courtyards on either side, lit with dozens of torches. Dayraven saw a massive shape looming in one corner and jumped. The creature flapped its giant ears and stamped its tree-like feet, and then raised its trunk and trumpeted. The sound echoed through the palace.

Dayraven stopped and looked, wondering if he were still dreaming. 'What's an elephant doing here?'

'It's the emperor's pet. It's called Abul Ahaz – merchants brought it here last year.'

Dayraven had spent many happy hours riding elephants near the duke's palace, where he had first met Halakh. The old man had helped Dayraven up after he had slid off an elephant onto a pile of straw, his cheeks burning with shame while the crowd laughed. Halakh's face was like lined old leather and his beard was long and white. He wore a black cap, a long robe lined with strange symbols and two metal bracelets engraved with Jael letters.

'Do you like solving riddles and puzzles?' Halakh asked.

'Yes.'

'I can teach you the greatest and most important of them. Would you like that?'

Dayraven had never thought that a person like Halakh could exist and felt drawn to him. The Magian heat had bitten deep and Dayraven's skin had peeled due to sunburn, but even the bright sun could not warm up the pool of loneliness inside him.

6

'Yes, I'd like that.'

Halakh held out a small bronze disc showing the sign of the Akhen: eight twisting arms around a central circle. Dayraven took it.

'Now we are friends for life,' Halakh said.

Friends for life, Dayraven thought years later as he and the soldier walked on down the gallery in the royal palace in Axo. A glow of happiness flowed through him at the thought of seeing Halakh again; there would be so much to talk about and to learn. The journey would have exhausted Halakh; he had been very thin and weak the last time Dayraven saw him. The thought flashed into his mind that this might really be the last time he met Halakh, but he pushed it aside. *People die, people change, Halakh always used to say. But a lot has changed in Faustia as well since I was last here.*

Crossing the plains of Faustia, Dayraven had seen bigger, richer farms with new, heavier ploughs and huge horses working the fields, rather than cows as he remembered. Sailing down the rivers of the empire, he'd passed more and bigger ships, many from far-off places. Everything looked richer and there was even an elephant in the palace courtyard. But then he must have changed as well, Dayraven knew, from the way people looked at him; young men in Faustia were usually clean-shaven, but it wasn't only his beard that made him different.

A pungent, sulphurous smell stung Dayraven's nostrils. He looked ahead and saw steam wafting out of a wide door.

The soldier stood to one side and waved him in. 'The emperor is expecting you.'

Dayraven nodded and walked to the door, then stopped. He'd waited so long for this moment, yet it had now come about in the strangest way. Hundreds of times, he'd thought of how it would be to meet the emperor again, but now everything was so different from how he'd imagined. And what would the emperor think of him now? And how would he fit into the changed empire? Could he fit in anymore after so many years?

The steam of the baths hung before Dayraven's eyes like a veil of memory. The last time he'd seen the emperor, had been at the far southern border the day that Dayraven had been given as a hostage to their rivals the Magians. Squinting in the fierce sunlight, Dayraven had looked out across the flat, open plain, towards the Magian army waiting on the other side. Beyond lay the vast horizon, shimmering in the heat. He felt a trickle of sweat run down his face and his tunic stuck to his back. He was proud to be playing a part in the great game of the world.

'It won't be for long,' the emperor said, clasping his shoulder, *'just until we can recover our strength, then we can make a new treaty with the Magians and bring you home.'*

In the palace in Axo, Dayraven wiped a hand across his eyes to sweep away the memories. *It's been fifteen years. The best years of my life.*

He'd watched the Faustian boys he grew up with at the duke's court return home and take their places one by one in the army, or become ambassadors or merchants. Dayraven had thought many times of trying to escape from Magia, but that would have shamed the emperor and his father's memory. All the time, he had waited for the call to come home, a call that never came. He had never dared form a serious relationship with a woman, because he always thought of his stay in Magia as only temporary. Now finally, he was back in Faustia, and felt like a stranger. Years before, he had dreamed of being welcomed like a hero, but it seemed like everyone had forgotten about him.

Dayraven walked through the door leading to the baths. At first, he couldn't see a thing, and waved his hand to clear the air. The smell choked him and he coughed. He heard a splashing sound up ahead and walked towards it, sliding a little on the damp tiles.

Once his eyes were used to the air, Dayraven could see a long pool filled with men, lit by torches hanging on the walls. Some lounged with their arms over the side, others floated on their backs and still others bunched together in small groups.

Dayraven stopped. In the duke's palace at Theodorica, the searing heat was kept at bay by the high, cool rooms, and the world outside never entered inside the white walls. With no paintings or statues for decoration but just geometric patterns, everything was ordered. The steam and smell here in these baths was something very different. Dayraven knew he was seeing the elite of the empire – the emperor and his closest companions and bodyguards.

The talk stopped as the men saw him. He walked on, while the soldier who had escorted him stepped back into the shadows between two of the hanging torches. Dayraven walked to the edge of the pool and stared across the steaming water at the man aged about sixty who was on his own, leaning back against the far side of the pool. Emperor Calvo the Great. His beard was silver now.

The emperor seemed to wake out of a daze and peered through the rising steam. 'Urland? Urland? Can it really be you?'

'I'm Dayraven, my lord – Urland's son.'

'Oh. You're so like him, even with that touch of southern sun on your face and that beard. I thought for a moment –' The emperor leant back and gazed upwards through the mist of vapour. 'We were all young and strong back then. Great days, with Urland at my side – and now his son is here. Welcome back to us, Dayraven.'

'Thank you, my lord. It's good to be home again.'

The words felt hollow as he said them. *Where is my home now?*

'Well, come on in, Dayraven – these days, I talk best in the bath.' Calvo sloshed his arms into the water, sending up foaming spouts.

Dayraven stood for a moment. The Emperor Calvo he remembered was young and decisive; now he was an old man who needed the bath to be able to talk and lived more in the past than the present. Dayraven undressed and handed his clothes to a servant who appeared out of the shadows. He slid into the water; for a moment, the clammy cold gripped him, and then the warmth closed over him like a deep, thick glove. His limbs seemed to hang looser in the hot water as he waded across to the emperor.

The emperor's companions and bodyguards had moved to the ends of the pool so he and Dayraven could talk without being overheard. Dayraven leant back against the edge of the pool; at least he was warm now.

'Ah, I love the feeling of being able to bathe whenever I like,' the emperor said.

'Even in the middle of the night, my lord?'

'Why not? If the emperor's not free to do what he likes, what sort of an empire would that be? And it's good for my joints – even the stupid doctors agree with that. They try and tell me I shouldn't eat roast meat at my age, but I do anyway. Now that you're in the bath, Dayraven, let's talk.'

Dayraven waited a long moment, but the emperor's thoughts seemed to be drifting away on the steam rising from the bath.

'What would you like me to talk about, my lord?'

'Remind me – how long have you been away, exactly?'

'Fifteen years, eight months, sixteen days and last night.'

The emperor's bushy eyebrows shot up like startled birds. 'So long? I could have sworn it was much less than that. For years now, I've wanted to bring you back to us, but it never seemed the right time. Then when we made a new treaty – oh, that must have been two years ago –'

'Three and a half, my lord.'

'Three and a half, is it already? Well, my advisers didn't think it was the right time. But now at last you're here.'

Dayraven felt the anger boiling up in him like the sulphurous springs of Axo. This old man sat in his bath, letting other people's lives drip away like water – Dayraven stopped himself. The emperor was still the emperor and he owed his loyalty to him, just as his father had. In time, he could forgive all the wasted years, he hoped.

The emperor wiped some condensed sweat off his brow. 'I'm sure you've heard about our successes in recent years. How we've defeated all the tribes in the east.'

'Of course, my lord.'

'Then you must have heard how we conquered the Siegrins and captured the gold of the Timurs. Ah, the gold of the Timurs!' The emperor splashed his hands in the

11

water. 'You should have seen it! Their great fortress – the Ring – was filled with gold and jewels. Wagon after wagon of it – I spent that gold in building this palace and in enriching the empire. And soon, I'll be head of an empire as big and as great as any there has ever been.'

'What about the Fifth Unmasking, my lord? That can't be far away.'

'Fifth Unmasking? What of it? I'm talking about my empire, Dayraven.'

Dayraven fought to hide his shock at this talk. Calvo had become an eccentric old man sitting in his bath, yet making the biggest plans ever heard of. The Faustian Era had already lasted as long as any in history and couldn't last much longer: the Akhen would soon send its Face to another part of the world and Faustia's time of greatness would be over. History showed that this was inevitable; the emperor should have been preparing for it by making alliances and strengthening the trade system, but he seemed to live in another world. The Face might Unmask in one of the parts of the world that the emperor had recently been antagonising; in that case, their revenge would be terrible. This was not a time to make new enemies, but the emperor seemed completely unaware of this. Someone else must be behind Calvo, pushing him on for their own reasons, but who?

'We have a great future ahead of us, Dayraven. Now you can be part of it and be one of us again.'

'Yes, my lord.'

Dayraven felt twisted up inside. For the emperor, it was just a matter of a few words to wipe away the years, so that everything went back the way it would have been. *I need time to be 'one of us' again, and maybe the rest of my life won't be enough.*

12

'Anyway,' the emperor went on, stroking some water out of his beard, 'I didn't want to see you just to chat over old times – I have a job for you.'

Dayraven saw out of the corner of his eye that the young soldier who had brought him there edged a bit closer. Dayraven turned to see, and the soldier made as if he were looking the other way.

'A job, my lord? Tell me what you want me to do.'

'It's better if my chief adviser tells you – he knows more about it.' The emperor turned to the soldier standing outside the pool. 'Call High Priest Astolf.'

Dayraven shivered despite the hot water. *Astolf?* He hoped it wasn't the man he remembered from so long ago, but had a sinking feeling that it was. If the emperor had surrounded himself with people like that, it was a bad sign for the empire. *And for me.*

'But of course you know Astolf,' the emperor said. 'You were both hostages in Theodorica for a while, weren't you?'

So it was him. 'Yes, my lord – Astolf has been back for years, though.'

'Well, since then, he's made himself indispensable to me.'

Dayraven heard footsteps and turned. The man who came into the baths was dressed as a high priest in a gold-lined cloak, but it was the Astolf he remembered. Dayraven saw his deep-set eyes glaring out of their black holes, and his dirty, crooked teeth. Dayraven shivered despite the hot water of the bath. He would never forget his first meeting with Astolf in the square of Theodorica the day after he arrived. Astolf had been armed with a sharp elephant stick and surrounded by followers.

'Hey, orphan boy!'

13

'Are you talking to me?' Dayraven asked.

'Yes, orphan boy. You.'

'My name is Dayraven. I know yours is Astolf.'

'Very smart, orphan boy. Your father was always smart enough to know when to run away from a battle, I've heard.'

'My father was a hero!'

'Can't have been much of a hero – got himself killed.'

'Only because your father betrayed him.'

'That's enough, orphan boy. Run back to your mother – oh, I forgot, she's dead as well.'

Mist clouded Dayraven's mind and he charged his older and bigger opponent. When the mist cleared, Astolf was lying in the dust, wounded by the elephant stick, and his followers had changed sides.

Fifteen years later in the palace at Axo, Dayraven shook his head to clear away the memories. Now the same face he had wanted to smash all those years ago was there again.

'Astolf is a new high priest,' the emperor said, 'but I've come to rely on him. He seems to know everything that's happening in the empire, and he always has gifts for his emperor and gold for new buildings and new projects.'

In the old days, the emperor would have distrusted Astolf as well. Now he values only baths, spies and gold, it seems, and the son of a traitor is advising the emperor.

Astolf paused for a moment and then took off his clothes and handed them to a servant. Dayraven saw the scar running right across his chest. Their eyes met and Dayraven knew they were both remembering the palace courtyard in Theodorica and the fight with the elephant stick. Astolf slid into the water.

'Now, Astolf,' said the emperor, 'tell Dayraven what we need him to do.'

'My lord,' Astolf said. 'I must speak plainly.'

'Go on.'

'I don't think we should bring Dayraven into this.'

'Why not?'

Astolf glanced at Dayraven. 'Well, he's only just come back from Theodorica, and –'

'And what? I knew him when he was a boy – I knew his father. He's already shown his courage and loyalty in all the years he's been in Theodorica, and he might be one of our great men one day.'

Dayraven felt Astolf's glare on him. *Anything to do with Astolf is best avoided.*

'My lord,' Dayraven said. 'Astolf is right. I've been a hostage of the enemy for many years. My baggage has not even arrived yet. Let me go back to my lands or give me a place in the army – or something else – until I can prove myself to you again.'

'Nonsense.' The emperor's face took on the stubborn look Dayraven remembered so well. 'You're the only person for the job – you speak Jael and Magian, don't you?'

'Yes.'

'You know as much about Jaelite mysticism as anyone, don't you?'

Dayraven thought of all he'd learnt from Halakh. 'I suppose so.'

'Listen to that, Astolf,' the emperor said. 'If anyone can get close to this – Halakh – and find out what he's doing here, it's Dayraven. An emperor has many enemies and needs many friends.'

Dayraven shivered under the hot water. *Halakh?* So, they knew he was there. He glanced over at the young soldier standing guard outside the bath, who was watching the steam rise up to the roof.

'Perhaps you know this Halakh? Oh, be quiet, Astolf – I've made my choice.' Dayraven could see that the emperor was not going to turn back now. 'He's an old Jaelite – he's spent time at Theodorica.'

Know him? He's been like a second father to me. But surely, Astolf already knows all that. Why is he pretending not to?

'I knew Halakh,' Dayraven said.

'Well, he's arrived – you tell him, Astolf. Go on.'

'Very well, my lord.' Astolf's deep eyes glittered. 'My spies say that Halakh has arrived in the empire. We have reason to believe that he's going to the city of Trevi – that has the biggest Jaelite community. We've known for years that Halakh has powerful connections among the Jaelites all over the world. He's gone on missions to them in many places, on behalf of Faustians and Magians. Arranging trade and treaties, things of that sort.'

'And what is he doing this time?' Dayraven asked.

'We don't know for sure. We think he's meeting someone to pass over something very important – a secret. All we know is that it would be extremely valuable to the empire.'

'So, what do I have to do?'

'Find Halakh, gain his trust. Find out what he's doing here and what the secret is. Get hold of it and bring it to me – to the emperor.'

'I'm happy to serve the empire, but this job is not for me.'

'Dayraven,' the emperor said. 'No one else can do this job like you. You know Halakh, and if there's a need for fighting, you can fight as well as anyone, they tell me – it has to be you.'

This is crazy. There must be some reason that Halakh has come all this way to see me, but now I'm supposed to spy on him for the emperor. Does Astolf know about our planned meeting in the Octagonal Temple and this is some sort of trap? But it should all become clear when I meet Halakh tonight. I just have to play for time.

'If this is what you want, my lord, I'll do my best,' Dayraven said.

'It's what I want. Now you'd better go – Astolf thinks you should leave for Trevi early in the morning.'

'You'll be well rewarded,' Astolf said, showing his crooked teeth in a smile.

'I will go and prepare myself, my lord.'

'Yes, do that, Dayraven – and good luck.'

Dayraven heaved himself out of the water and sploshed over to the bench where a servant held out a cloth to dry himself with. The young soldier glanced at him and then looked away.

***

The Twister held the thin copper scroll in his thin fingers. The metal felt warm from the old Jaelite's body. *Warmer than he will be soon.* The Twister felt an itch on his hump, reached with the scroll to scratch it and sighed as the smooth copper calmed his skin.

He held the scroll out in front and turned it round in the candlelight. It was bound together with braided copper string and closed with a heavy seal. His fingers wanted to

17

open it, but then he thought of what High Priest Astolf had said.

'*Follow the Jaelite. Wait till he gets the scroll from its hiding place and follow him again. Wait until he's alone at night, then kill him. Do not open the scroll – bring it to me.*'

Astolf glared out of his deep, black-ringed eyes that looked like holes in snow. The Twister glared back; he knew he was made wrongly on the outside, but Astolf was crooked and bent on the inside.

'*You hear me, Twister? I got you out of that prison of a hermitage – I. Otherwise, you'd still be rotting in there like a broken stick.*'

The Twister shivered; just the thought of the hermitage made him feel sick. He remembered the icy nights without sleep, the dousings in cold water, the handful of slimy food, the beatings.

'*I see you haven't forgotten the hermitage. I can send you back there whenever I like.*'

'*You said you'd see that I got back power, wealth – everything that was taken from me.*'

'*And so you will. But remember why I freed you – not to look at your great beauty but to work for me. Do that and you'll get what you want.*'

'*I guess I've got no choice.*'

'*You knew that already. So, bring me the scroll straight away – and don't open it.*'

The Twister lowered the scroll and looked up at the ceiling way above him; the memory of Astolf melted away like the oily smoke from the candles. The Octagon was beautifully made and shining, not like the small, creepy temple at the hermitage. Memories of the cruel hermits – mostly escaped criminals – flashed into his mind again. Years before, he had come to places like this finely dressed, adored by the crowds. They hadn't cared then about his hump but looked at his handsome face and at all the slave-like followers swarming around him.

The Twister glanced down at his white tunic covered with golden bees. Now he was finely dressed again, and soon he'd have thousands of slaves again. First of them all would be Astolf.

The Twister picked up his black cloak from the floor and turned it around to check for bloodstains, but it was clean. With a wash of cool air, he threw it round his shoulders and fastened the clasp, then thrust the scroll inside his tunic.

Astolf's not here. It's just me and the old Jaelite. Now I'm free – free to get revenge on all of them. Including my father.

The Twister used to love his father and his father had loved him. When his father clasped him on the shoulder, he might even have touched the hump, but neither of them minded; the Twister had been just the same as the other children. Why, then, had that same father thrown him out into the cold years later? He was the eldest, but when he was eighteen, his father had replaced him with the next son in line and had even given his name to another child – as if he didn't exist.

The Twister looked down at the dead old man on the floor. The murder was his father's fault in the end; if his father hadn't cast him off, he could have lived as he always had, but instead, he'd ended up in the hermitage. He shivered at the thought of the brutal work, the harsh laughter and jokes about his hump. Astolf had promised him wealth and power again if he killed the Jaelite and stole the scroll.

19

The Twister had killed in battle when he was very young and never regretted it, but this had been different. This old man had looked at him in a friendly way, not seeing anything evil in his face; still, he had to die, and anyone else who tried to stop him would die as well. He would have to go on killing until he could have his old life back. *My father caused this.* One day, his father would know what it meant to cast out his own son.

The Twister choked back his rising tears and turned towards the eastern tower, through which he had entered. He stopped and took out the scroll again. Astolf wanted this thing badly, he knew, and the Twister's fingers itched to open it. What if Astolf planned to cheat him? Once he gave him this scroll, perhaps Astolf would try and send him back to the hermitage. *No!* The Twister clenched his fist until the nails bit into his palms.

What if he held on to the scroll? Astolf would have to bargain then. He would have to show something more than just empty promises. But that risked making Astolf angry, and then maybe Astolf really would send him back to the hermitage. The Twister's mind flooded again with the darkness, the silence, the cold of that isolated place. *No! They won't shut me up again in there.*

He staggered as the fear grasped him. The high ceiling seemed ready to crash down on his head, and the golden lion in the mosaic reached out to grab him in its giant paw. The Twister almost shrieked but choked it down. Panic began to rise in him. *No!* If the fear seized him here and he collapsed, they would know who killed the old man, and then they'd really lock him up for ever.

Footsteps rang in his ears, and the Twister covered them with his hands. He looked at the dead body lying in its pool of blood. The great lion on the ceiling had leapt down and torn the life out of that old man, and now the lion was after him, too. The footsteps were coming closer and closer – he had to escape.

The Twister spun around under the bright dome of the ceiling. *Up!* He had to go up! The lion was somewhere on the ground now, near the blood. *Up!* Up he would go. The Twister stumbled to the stairs leading to the upper story. Somewhere behind him, he heard the scrape of feet and a noise at the tower entrance, and imagined the golden lion fumbling at the lock with its great paws. *It won't find me upstairs.* The Twister blundered up the marble steps, supporting himself with one hand, while the other clutched the scroll.

***

Dayraven walked back along the corridor, his skin glowing with the heat of the bath. Somewhere out in the courtyard, the elephant stamped its feet.

A wild mix of thoughts whirled through Dayraven's mind. Joy at meeting Halakh was mixed with concern for his old teacher and with speculations about what Astolf's plans might be. Dayraven had thought so often about his return to Faustia, but he could never have imagined that it would be anything like this. Halakh's letter asking to meet him in Axo had been strange enough. The letter had been waiting for Dayraven when he arrived at the royal palace. Halakh had been away travelling when Dayraven left Magia, and something serious must have happened since then. The letter said that there was a scroll which would explain everything. At this meeting in the middle of night, there would also be a woman; she would have something to identify herself. *Who is this woman? What does it all mean?*

Dayraven recalled one of the hundreds of times he had walked together with Halakh in Theodorica, learning. The sun shone on the gleaming white arches of the palace, and Dayraven supported the old man by the elbow. The air was cool under the passageway that they followed around the courtyard. Dayraven's senses sang to the sweet smell of fruit in the air and the tinkling ripple of the fountain in the centre. Halakh wore the expression that always made Dayraven think of a locked treasure chest. *Full of mysteries.*

And now he was supposed to spy on Halakh for the emperor, as if his old friend were an enemy. But anything to do with Astolf promised no good to anyone except Astolf himself.

There was only one way to find out what was going on, and that was to get to the Octagon. Dayraven knew he was late; the bath with the emperor had wasted time. He hoped that Halakh was still there and told himself that everything would work out when they met.

Dayraven turned at one of the high archways leading into the courtyard, and the cold night air of Axo draped around him like a robe. The guards tensed for an instant and then relaxed when they saw who it was. They evidently knew him well already – he was still the son of Urland.

Dayraven turned towards the Octagonal Temple, feeling the ground fall away under his feet as he headed down the slope. The moon was wrapped in clouds and the only light was thrown by the line of high torches outside the palace. The temple was usually closed, the soldier had said, but Halakh had asked to meet him there. *The sun tower will be open*, the letter had said. That must be the most eastern of the eight towers around the temple.

The clouds drifted away and the copper dome of the temple rose out of the darkness, gleaming in the moonlight. Dayraven caught his breath. They'd said in Theodorica that the Octagon at Axo was a fantastic piece of work. *And it is. It really is.* Dayraven had seen a lot of wonderful buildings in Magia, but this was as great as any of them. The great dome was held up by the stone walls of a giant polygon, with rounded arches cut into every side. And in there, among all the treasures, were the sword and hunting horn of his father, the hero, to make a sort of shrine to him here in Axo.

The moon slipped back behind the clouds and Dayraven walked on. A cold breeze stung his face but also carried the warm smell of the first baked bread of the day. He hadn't smelt Faustian bread like that for years until the journey back, but this was no time to think of food.

Dayraven crossed to the eastern tower, reached for the handle of the door and turned it. The door opened with a faint squeaking noise. *If the door's unlocked, Halakh must be here.* He walked up the smooth stone steps, hearing the sound magnified in the narrow space. The smell inside was close and musty. Up ahead, two torches hung from the walls, but the steps in between them looked like deep puddles of blackness.

Dayraven reached the top of the steps and listened at the door. He thought he heard something above the pounding of his own heart, but it was too soft to be sure. Dayraven steeled himself and pushed open the door. His eyes blinked in the bright candlelight and then followed the double levels of soaring arches and marble pillars up to the domed ceiling. The glittering mosaics hung there like a giant canopy, telling the story of the Fourth Unmasking.

He had studied all the Unmaskings intensively with Halakh. In the Fourth Unmasking, the Face had transformed Faustia from a cold, backward provincial kingdom into the most powerful empire on the planet. The Face had done the same for the ancient, magnificent Magians one thousand five hundred years earlier, in the First Unmasking. Six hundred years after that, for the Second Unmasking, the Face had appeared in the form of a woman to the clever philosophers of Periclea in the south-east. Then he had appeared as a man to the well-organised soldiers and engineers of Apollinia in the south four hundred and fifty years later in the Third Unmasking. It had been the turn of the Faustians five hundred and seventy-five years ago, in the Fourth Unmasking. Once every five hundred years or so, the Akhen elevated one of the areas of the world to greatness by sending the Face down to earth. The effects of the Unmaskings were never permanent – the favoured people always lost their pre-eminence after four or five centuries – but they all kept the memory of the Face's intervention in their own book of the Unmasking, four in all by now. In this way, the religion of the Akhen had gradually taken over most of the world.

In all the Books of the Unmaskings and in the mosaics, statues and paintings, the Face's human appearance was never shown or described. The writers and artists seemed incapable of doing so; the Akhen would not allow it, apparently. The head was always shown by a shining disc, sometimes with the eight pulsing arms of the Akhen symbol. Was the Face reincarnated each time? No one really knew, although some believed that reincarnation happened occasionally, and not only for the Face of the

Akhen. The Books of the Unmaskings never explained precisely how the Face was able to change the world at each Unmasking: it must be some kind of magic, but no one seemed able to say. *So many mysteries. A face without a face – an unmasking that leaves the mask.*

Dayraven found himself staring at the great lion in the mosaic far above, and the creature stared back, as if asking where he'd been all this time. He tore his eyes away and glanced around the lower level of the temple, where he was standing. There was no one there. *Perhaps Halakh is waiting on the upper level.* That was where his father's sword and hunting horn were kept, he remembered. Dayraven moved towards the stairs but then saw a candle lying on the floor near the altar.

Dayraven moved closer. 'Halakh?'

His voice echoed all around the high ceiling.

Dayraven stopped and then went forward again. 'Halakh?'

All his senses screamed that something was wrong and his heart was thumping. Dayraven jumped at a noise behind him and grabbed a heavy metal candelabrum from the altar.

'Halakh?'

Something must have happened to Halakh, or he would have answered by now. But he could see no one.

He moved toward the shadows, holding the candelabrum. Someone was there. Dayraven stood listening to his own heaving breath. A shape moved out of the shadows off to the right and Dayraven tensed.

'Dayraven,' said a hoarse whisper that Dayraven was sure he'd heard before.

The speaker stepped out into the light and Dayraven gasped; it was the young soldier from the baths. Dayraven started forward, lifting the candelabrum, and the soldier whipped out his sword and raised his shield. Dayraven stood still.

'I followed you here,' the soldier said.

'Why?' Dayraven held himself ready.

'I came here to meet Halakh, like you.'

'How do you know his name?'

'I don't know him, but he knows me. He sent me a letter.' The soldier put his sword back in its scabbard and slung his shield over his back. 'Halakh said to bring this to show you.'

The soldier held out a small bronze disc showing the sign of the Akhen, and Dayraven recognised it. Halakh used to give them as gifts; he had given Dayraven one just like it when they first met.

Dayraven saw a red mist rising in front of his eyes. Anger made his arms tremble and he fought to control it. He walked towards the soldier, feeling the hard weight of the candelabrum.

'It's a lie,' Dayraven said, getting within striking distance. 'You killed Halakh and took that from him – in Halakh's letter to me, he said the other person I'd be meeting was a woman.'

'I am a woman.'

'What are you saying?'

The soldier swept off his helmet and tugged a little at the back of his head, and a flood of long blond hair tumbled out, gleaming in the candlelight. Dayraven's brain was whirring with confusion.

'Does any man have eyes like these?' the soldier said in a sweet female voice.

Dayraven found himself looking into her deep blue eyes. It was funny how he'd never noticed how nice they

26

were; the soldier must have kept her eyes squinted and lips pressed tightly together before to hide their beauty.

'You're a woman!'

The full lips smiled. 'I'm Sunniva.'

Dayraven knew he was staring at her, but he couldn't stop. Then a thought shoved itself into his mind and he felt himself going red.

'You – you were at the baths! You saw – everything?'

'Just enough to want to get to know you better.'

What had Halakh said once? *Fill the mind with wonderful things, but don't be ashamed of the senses.*

'But why the disguise?'

'It's the only way a woman can have any freedom in this empire. The reason I need to travel freely – well, it's sad.... Maybe I'll tell you later. I use my brother's name and insignia when I'm a soldier. I always make sure I'm on guard duty when the emperor takes his bath, so I don't have to get in there myself.'

Dayraven looked at the hilt of her sword. It seemed a good weapon.

'Can you fight well?' he asked.

'When I have to – I've practised most of my life. I prefer bow and crossbow, but they don't fit with my soldier disguise. Anyway, just imagine I'm a man. Shall we look for Halakh?'

Dayraven nodded. This had not been what he was expecting, but the world was a strange place and getting stranger. Halakh had arranged for this warrior woman to be there, so he would have to trust her.

'Yes,' Dayraven said. 'Let's look for him. We'll split up, but be careful – something is wrong here.'

'I'll try over this way.'

Sunniva moved off. Dayraven looked at the upper levels; it was so quiet, but the feeling of uneasiness didn't go away. He walked around the altar and saw the body on the ground. His throat locked up with shock. No one else in the empire could be dressed in robes like that; it could only be Halakh. Dayraven didn't want to believe it, but he felt an icy grip seize his limbs.

'Halakh?' he whispered.

Then the ice melted and Dayraven rushed forward and knelt by the body. He could see that his old teacher was dead. A small throwing axe was dug deep into his chest. The blood on his robe and on the floor all around was only just starting to dry. Dayraven absently traced with his finger one of the golden stars on Halakh's robe as he arched his neck back to look at the lion on the ceiling; it had seen what happened but would never say. He imagined Halakh's soul, star-shaped and glowing, drifting up and vanishing into the lion's mouth; what would happen to his soul now? Halakh had taught Dayraven many theories of the afterlife. *Now he knows which one is true.*

Dayraven looked back down at what was left of Halakh and fought back his tears. *One day, I'll be gone*, Halakh had said long before in the courtyard of the Duke's palace. Dayraven could still smell the spring flowers that waved in the cooling breeze. *But you'll carry away what I've taught you until you need it, like a camel crossing the desert.*

And now you are gone, Halakh. But why like this? Who killed you? And what secret were you bringing me? Goodbye, old friend.

Sunniva walked towards the darkest part of the temple, where the shadows hung like a heavy cloak. She stopped and listened as a sound came, her hand moving to the hilt of her sword. It was only the scrape of Dayraven's feet behind her, she realised. Sunniva raised her head up and up, taking in the rising layers of arches and columns. She had seen this building so often and heard so much about it from her father, yet seeing it now was a new feeling. All the secrets of the place that had always seemed just part of a game now made her tremble. Something in the air told her that this was no game. She felt even more the shield hanging on her back, the dead, cold weight of the sword stretched along her thigh and the heavy mail coat pressing on her shoulders.

A thought flashed into Sunniva's mind of the gentle, easy life that she could have. She felt for a moment the caress of silk on her skin and the touch of jewels on her wrists and neck. But all that was gone. One day, when the quest was over, she would hang up her armour and weapons. Sunniva tucked up the last of her hair under the helmet. First, she had to complete her task. Finding Halakh was part of it, she felt sure, whoever he was. The name meant nothing to her, but there had to be some importance in this strange meeting in this temple, of all places. Her search had taken her to many places in the empire, without success. Only she could do it. Her sisters were married and lived far away. Her brother was in a garrison somewhere. His letters told the usual story of drunkenness, gambling debts and women; he would never miss the palace insignia that Sunniva was using to move around here. Returning to the palace, where she had started her search, had been more desperation than anything else, but it might be the key. The letter from Halakh that had been waiting for her promised – she didn't know what, but it had to lead somewhere.

And what about Dayraven? Like her, he was not what he seemed. He was a Faustian like her, and the son of Urland, but she knew that he must be at least as much Jaelite or Magian; his tanned skin, his clothes, beard and hair suggested that. The slight lines around his eyes from squinting in bright sunlight showed that he had lived in a hot climate for a long time, and he talked so differently. Could she trust him on the quest? She didn't know. The scene of him undressing and slipping into the bath flashed in front of her eyes, and she saw again his tight backside, strong thighs and the rippling muscles in his back. *But no*, Sunniva told herself, straightening her back like a soldier. Fate had thrown them together – why, she didn't know yet – but if needed, they'd fight together like comrades, that was all. She gripped her sword hilt tightly.

Sunniva heard Dayraven gasp back near the altar, turned and strode that way. Dayraven swung around as she approached. A shock ran through her as she recognised the old man on the ground.

'That's Halakh?' she asked.

'Yes.'

'That's not what he called himself when I saw him.'

'So, you did know Halakh? How?'

'Years ago, when I was very young, he came to visit my father at Trevi – three times that I remember.'

'Do you know why Halakh would come all the way to see your father?'

'No, I was just a child. It didn't seem strange to me at the time. When I got that letter telling me to meet someone called Halakh here, I couldn't understand it.'

Sunniva had been playing with two wooden soldiers in the hall of her father's house many years before when she first saw the strange old man. She often sat on a rug dreaming of battles and acting them out with her wooden soldiers. The Faustian foot soldier was her oldest toy; the point of his spear was broken and his armour was battered. Her favourite was the Magian warrior. His clothes and weapons were strange, and she used to lie awake at night, thinking of the distant lands where he came from, imagining herself there having adventures.

She got on well enough with her brother and sisters and the children of the servants, but the best games were those on her own with the soldiers. The girls soon became bored of battles and tried to involve her in embroidery and such things, while the boys became rowdy and stupid and tried to boss her around just because she was a girl. She and the wooden soldiers had a wonderful time on their own; they were always brave and generous, whether they won or lost. Her father would watch her playing sometimes and smile. He had always wanted her to be different, as if he wished she'd been a son, and had involved Sunniva in his research from very early on. Sunniva's brother had always been a disappointment to their father and only seemed to want to annoy him.

It was in the middle of one of these games that the strange old man had arrived, looking like a kind wizard out of a story. Every time she saw him, he always had gifts that seemed to come from another world. Sunniva never dared talk to him, although she so much wanted to ask about other empires, kings and battles. For weeks after he had gone, even her soldiers were forgotten as she talked about him all the time with the servants, her brothers and sisters and even her father. The Jaelite Uncle, they used to call him.

And now, when I've finally learned who he really is, he's dead.

Dayraven stood up, his mind whirling with everything that had happened.

'Halakh's killer must have escaped by now,' he said. 'How many other ways out are there, do you think?'

Sunniva's brow wrinkled a little as she thought. 'Apart from the tower we came in, there are seven others – all of those have access to both the upper and lower levels. From both levels, there's a covered passageway leading back to the palace. Then there's the main door on this level as well.'

Dayraven could feel himself gaping in surprise. 'How can you know all that?'

'I should know it – I feel like I've lived in this place.'

'I don't understand.'

'My father designed this temple.'

Dayraven knew that he was staring even more. 'You're Ado of Metos's daughter?'

'Yes. You've heard of him?'

'Of course – he's one of the world's greatest architects and scholars. The duke used to dream of getting Ado to design a building for him. I remember them talking about it when Ado came to Theodorica.'

Now he saw Sunniva's face flood with surprise. 'My father went to Magia? He never told me that. I thought he was in Apollinia or Periclea.'

Dayraven felt thick layers of mystery cloaking his mind; there was no starting point where they could even begin to unravel it all.

'Where is your father now?'

'Vanished.'

'Why would your father vanish like that?'

'I don't know. Something must have happened to him, so I promised myself that I would find him. That's why I dress like a man – I'll keep searching until I find my father.'

Dayraven could see from her set face that she meant every word.

Sunniva looked down at Halakh. 'When I first heard that my father had disappeared, I thought that maybe the Jaelite Uncle – that's what I used to call Halakh – had something to do with it. I wondered whether he and my father had gone off together on some secret work. Now I see what happened to the Jaelite Uncle.'

'But we don't know what's happened to your father. Or to Al-Suli.'

'Who's Al-Suli?'

'My Magian tutor – he taught me the Magian language, philosophy, *shatranj* – he was one of the supreme masters of the game. On my way to Axo, I heard that Al-Suli had vanished while on a journey for the duke of Theodorica.'

'So, three great scholars – Ado, Halakh and Al-Suli – a Faustian, a Jael and a Magian, all dead or vanished at about the same time.'

'A sad coincidence.'

'Yes.'

Dayraven looked up at her and she met his eyes. He knew they were thinking the same thing: it didn't feel like a coincidence.

'But why would Halakh want to meet you now?' Dayraven asked. 'It must have something to do with your father – maybe he wanted to tell you where your father was or what happened to him. Perhaps that is explained in the scroll he mentioned in his letter, but Halakh's killer must have taken it.'

'Why did Halakh want you to be here as well?'

'I don't know. I've been wondering that myself. Whatever Halakh wanted to tell me or give me – well, he could have done that in Theodorica before I left. Unless –'

'Unless?'

'My thirtieth birthday passed while I was travelling back here. Halakh very strictly followed the Jaelite belief that certain things couldn't be told to a person under thirty years of age – the age when the Face of the Akhen has always revealed itself. Halakh always said that there were a lot of very important things he would tell me after I reached that age, but I was brought back to the empire just before I was old enough. Halakh must have been looking for me for that reason. Whatever he wanted to tell me, it must have been extremely important to risk his life coming all this way at his age. Maybe something happened suddenly that made him act so fast.'

'My father always said that one day, the time would be right for me to be told a lot of great secrets. I won't be thirty for another five years, but Faustians aren't so strict about age.'

Dayraven studied Halakh's face once more. *You've asked me too many riddles this time. If only you'd left me even one clue.*

34

***

Astolf hurried up the hill, shivering in the cold. The small temple where he'd arranged to meet the Twister was just inside the city walls.

Dayraven! Dayraven! The name thundered in his head like a beating drum. *Maybe Dayraven hopes to avenge his father's death all those years ago. But the great hero's son will be destroyed, just like his father was. I have to get rid of Dayraven in the same way, once he has served his purpose. I can't just wait for him to take his revenge when he wants.*

Astolf looked around. The street was very dark and he knew that dawn was still some time away. Astolf heard the sounds of the waking city; horse's hooves, millwheels clanking.

He unlocked the temple door, and the stale and musty smell hit him. No one ever came there, which made the place perfect. He lit some candles, and while their smoke filled the temple, Astolf carried a tall candle on a stand to check that no one was hiding in one of the dark corners.

He knelt in front of the altar and pressed his hands together as if to pray. *It's always useful to look as if you are praying.* Even if someone were to come in, they would never suspect a man who was praying. *And not if he's a high priest, above all.* Astolf smirked and then set his face in a pious look. The only person who would come to this place in the middle of the night was the Twister. *He should be here already.* If the Jaelite had gone to the Octagonal Temple, he should be dead by now and the Twister should have the scroll.

But of course the Jaelite went to the Octagon. Astolf's spies were never wrong. They had intercepted the letter to Dayraven, but it had been written in Jael and probably coded. There had been a second letter in plain Faustian language addressed to a soldier in the royal palace, and that second letter had told Astolf what he needed to know. Presumably, Halakh had been compelled to write the second letter in Faustian because the recipient did not read Jael. That detail had lost the game for Halakh; he had been in too much of a hurry. Astolf smirked again. *All of Halakh's problems should be over now for good, anyway, but where is the Twister?*

What was life, Astolf thought once more, if you didn't make yourself stand out from the rest? Power could do that – now he had it, but he wanted more. Money could do it, and he needed much more of that. With those came praise, admiration, the love of women, the things the heroes always got but couldn't keep because there was always someone smarter to take it away from them. *The things that Dayraven has always had. Dayraven. Dayraven.*

Since that first day in Theodorica many years before, Dayraven had made Astolf's life a misery just by being who he was. The boys all followed him, the Faustian girls admired him, the duke valued him. And all the time, he, Astolf, had to look on. Dayraven had often mentioned his father's death and how one day he would definitely find out the truth and take revenge. In Magia, Dayraven could do nothing so as to not create problems for the emperor, but now he was back in Faustia. Astolf clenched his fists at the thought of Dayraven taking his place close to the emperor. Even worse, given time, he would learn exactly what happened to his father. Astolf would not allow him enough time for any of this, though. Dayraven would die and his death would stir up new troubles between the emperor and the duke – he who wanted the scroll wanted that as well, if possible. It would weaken the emperor's position even more. And what did it matter to Astolf who was emperor?

Astolf had advised the emperor for years not to bring Dayraven back, but now that he was there, he was a perfect scapegoat for the murder of Halakh. Astolf would convince the emperor of his bad mistake in trusting Dayraven, who was clearly now a spy of the duke of Theodorica. He could invent some proof to show that Halakh had been on a mission for the good of the empire. The emperor could easily be made to believe that Dayraven had turned traitor in all his years away: he had killed Halakh for his master the Duke, Astolf would say.

Astolf smiled to himself and glanced up at one of the tall candles. He could tell the time by the amount it had burnt down; the Twister was very late. What could have gone wrong? If Halakh had not gone to the temple, surely the hunchback would have come back straight away. Dayraven couldn't have got there first – he had been at the baths.

Could the Twister have failed to kill Halakh? Surely not – Halakh was a weak old man. The Twister was bent out of shape, but the bubbling core of hate inside him made him strong and ruthless. *But where is the Twister? And the scroll?*

Once Astolf had the scroll, he would send in some men to search the Octagonal Temple. They would find Halakh dead and maybe Dayraven in there; if not, Dayraven couldn't run that far. As soon as he could, Astolf would take the scroll and its secret to those who wanted it.

But until the Twister came back, there was nothing he could do. If he sent soldiers into the Octagon now, who knew what might happen? Could the Twister be trying to double-cross him? But no – he was too terrified of being sent back to the hermitage, and he believed the promises of power and wealth.

Astolf bowed his head and waited. *Dayraven! Dayraven!* The name pounded in his head. Time passed.

Astolf stood up. *Something's gone wrong.* The Twister should have arrived long since. The tiny temple was as dark and quiet as ever, but who knew what was happening back at the palace and the Octagonal Temple? Had Dayraven somehow interfered?

Astolf walked towards the door; it was getting dangerous to stay there while the situation might be getting out of control. He went out into the cold, locked the door and hurried back up the slope to the palace, counting off the possibilities in his mind. If the Twister had run off with the scroll for himself, then the quicker Astolf found out about it, the better. If the Twister had been caught, then it was better to be there to handle the problem. Whatever had happened, Astolf decided, he needed to be close by. That way, he could work on the emperor as necessary.

And he could deal with Dayraven. *Dayraven! Dayraven! Always Dayraven.*

A blustery wind pushed at Astolf's back as he walked. One of his own spies could have done the job getting the scroll, but He had wanted the Twister brought out of the hermitage for this purpose. And who knew what had gone wrong now?

The guards around the palace stood to attention as he passed. Astolf was still toying with the idea of taking a group of soldiers into the Octagonal Temple. It was too risky, though, without knowing what was going on in there; maybe it was better to wait and see and not get involved.

Astolf reached the palace. *It's all the fault of the Twister. And Dayraven.*

***

Sunniva fought to keep the tears out of her eyes. She glanced at Dayraven and saw that he was doing the same. Whatever Halakh had been doing all these years, it was over now and they would never know why he'd been killed. It was so senseless. She turned away from the empty, pointless death stretched out on the cold floor, and her eyes fell on something small and gleaming on the floor. Sunniva laid her shield aside and bent down to pick it up on one finger.

'Dayraven.'

'Hmm?'

'Look at this.'

He turned and saw the tiny golden bee she was holding out. Sunniva watched his eyes bulge, as she knew hers must have done.

Dayraven strode over and took the bee in the palm of his hand. 'Where did you find this?'

'Over there – on the floor.'

'This is the symbol of –'

'The Clovian Dynasty. Yes.'

'But they've died out, haven't they?'

Sunniva picked up her shield and gripped her sword tightly. Just saying the word had made the temple suddenly feel much colder and darker.

'It looks like they're still with us,' she said.

39

The strange events of the night swam in Sunniva's mind together with memories of her father. No Clovian had been emperor of Faustia for more than fifty years before she was born, but Sunniva had once seen one of them face to face, and she still shivered at the memory.

When she was just nine years old, Sunniva's father had taken her to see the tomb of the Clovian king Merech that he had rediscovered after centuries. A mummified man with a long black beard and hair was sitting on a throne at the back of the tomb, staring straight at her. In one hand he held a crystal ball, and the other was resting on a bull's head made of gold. His fingernails were long and curved like the roots of a tree. His long white robe was fringed with tassels and covered in golden bees. Propped on the wall behind him were stacks of weapons inlaid with jewels, and alongside him stretched the skeleton of a horse. There were hundreds of gold bees inlaid with jewels piled everywhere.

King Merech slowly turned to look at her. His tight, leathery face was crinkling as his mouth opened to speak. Sunniva could feel the soul inside her coming loose – it was going to be sucked into the dead king's head. Then he could come alive and climb down from that throne where he'd sat unmoving for so long. She crossed her arms over her chest to stop her soul from slipping out, but at the same time, she couldn't help being drawn to him. He was calling to her, he needed her, needed her soul. She could hear the rattle of the golden bees on the tomb floor behind her as the king stood up.

She pulled herself back and screamed, running from the tomb, through the crypt and outside. The air tasted clean and fresh and Sunniva gulped it down. She ran and ran and then fell face first in the mud. She screamed again but her mouth was full of dirt. The dead king was next to her, pulling her up. He would take her soul, but she would miss her father and the Jaelite Uncle and all the adventures she was going to have when she was grown up.

Sunniva raised her head from the mud. Her father was next to her, scraping the mud and matted hair from her face. He was crying and apologising and worried for her all at the same time.

'I should never have brought you here, Sunniva - I'm sorry. You're safe now.'

'He was coming to get me, Father.'

'No, no – he's dead. They're all dead. All the Clovians – long ago.'

In the Octagonal Temple in Axo many years later, Sunniva put up her hand to wipe away the mud, tears and rain, but they were gone. *Like my father. But the Clovians are still here.*

She shivered and glanced up at the ceiling far above. The golden lion twitched its tail. Ever since that day in the tomb, Sunniva had felt a strong connection to her father's research. Now, while she was looking for him, she had found the Clovians again.

***

The Twister sat up with a start. He had been daydreaming about his wonderful past life and didn't know where he was for a moment, but then it came back. He remembered that the lion had chased him up the stairs and shivered with fright. The Twister lay still, listening. Maybe the lion was stalking him now somewhere in the dark, and he'd never know until it was too late.

41

He looked around. Candles were burning somewhere, so it wasn't really all that dark. He saw that he was huddled at the base of the emperor's pale marble throne, and a wave of hate rose in the Twister's chest. Soon, the emperor would no longer be sitting on it; it was just a matter of time.

He could see the simple stone shape of the throne, so if the golden lion were there, he'd see it as well. Maybe it had found someone else to eat. The Twister lay back a little. There was still something else he had to remember, he knew, but it hid itself away in the deepest part of his mind. He looked around again and saw the great sword and hunting horn of Urland hanging on the wall. But no, that was not what he needed to remember.

The hermitage! Were they after him? No – Astolf had said he was safe from them as long as he did what Astolf wanted. *Astolf.* The Twister thought of him and shivered again. Had Astolf sent the lion after him? No – Astolf had sent the Twister after something.

Then he remembered the scroll. Where was it? The Twister found the copper cylinder and hugged it to his chest. *As long as I have this, I'm safe from the hermits.*

Then he heard voices; a man and a woman. The Twister strained his ears but couldn't make out the words. *Who are they and what are they talking about?* He clutched the scroll tighter and edged along the floor, closer and closer to the stairs. His hump was throbbing; that was a sign of danger that had never let him down. When his father had sent the soldiers to drag him off to the hermitage, the hump had told him something bad was going to happen, so he'd been ready, but there were too many of them. They'd laughed at his furious shrieking as they took him away, but soon he'd be laughing at them all. For now, though, he had to get away.

The Twister listened. The man downstairs was the son of Urland and the woman was the daughter of Ado of Metos; the past was after him once again. It would be easy enough to hide in a dark corner and wait for the chance to strike. All his life, even in the hermitage, he had trained and exercised to be as agile as he could despite his hump, so he could fight well. Two quick stabs of his knife and it would be over. But no, the Twister told himself – he had to get away with the scroll. *The scroll.* That was the key to power.

The only way out he could see was down the stairs, and that was too dangerous. But no – the woman had said that both levels led to the passageway. There was the door; he could open it from the inside. It would be noisy, but by the time they got up the stairs, he'd be gone.

He stood up and tucked the scroll back inside his tunic, but it got stuck. The Twister scowled – what was blocking it? He shoved the scroll down harder, and one of the tiny gold bees on his tunic was torn off and slipped down the inside of his cloak onto the floor. It clattered down the stone steps, and with every plink of the bee, the Twister's hump throbbed more and more.

Dayraven heard a faint rattling sound from the stairs and tensed. He knew that Sunniva was staring at the last stone step just as he was. A small golden thing bounced down the stairs and lay still. Sunniva stooped to pick it up; another golden bee.

She held it out on her palm, her face pale. 'They're back.'

43

Dayraven snatched up a heavy metal candelabrum from the altar and raced for the stairs, hearing Sunniva running behind him. He saw a short figure in a black cloak and hood at the top. Dayraven slowed a little, shoulders heaving, watching for the flash of a throwing axe, but it looked as though the enemy had no more axes and not even a sword. Dayraven saw him lunge for the wooden footstool at the base of the throne and throw it. Dayraven ducked but heard a dull thud as the stool hit Sunniva and knocked her down the stairs. He turned back; Sunniva was sprawled on the ground, clutching her chest.

'I'm all right!' she gasped. 'Hurry – before they get away!'

Dayraven turned back to the stairs and ran up them two at a time. He reached the top step and rushed into the open space, thrusting the candelabrum in front. The man in black was armed only with a knife hanging at his waist, but sprang for the sword of Urland hanging on the wall behind the throne, wrenched it out of its mountings and slid the blade from its scabbard.

Dayraven fought against a new fear. His father Urland's sword had been sacred ever since the great hero died, and he had grown up with stories of the sword's power. No one ever dared to even touch the sword, but now he had to fight against it. He went forward, holding the candelabrum ready. Dayraven had fought a lot with spears and swords in Magia, but never with anything as heavy as this; he thought that big swings would be too slow, so he thrust at the man's face as if using a lance.

The man in black was very fast. He stepped aside and swung the sword at Dayraven. He blocked with the candelabrum, but it was knocked out of his hands and his opponent giggled. Dayraven kept an eye on his enemy while backing away, until he reached the emperor's marble throne. The enemy shrieked and swung the sword downwards. Dayraven dodged and a puff of dust and fragments flew up from the throne as the sword hit it.

Dayraven looked around for another weapon. *Urland's hunting horn!* He ran along the wall and pulled the horn off the wall. It was long and heavy, and its hard ivory set with thick metal mountings made it a good weapon. Dayraven stood and faced the man in black; now it would be his father's sword against his hunting horn.

The enemy swung a great overhead blow. Dayraven gritted his teeth and blocked, hoping the ivory was strong enough. The blade landed with a heavy thud and the force pushed him back against the wall.

Dayraven thrust the man back with his foot and advanced, swinging the horn. The enemy swung again from the left. Dayraven knocked the blade away and chopped at the man's elbow. There was a loud crack and the man hissed in pain and the sword clanged to the floor. Dayraven planted his foot on it and swung the horn, keeping the enemy back. The man drew a knife with his other hand as Dayraven moved closer. He could hear the man's rasping breath. The knife thrust forward. Dayraven spun away and hit the man hard in the body with the horn. The enemy staggered and a scroll fell out of his cloak onto the floor. Dayraven moved to get in front of it.

The man in black shrieked and ran for the door, flung the bolt open and rushed down the passageway, yelling.

***

Astolf paced along the corridor, his mind whirring. There was still no way of knowing what was going on in the Octagonal Temple, or what Dayraven was doing, and until then, he couldn't take any definite action. One thought above all prodded at him: if the scroll wasn't found, he'd have to tell Him it was gone, and that didn't bear thinking about.

'High Priest Astolf,' said a voice.

Astolf looked up. A soldier was standing in a doorway.

'Yes, what is it?'

'The emperor wants to see you.'

Astolf sighed. *Right in the middle of all this?*

'Let's go, then,' he said.

The soldier led the way to one of the emperor's private rooms. Astolf put on his most pious face and stepped in. The emperor was seated at a heavy desk, looking at some documents in front of him and holding a knife in one hand and a big chunk of meat in the other. The smell of roast boar filled the air, and some of the crowd of scholars and doctors gathered around the emperor's chair were licking their lips.

'Ah, Astolf – come in,' the emperor said. 'Let me cut you some meat.'

'No, thank you, my lord. Not at this time of night.'

'What do I care about the time of night? My idiot doctors even try to tell me I shouldn't eat roast meat at all, but I eat as much of it as I like, when I like.'

Astolf watched as the doctors laughed and bowed. *Flatterers.*

'You wanted to see me, my lord?'

'Yes. I feel like hearing a ceremony of the Akhen.'

'A very good thing.'

'I mean right now – in the Octagonal Temple.'

46

A spasm of panic ran through Astolf. *Not now.*

'As I've said before, my lord, you must wait a little longer before using the Octagonal Temple again.'

The emperor stabbed the air with the meat. 'Wait? Wait? I never wait. If I waited for these stupid doctors, I'd never bathe, never eat, never do anything. Why can't we use the temple?'

'It is being prepared, my lord.'

'Still? You've been telling me that for a long time now, Astolf.'

'The work of the Akhen is slow.'

'Well, I've had enough of waiting.'

The emperor stood up and handed the meat to one of his servants while another brought up a golden bowl of water.

'My lord, please be patient,' Astolf said.

The emperor washed his hands and then dried them on a linen cloth held out by another servant. 'Patient! I'm never patient! Why should I be? I had that Octagon built, Astolf – not you. I want to sit upstairs on my throne and hear the praise of the Akhen, and you're going to say that praise, or I'll find someone who will.'

The emperor held out his arms for a servant to slip his cloak on, while another fastened the clasp. Astolf's thoughts were thundering through his brain. When the emperor was in this sort of mood, there was no stopping him. He would just have to hope that the Twister had already left, taking the scroll with him.

'Your desire does you great honour, my lord,' Astolf said.

'Ha! Fools all around me!'

47

Astolf followed as the emperor strode off at the front of the group. Astolf kept his eyes on the emperor's broad back as they walked down the corridor, trying to beat back the fears that flooded his thoughts, but they kept coming. He imagined the Twister being captured and telling everything in between mad shrieks. Astolf started praying genuinely for the first time in his life.

Off to the right, the elephant lumbered around, flapping its ears.

The emperor stopped and looked. 'Ah! My elephant Abul Ahaz – let's go and see him.'

'But, my lord,' said one of the scholars, 'what about the ceremony?'

'Oh, stop annoying people all the time! I want to go and speak to my elephant. What sort of empire is it if the emperor can't even talk to his elephant when he wants to?'

Astolf felt relieved. This would delay the emperor in reaching the Octagonal Temple. Astolf had always been afraid of the elephant, and it brought back bad memories of Theodorica and Dayraven, but now he was glad it was there.

The emperor crossed into the courtyard and walked up to the elephant's handler. 'How is he?'

'A bit restless, my lord. I think he'd like to have a run around.'

'Good. I'll be back in a while – untie him and put on his saddle.' The emperor stroked the elephant's trunk. 'What are you feeding him?'

'Just grass, my lord.'

'Grass? I've told you before – he likes these sweet things. Don't you, Abul?'

The emperor took up a wooden bucket of bread soaked in wine and honey and held out big pieces of it, and the elephant grabbed them in its trunk.

'Look at that!' the emperor laughed. 'He loves it.'

'My lord, too many sweet things are not good for him – they'll get him stirred up.'

'You're all against everything, aren't you? He's an emperor's elephant, isn't he? What sort of emperor's elephant is he if he can't eat what he wants?' The emperor passed the bucket back to the handler. 'Keep feeding him what he likes.'

Astolf drummed his fingers against his thigh. This delay was good, but at the same time, he was burning to know what was happening in the Octagonal Temple.

He turned as a soldier came running up.

'My lord!' the man said, out of breath.

The emperor wiped his hands on one of the doctor's cloaks and turned around. 'What is it now?'

'An intruder in the palace, my lord – a man in black running and yelling. He stabbed a guard who challenged him.'

'So, catch him.'

'We're trying, but he's got away.'

'Fools, all of you!' The emperor strode off, giving orders.

Astolf sighed in relief. So, the Twister had got away, but now Astolf needed to know whether or not he had the scroll. *And where is Dayraven?*

As the group walked along the corridor, Astolf hung back, and when the chance came, he slipped away. The first gleam of dawn was touching the Octagonal Temple. Astolf turned the other way; surely the Twister was heading back to the temple where they had arranged to meet. He hurried on through the cold air.

***

Dayraven set the horn down, his chest heaving. He turned at a noise behind him and saw Sunniva.

'Are you all right?' he asked. 'It's easy to fall heavily in armour when you're not expecting it.'

'No real harm done, I think, thanks to my helmet. My head aches a bit, though.'

'Let me have a look.' He lifted off the helmet and her hair flowed out. 'There's a big dent here on the left side.'

'The same for my head, probably.'

'Let me see.'

He felt along her scalp, his fingers tingling from the touch of her fine hair. Sunniva looked around once and then quickly turned away. She winced as he touched the sore spot.

'Sorry,' Dayraven said. 'Well, there's no blood, but you're going to have a bruise there.'

'What about you?'

'I'm all right. But – Halakh's lying down there dead.'

Sunniva put on her battered helmet. 'I understand.'

Dayraven felt that she really did understand what he was feeling, but it was too early for him to talk more about it with her.

'Well, the killer got away,' he said.

'That couldn't really have been a Clovian, could it? They're all dead, aren't they?'

'Well, in Magia, I heard stories that some had survived.'

'But their last king was just a boy – so were all the last ones.'

'Yes, but these Clovians are said to be descendants of their earlier King Guntro, the last strong Clovian king. All the ones after him were just puppets, like you said. But they say that Guntro had a son who survived him and went into exile in Seanor. The later Clovians died out, but Guntro's line is still alive. Their current leader is Dagon.'

'Do you believe it?'

'I thought it was just a story, but now I'm not so sure.'

'But why now? If there have been surviving Clovians for more than fifty years, why haven't they shown themselves before?'

'That's another mystery. Whoever that was I just fought, he knew how to use weapons. I could see from the way the throwing axe was thrust so deep into Halakh's chest that his killer was an expert who knew how to direct the blade.'

Sunniva picked up the scroll. 'This must be the scroll that Halakh mentioned in his letter. Do you think Halakh was killed for this?'

'He must have been. Let's try and find out why.'

Dayraven took the scroll and slipped off the band around it, sensing Sunniva watching him. His fingers shook as he unrolled the thin copper sheet.

As he stretched out the scroll and saw the letters etched into the copper, Dayraven sucked in his breath. 'The first part's not written in Jael, like I would have expected from Halakh. It's written in the Faustian alphabet, but it doesn't make any sense.'

His mind was whirling. There seemed to be no pattern, no meaning. Halakh had been killed for this and he

51

couldn't even understand it. Dayraven ran his eyes along the first two lines of letters:

SUN GIFT
SUN BIRD

Out of the corner of his eye, he saw Sunniva step closer and look at the letters stretching across the page.

'I can't understand the rest of it – it's written in a kind of picture code – but those first two lines are easy,' she said.

'Are they?'

'Yes. "Sun gift" is me – that's what my name means in Seanish. I have a family connection to Seanor.'

'So do I – not surprising when Seanor and Faustia have been allies for so long. What about "sun bird"?'

'That's easy as well – it's you. "Sun bird": "day raven". My father used the phrase "sun bird" in a puzzle years ago. He said one day I'd meet someone at a really important time, and then the name would make sense to me. But how could my father have known the name "Dayraven" so long ago? And how did this puzzle from my childhood end up on a scroll carried by Halakh?'

'Well, we don't have time to understand why, but whatever this scroll is about, we're both supposed to be involved in solving it. That's what your father and Halakh meant by putting both our names at the beginning, and that's why Halakh wanted both of us here.'

Some shouts came from outside. Dayraven jumped to grab Urland's sword and saw that Sunniva was reaching for hers. The noise grew fainter.

'Sounds like they're heading away from here,' Dayraven said.

'The guards must be chasing whcever that was you fought.'

'They might search in here later, and if they find us, they'll think we killed Halakh.'

'Dayraven – we've got the scroll now. We can't do anything more for Halakh, but if we get away, we can decipher his code later. If we stay, either the soldiers will find us, or the killer will come back for the scroll, perhaps with others.'

Dayraven's heart was thumping. Halakh must have known he was going to die; that was why he mentioned the scroll in his letter. He would have left a clue, so the answer had to be here somewhere. Halakh's death had shaken him, but Dayraven knew he had to stay calm to solve this. Even beyond death, his teacher was setting a puzzle for him. What had Halakh once said? *The whole world's a riddle, if only we know how to read it.*

'There's a reason why things are exactly where they are,' Dayraven murmured.

'What?' Sunniva said.

Dayraven looked around at the throne, Urland's sword and horn and then back at the scroll. 'I'm not leaving here till I find out why Halakh was killed and what he wanted to tell me.'

'Neither am I, then – but why can't we leave here? Like I said, we've got the scroll.'

'Yes, but there's a reason the scroll was here.'

'Halakh brought it to give to us.'

Dayraven shook his head. 'I can't believe that Halakh would make it so easy for his killer.'

'Maybe he didn't know they were after him.'

'Then why go to all the trouble of etching a coded message onto a copper scroll if he was going to meet us anyway? He could have told us whatever he wanted to say when we met him, without the risk of someone else finding it. No, there's something about this Octagonal Temple that he wanted to tell us.'

'Dayraven, you're not making sense.'

'We won't be able to solve the puzzle he's left without staying in here for as long as we can. Halakh spent his whole life finding patterns – codes – in everything. The whole world was an illuminated manuscript to him. To him, there were messages written in nature, in buildings – if you knew where to look. He spent years teaching me about them. "There's a reason why things are exactly where they are," Halakh said to me one day. I had just lost a game of *shatranj* to my tutor Al-Suli –'

'You said he was one of the great masters of the game, didn't you?'

'Yes, he was – is. I had never beaten him, but that day, I thought I was finally going to. It turned out that my pieces were well placed for attack, while Al-Suli's were placed for both attack and defence. Halakh was watching the game and pointed that out. I could see what he meant, but when I asked him how I could see it during a game, Halakh said, "Just remember that there's a reason why things are exactly where they are."'

'How does that help us now, though?'

'It means that Halakh specifically chose this building to meet me again. He probably knew he would soon be dead, and he would have left me a message – this temple must be part of it somehow.'

'Then let's find the message before somebody finds us.'

Dayraven's mind was clear now. *Just like a clean sheet of parchment.*

'I'll need something to write on,' he said.

He looked around, but there was nothing. Then he remembered.

'Halakh always carried a wax tablet on him – he said he never knew when an idea would come into his head.'

Dayraven went down the stairs, with Sunniva following behind. Seeing Halakh's body didn't hit Dayraven so hard this time; the sadness was still there, but the shock had lessened. By now, Halakh's soul would be safely placed wherever it had ended up. But what had Halakh wanted to say to him? He owed it to his old friend to find out why he had died.

Dayraven squatted down and felt the left side of Halakh's robe. There was no wax tablet there, so he reached over and moved Halakh's right arm, which was covering his body. As Dayraven gently grabbed the wrist, he felt the cold metal of one of Halakh's bracelets under his fingers. He lowered the arm and felt inside the robe until he found the wax tablet. The tablet was blank and the wooden writing stylus was tucked in a groove along the side.

Dayraven stood up and stepped over to the altar. He flattened out the scroll, laid the tablet next to it and picked up the stylus. He had seen Halakh write so often on this tablet that it felt strange to be doing it himself.

A horn sounded somewhere out in the city and the last shouts of alarm faded away. How much time did they have before someone burst in here?

***

Astolf heard the alarm cries trail off to the right, stopped for a moment to listen and then went on down the

55

hill towards the temple. The Twister was very agile, so there was a good chance he would get away from the soldiers, but did he have the scroll or not? Astolf bit his lip as he asked himself yet again. And Dayraven? Was it finally going to be the end of him? The hero's son caught in a trap, just like his father?

He turned the corner, out of the wind. Astolf thought of how close he might be to reaching his dreams.

Astolf heard a soft noise behind him and spun around. He saw the tail of a cat slinking around the corner and smiled a little. For years, enemies had tried to creep up on him from behind. But he knew what they were up to before they'd even thought of it.

A flapping sound came from somewhere above him. Before Astolf could see what it was, he was shoved back against the wall with a knife at his throat. His heart pounded as he looked into the gleaming eyes of the Twister. The hunchback's face shone with sweat.

'You! Are they still after you?' Astolf arched his neck away from the point of the knife. 'What are you playing at? Put that thing away.'

'This knife's in just the right place. Maybe a little bit farther forward would be better.'

Astolf fought his rising panic. 'Did you kill the Jaelite?'

'He's dead.'

'Did you get the scroll?'

'No. I lost it.'

'And Dayraven?'

'Still in the Octagonal Temple – he has the scroll. The daughter of Ado of Metos is with him, disguised as a soldier.'

'Well, we can get the scroll back. Now stop fooling around and let me go.'

The Twister's eyes blazed. 'No.'

'You have to go back and get the scroll.'

'No.'

'Do you want to go back to that hermitage?'

'I won't be going back there. If I kill you, there'll be no one to keep me there, then I have the whole empire to hide in.'

'Why kill me? I set you free, and without me, you'll never get anything.'

Astolf saw the Twister's eyes cloud over and heard his voice become more distant and distracted.

'You tried to have me killed, so I'll kill you. A good thing my hump warned me – it tingled and then whispered to me.'

'What are you talking about?'

'The lion killed the Jaelite, then you sent it to kill me. After I fought Dayraven, it chased me down the corridor. I could hear it snarling and its tail lashing the walls.'

'What lion?'

The Twister went on as if he hadn't heard. 'The lion jumped off the ceiling, but then it couldn't get up the stairs. Maybe the soldiers are chasing it now, thinking it's me. So, you see, I have to kill you.'

Astolf's thoughts were bounding on ahead. He knew he had just seconds to save his life.

'Killing me would be a big mistake, Twister. I control the lion – if you kill me, the lion will hunt you down, wherever you go.'

The knife wavered a little. 'I escaped from it just now. It couldn't catch me.'

Astolf managed a small laugh. 'I sent the lion this time just to show you my power. Do you think you could have escaped if I'd ordered it to kill you?'

'And you sent the lion to kill the Jaelite?'

'Of course – I only needed you to get the scroll. You've failed me, but I won't send the lion after you. Now let me go.'

The Twister withdrew the knife. 'I'll never go back to that hermitage!'

He turned and ran off, and Astolf breathed a deep sigh of relief. The Twister had gone crazy. He would probably be back sometime, so Astolf had to stay vigilant. When the immediate crisis was over, Astolf would send some killers to find the Twister and finish him off. At least He could not blame Astolf for the Twister's madness and failure.

Astolf turned and looked back at the Octagonal Temple. Now at least he knew the situation: Dayraven had the scroll, but he couldn't have gone far yet. Astolf could get a group of his best men, search the temple and track him down.

In an hour at most, he'd have the scroll and Dayraven would be dead or wishing he were. Astolf strode back up the hill towards the Octagonal Temple and the palace.

***

Sunniva watched as Dayraven copied out the picture symbols that came after the words. They sat in a block like an army confronting her.

'On the first line – a dagger or sword, then a cow,' Sunniva said.

'Then the second line reads like this: window – cattle prod – cow – window – fist – cow – cattle prod – water –

eye – prop – hand – nail. Now I'm sure what the basis of this code is. The pictures represent Jael letters.'

'Jael? I can't read Jael, but I know it doesn't look like that.'

'The Jael letters each have a sound, a name and a meaning. Take the two letters in the first line. The first picture we said is either a dagger or a sword. If I'm right about these being signs for Jael letters, it will be a sword. That's the letter which represents the "z" sound.'

'*If* you're right. And the cow?'

'It's probably more an ox, which represents the first letter of the alphabet – "A".'

Sunniva ran her mind over the earlier codes they had solved, and they swept through her brain like a storm.

'Dayraven – if these are really Jael letters, won't they be written right to left?'

'Yes. We need to reverse the order.'

'Which gives us "A-Z" on the first line. What does that mean?'

'I don't know. Let's get all the letters in the second line and try to interpret them.'

'All right. What are the letters in the second line?'

Dayraven looked at the wax tablet and wrote them down as he read. 'From right to left, we've got the Jael letters for: V-I-S-A-M-L-A-K-H-A-L-H.'

'What does that mean?'

'I recognise this sequence of letters from the Book of the First Unmasking. That book is mostly written in Magian, but some passages are in Jael – the language of the original prophecies about the Face of the Akhen. This passage contains precisely two hundred and sixteen letters – each verse contains seventy-two letters. Jaelite mystics use those letters to try and construct the seventy-two-letter title of the Akhen – its secret name. Discovering that name is one of their greatest goals. Each mystic rearranges the letters in their own way and uses them for meditation and to gain spiritual insight.'

Dayraven smiled and Sunniva stamped her foot. 'You can be so annoying – I hate it when you look smug like that. You obviously know something I don't.'

'Jaelites make two bracelets using the seventy-two-letter title. They divide the title into two lots of thirty-six and wear one half on a bracelet on each arm.'

Sunniva could feel herself smiling now. 'And I hope you're going to tell me that Halakh is wearing these bracelets.'

'He always did, which means that he will have already applied all the techniques to create the precise order of letters. Halakh wants us to take his bracelets – they must be what all of this is about. So, we grab the bracelets and get out of here before anyone finds us.'

'Which means something else.'

'What?'

'I'm getting there first.'

Sunniva turned and raced down the stairs, hearing Dayraven's feet pounding behind her. At the bottom of the stairs, Sunniva tensed and reached for her sword, but everything was just as they'd left it. How much longer did they have?

She slowed down out of respect for Halakh's body and walked up to it. As Dayraven approached, Sunniva knelt down and lifted Halakh's right sleeve. Around his wrist hung a wide copper scroll inscribed with many lines of symbols.

'Here's one bracelet,' she said, slipping it off the old man's thin wrist and passing it to Dayraven. 'Now for the other one.'

Sunniva reached over and felt Halakh's left wrist. There was nothing there. She lifted up the sleeve and looked.

'Dayraven.'

He looked up from the bracelet with a puzzled expression. 'Hmm?'

'The other bracelet – it's gone.'

'Don't joke.'

'I'm not – see for yourself!'

Dayraven looked shocked.

He knelt down at Halakh's side and searched. 'Check the floor – maybe it fell off.'

'I've done that.'

'Maybe it's underneath Halakh. Help me lift him.'

Sunniva put her hands under Halakh's body and together they lifted. He was very light.

'There's nothing here,' Dayraven said.

They lowered the body back down and Sunniva drove her thoughts on. 'There's only one possible explanation. The killer took it.'

'But if the killer knew the bracelets were important, why would he take just one of them?'

'Maybe we came in just as he was about to take the second one.'

'I don't think so – we would have heard him going up the stairs. Besides, the killer was after the scroll. He can't have deciphered it and the rest of the clues by the time we got here, can he?'

'No, you're right.'

'So, what happened to the other bracelet, then?'

'I don't know.'

'And the funny thing is, the bracelet itself is very unusual. I didn't notice before, with the shock of seeing Halakh dead.'

'I thought you said Halakh always wore these bracelets.'

'Yes, but not like this one. I've never seen one of these before.'

'Let me see – I didn't really look at it before.'

Sunniva took the bracelet and turned it around in her hand. The letters were Jael ones, but the style and shape of the bracelet were strange. From many years before, memories were rising up like morning mist.

'I've seen a bracelet exactly like this before,' she said. 'Years ago.'

'You have?'

'Yes, no doubt. The mystery's solved.'

'What do you mean?'

'The second bracelet was never here.'

'Where is it, then?'

Sunniva stood up, still holding the bracelet. 'My father's house in Metos.'

***

Astolf strode towards a secluded part of the city. He could hear his breath coming in gasps. The first signs of dawn were peeping out in the east. Astolf scowled as he thought of the token he'd just found in his rooms and now carried with him; a flat ivory disc inscribed with a black square. Why now? He was close to finishing things off with Dayraven, but to refuse this summons would be fatal. He glanced around, wondering if the Twister would come

62

back; he could be dealt with later, but there was a more urgent matter now.

Astolf turned into a courtyard surrounded by a covered walkway. The roof was held up by white marble columns that gleamed like a giant skeleton in the moonlight. The air was still in here, and cold. *Like a tomb*, Astolf thought with a shiver. He walked on, wearing the face of a holy man just back from prayer in the middle of the night.

There was no one around and Astolf's footsteps rang out. He was approaching a deserted area of the city that had not yet been built on; no one ever came there, he knew. Astolf could feel his heart race. He wished he were heading back to the palace, where there would be torches, warmth and people.

He turned a corner and stopped. There was a man standing up ahead. Astolf flattened himself against the wall in the shadows and waited. The figure was too tall to be the Twister. The man turned his head to listen, evidently having heard the footsteps stop. Astolf heard his own breath rasping and tried to quieten it. The blood was pounding through his veins as the man started walking towards him. Now Astolf saw a thin young face, with a strip of light blue cloth wrapped around the eyes.

So, it's the blind man. There was something sad and chilling about a strong young man who was blind.

Astolf flattened himself against the wall, feeling like a squashed fly. The man came nearer, carrying a long, sturdy stick and walking freely despite his blindness. Astolf waited, almost choking on his breath. The man stopped right in front of him and looked straight at Astolf, as if he had perfect sight.

'What are you doing standing there, Astolf?' he said.

Astolf tried not to breathe. The man thrust with his stick at great speed and shoved Astolf in the stomach. A wave of red-hot pain flashed over his body and he bent over and gasped.

'You think I can't hear your scared breathing, Astolf? Or your rattling money bag? Or smell your greed?'

Astolf stood up, fighting for breath.

'She's waiting,' the blind man said. 'You don't want to keep her waiting any longer, do you?'

Astolf trembled with fear. If anyone had ever kept her waiting, they were dead now, he was sure of that. He forced himself to stand up, despite the burning in his stomach.

'Down there.' The blind man pointed with his stick.

Astolf walked into the shadows, hearing the blind man behind him. *Right at this moment, Dayraven might be escaping with the scroll.* But there was nothing to be done for now.

Up ahead stood a giant sort of carrying-chair covered by a tall, pointed white canopy. Eight handles stuck out of the couch at the front, back and sides. The eight men who carried the couch stood in the shadows, all dressed in black and armed with swords.

Astolf stopped. The blind man stepped in front of him to one side and waved Astolf forward. He walked up to the canopy.

A big *shatranj* board on high legs stood in front of the canopy, and a pile of cushions sat next to it. Astolf felt a thrill run through him as a woman's hand appeared through the opening and began setting up the *shatranj* pieces on the board. The hand was perfect, with long, elegant fingers, and wore an ornate ring on the middle finger. It was all he had ever seen of her. Astolf imagined yet again how perfect

64

the body and face must be that belonged to that hand. Apart from the ring, there was no jewellery on the hand, no sleeve at the slender wrist that might have helped him even guess where she was from. He could just see her outline through the thin material.

'I got here as quickly as I could, Malombra,' Astolf said.

'Sit down,' said the woman's voice from behind the canopy. 'Now we can continue our game – I remember exactly where all the pieces were.'

The voice sent flames of lust racing through Astolf's body as it always did. It promised all the pleasures of the world. Astolf hesitated. The voice giggled in a way that thrust shivers of desire through him.

'Hurry up, Astolf. You know you have to hurry if you want to play with me.'

'I have no time now, Malombra.'

'You should always have time for me. I made you a high priest; I made you rich. You think you could control Calvo without my potions that make him your slave?'

Astolf sat down on the cushions behind the white pieces. Malombra moved a piece on the board and they began to play. Malombra was one of the great masters of the game, he knew.

'I haven't forgotten all you've done for me, Malombra.'

'Really? I know who you are working for.'

Astolf jumped. She knew about Him.

'From now on, you will work for me,' Malombra said. 'I want that scroll – oh, yes, I know all about your scheme. I hear things from my spies.'

'But if you know who I'm working for, then you know what He would do to me if I betray Him.'

65

She laughed. 'You must know what I will do to you if you refuse me. Now tell me what is going on. I'm sure you don't want to displease me.'

Astolf wondered yet again what lay on the other side of the curtain. "Malombra" meant "evil shadow" in Apollinian. Did that mean she was from the old empire of Apollinia in the hot south far away? No one knew. They said her beauty defied belief and that it was worth a man damning his soul forever to possess her just once. Any man who could beat her at *shatranj* was allowed on the other side of the white veil. And any man who lost a game to her owed her his life. Astolf gulped and moved again.

A sweet sort of fragrance always hung around Malombra, but Astolf could not identify it. Her voice was somehow indefinable – she could have been from anywhere. There were many stories about the unimaginable delights Malombra could give to any man she allowed behind the veil and onto her couch. Not just with her beauty but with her matchless skills in the arts of love and the pleasure potions she concocted. But there were also stories about the tortures and poisons she inflicted on those who angered her. Astolf shuddered. He had no choice; somehow, he would have to play for time with Him.

'The hunchback – the Twister – had the job of getting the scroll,' Astolf said. 'He killed the Jaelite but did not get the scroll.'

'Where is it now?'

'Dayraven, son of Urland, has it. The daughter of Ado of Metos is with him, dressed as a man. The Twister has gone mad and run off.'

'That's better, Astolf – tell me everything, always. You know better than to make me angry. Your plan is not going well, is it? You need my help.'

The hand moved an elephant. Astolf felt his heart thudding inside him. He jumped in fear and knocked one of his chariots off the board. Apart from her tortures and poisons that kept the victim alive in agony for days, Malombra kept prisoners in tiny holes under the floor in various places. She loved to sit above, listening to their screams and groans, they said, and Astolf had no doubt it was true.

'But, Malombra – we're only fighting Dayraven. If I go and get some of my own men now, we can finish this and get the scroll.'

'You think it will be so easy to beat Dayraven? He is the son of Urland and a great fighter with powerful knowledge. You've always overvalued yourself, Astolf.'

'I've known Dayraven for years and I'm sure I can get the better of him.'

'And I'm sure you can't. Not without help – the sort of help I can give you. Go to the tombs outside the north wall.'

'The tombs?'

'Someone's waiting for you there. Explain the situation as clearly as your clumsy mouth can, and don't get in the way when they go to work. Remember, you're just a tool in all this.'

Astolf made to speak but stopped. He wanted to ask who was waiting for him, but decided it was better not to.

Astolf turned to go. 'I will not fail you, Malombra.'

'We will go on with our game next time. When all this is over, if you've pleased me, I'll let you see me, whether you win this game or not.'

The ice in Astolf's veins turned to molten fire. No man ever saw Malombra unless –

'See you, Malombra? You – you mean –'

'I mean see me.'

Astolf started to sweat again, this time with boiling lust. To see her, to get behind that canopy, on Malombra's couch – that was worth more than any amount of wealth, power or revenge. Now he wasn't afraid of anyone or anything. He strode off, feeling like a giant. From behind the canopy he heard the distant tinkling of silver laughter.

Astolf hurried on. A cold wind blew in his face, but he hardly felt it. When he finished the task, Malombra would let him see her. *See her.* The other times he'd done jobs for Malombra, he'd always been well paid with money and power, but now she was prepared to pay with herself. Whatever was at stake here must be immensely important.

Astolf felt a stab of fear – by working for Malombra about the scroll, he was betraying Him. But Malombra was offering herself! He would take the risk. He had no choice, in any case.

He turned onto the path leading to the tombs. Dawn was near, but here outside the city, it was very dark. The *clop-clop* of a horse's hooves and the barking of a dog seemed a long way off.

For the first time, Astolf felt the cold. Who was waiting out there? He slowed down as the thought hit him that it might be a trap; maybe Malombra was secretly displeased with him.

His thoughts filled with scenes of sudden death jumping at him out of the darkness, followed by a quick burial in an open tomb already waiting for him. Astolf shuddered. He could already smell the damp, freshly dug soil, hear the crunching slide of the shovel as it filled in his grave and feel the cool, moist earth running over his lifeless body as it sprawled at the bottom of the open grave. *Don't be stupid*, he told himself. *If I were dead, how could I feel anything?* He walked on and then stopped again. *So, they mean to bury me alive!*

But why would Malombra come all the way here for that? She would just send a killer, as she had done so many times before to other people. *With my help.* And if he didn't go now to the tombs, Malombra's killer would find him somewhere else. Astolf tried to warm his thoughts by picturing the delights waiting on the other side of Malombra's veil.

He reached the edge of the graveyard. The cold licked his face like a giant slimy tongue. He glanced around. The tombs spread out all around him. The moon was hidden by the clouds, and the tombs shone dully in the darkness. There was no order or plan to the way these slabs of rock lay about; they were scattered like boulders on a hillside, rising up out of the clinging grass.

Astolf walked on, shrinking away from the towering statues that soared above some of the tombs. Other graves were covered with high arches. The swampy ground had made some of them lean over in time. Astolf edged away from them, as if they were about to fall on him.

He stopped in the middle of the field of the dead and looked around; the wind tousled the grass, but there was no other sound or movement. The tall statues made him shiver. He was alone there with the dead. Then the clouds covering the moon slid aside and the graveyard was bathed in white light.

Astolf shivered in fear – one of the statues was alive. He fell backwards and felt nothing more.

***

In the deep shadows near Malombra's canopy, the Twister turned onto his other side. His hump had been a comfortable cushion as he lay on the hard ground, but now it was pulsing after everything he had heard, and he wanted to enjoy the feeling.

He had followed Astolf to Malombra's canopy and it had been worthwhile for the information he had gained. He had been working for Astolf who was apparently working for some unnamed person – "Him" – but now Astolf was working for Malombra. The Twister looked up at the stars that poked through the dark clouds. The moon would come back out before too long, he knew, and then it would be time to be on the move again. But not for the moment.

The Twister let his mind drift into his hump, feeling what it felt. It burned red-hot. This woman, Malombra, was so close, he almost felt he could touch her. He looked across at the white peak of her canopy and then lay back again.

So, she really existed! In the dark nights at the hermitage, he had heard stories about this woman of legendary beauty. He and his hump had listened as eagerly as any of the hermits, but he hadn't really believed the stories were anything more than products of the hermits' overactive minds. But she was real and reclining on her couch just a short distance away. His hump was scorching now.

Years before, the most beautiful girls had been happy to share his couch, the Twister remembered, and he'd made them all love his hump. Back then, they'd loved even that, but that was before the nightmare of the hermitage. He thought of one of the many girls, one of the first.

During love-making, he had taken her hands and placed them on his hump. The girl recoiled and pulled her hands away, but she must have seen the anger in his eyes, because she replaced her hands and began stroking the hump.

Afterwards, lying together on the rich couch, she had kept absently touching it. The Twister had felt his hump glowing, and the same feeling spread over his whole body. He could make women do anything he wanted; now this girl would even pretend she liked the hump.

'*Are you wishing I didn't have that?*' he said.

She woke up from her daze and looked at him. '*What?*'

'*That – the hump. I wish it were gone.*'

'*I don't.*'

'*You don't?*'

'*No – it makes you different from other men.*'

'*And you like that?*'

'*Of course. The rest of you is perfect – but this*' – she caressed the hump, digging her nails into it – '*this makes you special. In the dark, it could only be you. It excites me.*'

The Twister's hump glowed even warmer with pleasure, and he turned towards the girl for more.

The Twister came to with a start. The girl and the couch were long gone and he was freezing in the darkness in Axo. Back in the old days, he had had fine couches, wealth and power. Now girls like that would run screaming from his hump; children shouted out names and farmers threw rocks at him. But soon he would have all the good things back and the women would return to his bed. First of them all would be Malombra; he would make her stroke

71

his hump and say how much she adored it. His hump glowed hotter in agreement with this.

He felt like jumping straight through the thin covering of the canopy and onto her couch. Or he could kill her guards and the blind man, and then she would be his, but there were too many of them. There would be other chances, his hump told him. Wherever the scroll was, she wouldn't be far away, so where it went, he would go.

Astolf was working for her now – perhaps he should follow Astolf and kill him. The Twister's fingers itched at the thought. But no! If he could get the scroll for himself, he could sell it to Malombra for whatever he wanted. His hump was sizzling now. Part of the price would be getting under her canopy and onto her couch; he would make her adore his hump. And if he got the scroll, then Astolf could not, and then Malombra would have Astolf killed in the most horrible way. The Twister's hump glowed.

He heard some orders given from inside the canopy and looked around. The eight men picked up the canopy and carried it off, with the blind man following behind with his stick.

The Twister watched them go. Part of his hump was telling him to follow Malombra, but the other part told him to keep an eye on Astolf, Dayraven and the scroll. Then he might get Malombra as well as everything else.

He stood up and patted his hump. *Patience, patience.*

***

Astolf sat up with a start. He didn't know how long he'd been lying on the damp earth. He glanced around; the living statue was still there. It was a dark man sitting on a horse, holding a long-handled axe. The man's hair grew

72

long on his right side, hanging down straight to his shoulders. On the left side, his head was completely shaven. Above the waist he wore only a sort of leather harness that left his chest and arms free. From it hung a lot of axes of different shapes and sizes.

Astolf tried to remember a prayer, or anything at all, but his panic blocked everything. He wanted to run but couldn't. The man on the horse sat staring at him.

The moon vanished for a moment and then reappeared even brighter than before. Now Astolf could see that the man's body was covered with tattoos. They grew thickly, like a forest; the colours and shapes dazzled his eyes in the moonlight.

He saw that the horse was a pale, sickly colour, like a corpse after a few days in the earth. The man jumped off his horse and led the horse closer. He sniffed the air like a hunting dog.

Astolf shivered; he knew who this was now, but tried to take heart. *If he were here to kill me, I'd already be dead.*

The man pointed to a tattoo in the middle of his forehead. It showed a skeleton riding a horse and armed with an axe.

'You're Death, the bounty hunter – one of the Riders,' Astolf said with a shudder. 'I'm High Priest Astolf.'

Death pointed to a tattoo on his left arm. Astolf looked, his heart thundering.

'Malombra,' Astolf said, looking at the tattoo. 'Yes, she asked me to meet you here. She wants a scroll that an old Jaelite brought here to Axo. Malombra's paying you, isn't she?'

Death nodded and pointed to a line of figures spread out across his chest.

Astolf squinted at it. 'How many people are there? Just two.'

Death pointed at his belly.

'A city? You mean which city are they in? Right here – in Axo. At least, they were earlier tonight. In the Octagonal Temple. I'll take you there.'

Astolf made to turn away but his legs trembled too much. Death slipped the big axe into a slit in his horse's saddle. He unravelled a knot on the leather saddlebag and a long flap tumbled down, holding a row of axes; Death took a middle-sized one in either hand and made some whirling swings, the blades gleaming in the moonlight.

Death nodded towards the city and Astolf turned towards the gate. He felt warmer now and his legs hardly shook at all. Astolf unlocked the gate and Death ducked under as he passed through, leading his horse.

As they walked through the empty streets, Astolf felt himself smiling. Soon he would see one of the Riders at work against Dayraven. He licked his lips.

***

Dayraven stood the candle on the altar. He could hear Sunniva climbing the stairs to tidy things up above.

Dayraven stood back to check that nothing was left behind. He looked down at Halakh sprawled in the pool of dried blood. *I'm sorry there's nothing more we can do for you, old friend. If you wanted to tell us something, we're trying to find out what it is. That's why we're going to Metos.*

'Goodbye, Halakh,' Dayraven whispered.

He walked back up the stairs to Sunniva.

'Have you got everything?' she asked.

74

Dayraven patted his tunic. 'Wax tablet – although there's nothing on it that we need at the moment. Scroll –'

'We've solved that.'

'Yes, so I think we can throw it away – but not here. And I've got the bracelet. I hope we can decipher that once we get to Metos.'

'It was many years ago that I saw the other bracelet there, but I'm sure it's the same.'

'Well, like I said, these bracelets are always made as a pair. So, if you remember only one of them, it must have been made together with the one Halakh was wearing.'

Dayraven picked up Urland's sword and hunting horn. They felt so heavy, so substantial, but the father who had owned them was just a misty memory.

'Are you taking those with you?' Sunniva asked.

'Hmm? No – I'm going to put them back on the wall.'

'They were your father's things, so they should belong to you now, Dayraven.'

'They were put in this temple to make a sort of a shrine to him. I think they should stay here.'

Dayraven slotted the horn into the bracket on the wall. The sword had been wrenched out by the killer in black, so it didn't fit back well into the bracket, but he managed to fit it in, slanting down at an angle.

'That's it, then,' Dayraven said, turning around. 'Let's grab our things and go to Metos.'

'This way.' Sunniva crossed to a door on the other side. 'This brings us out on another walkway.'

Dayraven followed as she opened the door. *Goodbye, Halakh.*

* * *

Death walked on behind Astolf, leading his horse. He saw Astolf shiver.

'There won't be many soldiers about,' Astolf said. 'They're out chasing an – an intruder.'

All around, Death could hear the city waking up. Dawn was tinting the roofs light pink and orange. Death snuffed the air and tensed for action.

'High Priest! Have you seen –'

Five soldiers came out of an alleyway and looked shocked when they saw him.

'It's Death the Rider – get him!' the soldier in front said, drawing his sword.

Astolf crept back against the wall.

Death let go of his horse's bridle and leapt into the middle of the soldiers with an axe in either hand. The first two soldiers swung their swords. Death swerved between them, slicing with his axes through the gaps in their armour, feeling the hot blood spray his face.

Death left the axes where they'd landed and whipped out two small throwing axes from his harness. With flicks of his wrists, he whizzed them into the throats of two more of the soldiers, and they slumped with a gurgling sound.

The last soldier turned to run, but Death pounced on him, grabbed the man around the head and twisted. A loud crack sounded and the soldier fell, his neck broken.

Death turned back and picked up his axes. Astolf squashed himself further back against the wall.

Death slipped his throwing axes back into his harness and glanced at the crumpled bodies of the soldiers. The smell of death was strong, but needless killing annoyed him. He wasn't being paid to kill those men. They should have stayed out of the way. Killing wasn't something he did for fun or out of anger; it was an art, a science, a way of life. Being paid a lot for doing it was a sign that he did it well. A person who killed out of jealousy or rage was a fool; he'd do it badly, most likely get himself killed, regret it afterwards and gain nothing from it. Pointless.

He led his horse and followed Astolf again through the streets. The smell of so many people was sickening. Death hated cities; he thought the high buildings were crowding in on him, waiting to crush him, and there were too many people. But a bounty hunter killed those he was paid to kill, and often they were trying to hide in cities, like ants in their nest, so he went there. It didn't change anything; they died just the same in busy towns as out in the open field, only more of them.

He watched Astolf's legs trembling as he walked. This man was trying to hide his fear, but Death had seen it too often to be fooled. There was the smell of fear as well. No mistaking that.

It had been the first smell he remembered. In the dusty village where he was born, nearly everyone stank of fear. He used to think the air itself smelt like that, and only later did he learn that that was what fear smelt like.

Where he grew up, the world was easy. Men shot arrows into squealing animals, spears into enemies, seized women. Those who did these things best and more often got the most out of life.

The army worked the same way. When they came to take him away from the village, he didn't know who he was fighting for or against, or where, but it didn't matter. He shoved axes into men and was paid for it.

He stroked the blade of the axe he carried. He had loved the axe from the moment he first saw one. So strong. An axe could tear shields and armour apart to get to the hot, beating flesh and blood underneath.

Death had loved fighting wars. Then the enemy caught him and tore at his flesh. He swore at them until they put a knife in his mouth and tore out his tongue and left him to choke on the blood.

Somehow, he lived. Strange people found him, looked after him. They tattooed their bodies and talked in grunting sounds. Death did not speak their language, but there was no need, anyway; talking was pointless. There was nothing new to understand and the world was the same everywhere. People smelt differently; that was all.

He killed these tattooed people's enemies; who they were and why they were enemies, he didn't know. In between killing seasons, they gave him tattoos. He learnt to talk through the pictures on his skin, so that speech was not necessary. Over time, he had the tattoos made to show all the things he needed to say: money, weapons, men, women, animals, food, drink, cities. He became a walking painting. The most savage beasts often had the most painted skins, he had seen; the animals that put claws and fangs into other animals.

Then one day he left. There were no more enemies to kill and the picture people had begun to fear him and his axes, so he went and killed elsewhere. It was always the same. Men died when he put axe blades into them; women screamed, some with pleasure, some with horror.

Over time, he met three others who understood him. They thought the same way and each was as good with their own weapons as he was with his axes. The Riders: the greatest bounty hunters in the world, and the most expensive. They never failed, either singly or together. With them, there was no need to talk. The others were far away at the moment, killing in different parts of the world, and he had his job to do here in this cold tomb of a city.

78

Death watched the buildings become denser around him; they were getting near the centre. He sniffed the air. There was fear there but not fear of him, just fear of death – but also of life. People crowded together in towns, trying to hide from both life and death, but every city wall had its cracks where they could both slip in.

They reached one of the towers of the temple, and Astolf shoved the key into the lock, shivering, and the key rattled as he turned it.

The stale smell of the stairs hit Death as Astolf pushed the door open. There was no lamp lit and the stairway was black. Death left his horse outside and walked towards the door, holding an axe in either hand.

Death stabbed one of the axes forward, telling Astolf to go on ahead. Astolf gulped and went in, and the clammy air wrapped itself around them. Astolf fumbled for the lamp and flint that were left at the entrance, and Death tapped him on the shoulder with the flat of an axe. *No light.* Astolf jumped.

They walked on in the dark. Astolf paused at the door leading into the centre of the Temple, and Death prodded him in the back with an axe. Astolf tensed and pushed open the door.

Nothing jumped out at them except the brightness of the candles. Death pushed past Astolf and strode towards the altar with one of his axes slung in his harness. An old man lay dead, killed by a throwing axe in the chest. It had been thrown well; the blade had dug far in to the flesh.

Death pointed at Astolf.

'Yes, I know him. He's Halakh, the Jaelite – he had the scroll. I sent someone to kill him. Someone else probably took the scroll, but I'll check whether he's still got it.' Astolf squatted down next to the body and searched. 'It's not here. Whoever's taken it is long gone by now.'

Death heard a faint noise above. He rushed for the stairs, taking out his second axe.

***

Sunniva staggered under the pile of things she was carrying. She had thought it was safer if Dayraven waited while she went to get their clothes and supplies. She was a soldier with palace insignia, so no one would stop her. She crossed a courtyard, peeping around the side of the pile. There was no one around. She and Dayraven could carry all of this to their horses, and then they would soon be out of Axo and in the open. It would be easier then; here there were too many enemies close together.

She thought of when she had seen the Jaelite bracelet in her father's study. It had just been there one day; she wasn't sure whether he had meant her to see it. Something else kept prodding at her mind, telling her to stay. Sunniva walked up to Dayraven.

'Now we're ready to leave,' Dayraven said. 'Let's get the horses – it's getting light.'

Sunniva dumped the pile on the ground with a loud slap. 'We can't.'

'Why not?'

'We have to go back to the Octagonal Temple.'

'Why?'

'Those clues Halakh left for us – we haven't used them all.'

'Yes, we did.'

'Some details we didn't use, but there's a reason they were there. It's the seeing game.'

'The what?'

'My father used to test how closely I observed things; he always said if a detail's there, it's got something to tell you. He would ask questions about something I had seen to encourage me to take note of details – I used to call it the "seeing game". Remember the cow and the sword in the pictures on the throne seat – the two at the very top, above all the other pictures. We solved the puzzle without those two pictures.'

'We didn't need them.'

'Then why were they there at all? Why would Halakh take the time to scratch pictures that we didn't need?'

Dayraven frowned. 'I don't know.'

'I do. They weren't meant to stand for Jael letters – they stand for the things themselves.'

'A cow? What are you talking about?'

'Urland's hunting horn was made from a cow's horn. That's what that picture stands for –'

'And the sword is Urland's sword! We have to take them with us.'

'Yes. Let's go.'

Sunniva led the way back to the upper part of the temple. How much longer would they be free to come and go? Sooner or later, someone would find Halakh's body, and then the palace and the whole town would be unsafe.

Sunniva stopped where the walkway met another passage, and Dayraven stopped behind her. She strained her ears so hard in listening that they started to ring. There was no sound other than the distant murmur of the waking city. Sunniva walked on and Dayraven followed.

She stopped at one of the doors leading into the inner part of the temple and turned to look back at Dayraven. How long had she known him? They'd only met that night over Halakh's body, but it seemed so long ago and so much had changed.

Sunniva stepped inside the upper level of the temple, her hand on her sword hilt. Everything was just the same as before. She nodded towards the wall where the sword and horn hung. Dayraven moved to get them while Sunniva guarded the stairs.

Behind her, she heard Dayraven trying to take the horn and sword out of the brackets where he'd hung them, but there was another noise below. She could feel the blood pulsing faster through her with the danger. Sunniva half drew her sword and glanced back at Dayraven. He had already taken down the horn and was struggling with the sword, but his face showed that he had heard the noise downstairs as well.

Sunniva listened again. There came a voice – Astolf's. So, Astolf had sent the killer in black! She could see from Dayraven's fierce look that he had heard that as well. Sunniva drew her sword fully and listened. It sounded as if Astolf were answering someone, but she couldn't hear the questions. Was it Halakh's killer down there with him? Maybe if she risked looking, they might know who he was.

She edged to the stairs and peeked down, then pulled her head back. Astolf was looking at Halakh's body. Seeing the man with him sent a chill down Sunniva's spine. The half-shaved head, the tattoos, the axe – it could only be Death, one of the Riders. Her father had told her about them, but they were just a myth, weren't they?

Sunniva turned back to look at Dayraven. He had taken down the sword and the scabbard, and looked like he wanted to charge downstairs and attack Astolf. Sunniva shook her head and Dayraven nodded and tied the sword around his waist.

She heard rushing feet coming up the stairs. Sunniva's mind was racing. There were two of them against Death and Astolf, but there might be more enemies coming. They had to get out of the temple; that was the important thing. Whatever secret Halakh and her father were trying to tell them, it could only survive if they escaped. She moved towards the door they'd come in by, but stopped. Death could cut them off before they got there, and someone else might be waiting outside.

Sunniva nodded towards a low, narrow set of stairs on the other side. Dayraven looked shocked, but she heard him following as she charged upwards. *There won't be anyone guarding this way out, because no one else knows about it. Or do they?*

She slung her shield over her back. As Sunniva ran, the stale, musty air choked her nose and throat. It smelt like the tomb of Merech that had terrified her as a child, but she blocked the thought as soon as it arose. Sunniva paused, her breath rasping and the blood pounding in her head. Dayraven rushed up next to her; she could hear other feet running down below. She looked around. They were in a dark, low room, and the little light that seeped in showed stacks of dusty old things. What Sunniva needed to find was something very different but much more valuable to them now. Her father had told her that there was a way out; he had designed it to allow large objects to be brought in and out without going through the temple. Sunniva whirled around, sensing that Dayraven was searching for the same thing. She saw a chink of light peeping out from behind some tables in the corner and rushed over to it; there was the door. She put her sword away, moved the tables and pushed the door open, knowing that Dayraven was behind her.

The door was stiff and raised up a cloud of dust when Sunniva opened it. She almost sneezed but fought against it. Dawn light streamed in, deep orange and red. After the darkness and closed space of the temple, Sunniva thought it was the most beautiful thing she had ever seen. The city of Axo stretched out ahead of her, the royal palace dominating the view. Around it sprawled colourful temples topped with gold Akhens and spacious stone villas that gradually merged with wooden houses and fields until the forest that stretched to the horizon.

The door was low and Sunniva stooped to get through. When she stood up, the emperor's capital city was far below, all around her. For an instant she was dizzy, but the fresh air tasted sweet. Sunniva heard Dayraven battling to get out as well. She drew her sword, took her shield on her arm and headed to the left, where there was an outside staircase on the opposite side to the palace. The great dome of the Octagonal Temple soared up on her left as she ran, trying to keep as low as possible. Against the rising sun, she could easily be spotted if anyone happened to look up at the top of the temple. It was quiet behind her, and the city spun below as Sunniva turned around and around to the left.

She reached the stairs, panting. They were narrow and steep, but going backwards, they should be easy enough. Sunniva slid her sword back in its scabbard, swung her shield over her back again and looked for Dayraven. He was gone. Sunniva sent her mind rushing on. Had he been caught? Surely, she would have heard the sounds of fighting, but there was no sound at all.

Everything Sunniva's father had told her about the Octagonal Temple, everything she had seen of it, flooded through her mind at the same time. Then it came to her –

there was another staircase, just like this one, on the other side. It was near the palace and therefore riskier. Maybe Dayraven had gone to the right when they got to this walkway, instead of to the left as she had. In that case, he would find his way down, and if they both kept walking around the base of the temple, they would meet. Maybe Dayraven was already waiting for her down there.

Sunniva looked around one last time; everything was still and quiet. She took a step backwards down the stairs, and the world lurched under her feet. *Don't look down. Take one step at a time.* She stared up at the great dome that seemed ready to fall on her. The wind felt stronger and tugged at her clothes. After a few steps, Sunniva felt the weight of her shield dragging her shoulders back, so she hunched them forward to get better balance. The heavy mail shirt and helmet pressed her neck and back downwards, as if trying to crush them. Sunniva gritted her teeth and kept putting one foot down, and then the other. *Don't look down.*

About halfway down, more thoughts pushed at her mind. What if Dayraven was trapped up there somewhere, and she was running away? Sunniva almost stopped and straight away felt dizzy. She blocked out the thoughts and kept going. Sunniva could feel the ground rising up underneath her and risked a look down. Not far now, but there was a horse by the door below, a horse the colour of a dead body. She shivered. Sunniva looked back up, steadied herself, and kept going.

Standing on the last step, Sunniva looked around. She was next to one of the doors leading into the temple, but Dayraven was not there. The worrying thoughts prodded at her mind again. *We'll find each other.*

She jumped to the ground. It felt very solid. Sunniva took a deep breath and looked up at the stairs stretching above her; it didn't seem possible that she had climbed down them, but she had made it.

Sunniva heard a rushing sound of feet and Death burst through the door, holding an axe in each hand. His tattooed face was twisted as if screaming in triumph, but no sound came out. Sunniva wrenched the shield off her back and drew her sword. Death swung an axe and Sunniva blocked with her shield. The blade tore deep into the wood of the shield, and the blow made her stagger.

Sunniva stepped back and caught her breath. Death circled, waiting for an opening. *He wants to enjoy it, killing a woman. That's why he's taking his time.* She had never faced two axes in battle before. They were deadly in attack the way Death used them, but without a shield, he had little defence. Sunniva knew she had to attack.

She jumped forward, thrusting her shield out as cover but also to hide which way she would swing her sword. An axe blade struck the shield, but Sunniva pushed it out and away from her and swerved to her right. She sliced with her sword, and Death raised the other axe just in time to block the sword. Sunniva could see the surprise on his face. *He must have thought this would be easier.*

She could hear voices and running feet. Soldiers were coming. Sunniva saw that Death heard them as well, and she could see that he didn't want to be found by them anymore than she did. She could also tell that Death would not be the first to run away from the fight. *And neither will I.*

Sunniva made the same attack again, but this time she sprang to her left to chop from the other side. Death blocked with an axe, and the other axe blade grazed

Sunniva's shoulder. Her mail shirt would avoid the worst, but there would still be a scrape and a bruise.

Sunniva circled away. Death's face was so twisted that the tattoos seemed to be coming alive. Sunniva kept her eyes on the axe blades as he came closer.

She heard again the noise of many people somewhere, but it had changed. There was an edge of panic to the sound now, and something else: a thundering rumble as if a hundred carriages were running out of control down a hillside.

A blasting noise rang out, then another on top of that, blaring like an army of trolls on the march. Sunniva had seen pictures like that in manuscripts; thousands of trolls rising up out of the ground, but that couldn't be happening today in Axo. *Could it?*

Death jumped back against the wall of the temple, looking for another opening. Sunniva's body was aching from the impact of the blows she had blocked. The roaring noise was getting louder, and so was the thundering; whatever it was, it was coming towards them. Death's horse was stamping, wanting to run.

The noise was deafening now. Sunniva risked a quick look. The emperor's elephant raced around the Octagonal Temple, trumpeting with its raised trunk; Dayraven was riding it on a high saddle, blasting on Urland's hunting horn.

Death's horse panicked and ran. Sunniva stepped back out of the way. Dayraven steered the elephant at Death, who pressed himself back against the wall, trying to get clear, but there was nowhere to go. As the elephant reached him, Death chopped at it with an axe. Dayraven blocked with his sword and the elephant ran on. Even over the noise, Sunniva heard the snap as one of Death's bones broke under the elephant's foot. He slumped back against the wall, roaring in pain and anger.

Sunniva glanced around; a swarm of soldiers was running towards them.

'Get on!' Dayraven shouted.

Sunniva looked back and saw that he had slowed the elephant down, waiting for her. She ran for it, hearing the roar increasing behind her. Dayraven reached down and helped her up the giant animal's side and on to the saddle. She saw that the elephant was loaded with all of their gear.

'Can you really ride this thing?' Sunniva called out.

'I've had a strange life. Now let's see what he can do.'

Dayraven dug with a sort of stick behind the elephant's ear and blew the horn again. Sunniva's ears rang and she felt the great beast pick up speed.

The shouts of the soldiers faded behind them. She covered Dayraven with her shield and looked around. Astolf was standing at the edge of the square, shouting orders to some of the men. She couldn't see Death.

The elephant charged out of the square, getting faster all the time. Sunniva felt herself hurled around but then found a way of sitting more steadily.

Two soldiers ran out of a side street on their left. They thrust with spears at Dayraven, and Sunniva stuck her shield in the way and hacked off the point of one of the spears. Dayraven turned the elephant to the right and blew on the horn again. The elephant lifted its trunk and replied.

'This is the longest way out of town!' Sunniva shouted.

'It's downhill, so we'll really get some speed up!'

The street began to dip. The elephant was going faster and faster, and the buildings went past in a blur.

'This elephant's gone crazy!' she shouted.

'The rubbish the emperor feeds him has stirred him up. Hold on!'

Sunniva clasped her helmet with one hand and looked past Dayraven towards the gate at the bottom of the hill. The guards were pointing and running around like ants, trying to shut the gate. Dayraven blew the horn again and the elephant went even faster. Sunniva no longer felt the juddering there was before; the elephant was racing along smoothly.

The gate was swinging closed. Sunniva knew how heavy it was, made to withstand a siege; maybe even the elephant wouldn't be able to break through once it was fully shut.

Dayraven blew the horn again and the elephant trumpeted and picked up even more speed. Sunniva saw a group of soldiers take a stand in front of the closing gate. The elephant went straight at them and Sunniva saw the soldiers leap out of the way.

The gate was almost closed as the elephant reached it. Dayraven crouched low and she did the same. The impact jolted Sunniva back in the saddle, and there was a crash of broken wood and wrenching metal.

When Sunniva raised her head, they were out of the city and thundering into the country, and she relaxed.

'Easy!' Dayraven said with a grin back at her.

Sunniva smiled in return. *Easy enough for now.*

PART TWO

The Royal Palace, Axo. Later that morning.

Emperor Calvo felt the hot water hold him in its grip. He opened his eyes and looked around through the rising steam; he was alone in the giant bath to which he had returned. A few servants and guards hung back in the shadows, but everyone else had gone. *All chasing the intruder, or trying to find out the cause of all the noise. While I, master of everything and everyone stay in the comforting hot water.*

The thought rose yet again in Calvo's mind that something was very wrong in the empire when the emperor stayed in the bath and let others take charge. Things had been very different in the past. Now he couldn't keep his thoughts on one thing for long. He managed to concentrate on important business for a while, but then seeing his elephant or the Octagonal Temple suddenly became the most important thing and he couldn't concentrate on anything else. After a while, he could only think of getting back in the bath. A fog almost always covered his mind.

Calvo tried to steel himself to action, but the soothing water held on to him and he subsided. *It won't hold me for much longer, though.*

'It can't hold you unless you let it, my lord.'

Calvo looked around. Through the steam, he could see a tall figure with a much smaller one next to it.

'Who's there?'

The shapes moved closer and Calvo saw a clean-shaven man holding a young boy by the hand.

'Urland? But it can't be –'

'You remember my son Dayraven, my lord – he must have grown a lot since you last saw him.'

'How – how old is he now?'

'Tell the emperor how old you are, Dayraven.'

'Five,' the boy said, and then hid his face.

'He only pretends to be shy, my lord.'

'He looks exactly like you, Urland.'

'So everyone says.'

'You are dressed for travelling, Urland – where are you going?'

'I came to ask your permission, my lord. Ganelo has sent me a message.'

'Ganelo?'

'He is camped near Ronca, on the far side of the valley, and requests urgent reinforcements. I plan on going there quickly with a small force and having the others follow once they are gathered.'

'Why Ronca?'

'Ganelo says there have been raids by border tribes from the hills, and towns have been burned.'

'I am surprised that Ganelo would ask you for assistance – you know he has always been your rival.'

'Oh, I know that, but probably no one else is close enough with an armed force.'

'Someone else could lead the men.'

'Ganelo would say I declined to help him personally when I was needed.'

'I don't like this, Urland. So sudden, and Ganelo –'

'With respect, my lord, there's no time to lose.'

'Very well, you may go. And good luck to you.'

'Thank you, my lord. The boy – you know that without his mother, he has only me....'

'Don't worry about that, Urland. He will always be looked after, no matter what happens.'

Calvo closed his eyes for a moment. When he opened them again, he was alone. *Of course I am. That was just a memory from a quarter of a century ago. I could have stopped Urland from going, saved him. Instead, he died in an ambush in the Valley of Ronca. Caught in a trap set by Ganelo, father of Astolf. That was when things started to go wrong. Ganelo is dead now, but Astolf has taken his place and the same thing is happening again. I promised to look after Urland's son, but instead, I let him stay a hostage for fifteen years. And maybe I have let Dayraven fall into a trap as well.*

He looked around once more. There had been a time when he had a dozen people he could trust completely. Above all, there had been Urland. Now Urland's son had come back, a son who looked so much like his father. And he, the emperor, had sent him away, into what sounded like a trap of some kind. *Astolf's trap.* Generations of traitors surrounded him, from father to son. While he was left alone in the bath, coming out only to feed his elephant. And if he called out, no one would come. Except one – Astolf. Calvo no longer trusted the medicine Astolf gave him for his health. He had poured it away that night without drinking it and would never drink it again. Calvo filled with shame at the thought of how low he had sunk in these years. He had even been cruel to his own family.

But now it was time to come out of the bath and take back his empire. Dayraven had been right: the Fifth Unmasking must be close and a lot of preparation was needed. Everyone had to play their part. Including the emperor. He needed to get away and clear his mind of Astolf's influence.

Calvo heard footsteps approaching.

'Who's there?' he called out into the steam.

A black figure stepped forward. *Astolf.*

'Just me, my lord.'

Astolf lifted his shoulders a little to raise his habit off his shoulders, where it hung soaked in sweat. A trickle of moisture ran down his forehead. His face was not as composed as usual, and the emperor saw a flash of fear and deceit. Deceit above all. *How could I not see it before? But I have to be careful. By now, the empire is full of my enemies and Astolf's friends. Maybe it's just my imagination.* The emperor glanced again at Astolf's sweaty face and felt sure that he was not imagining things. *He's been running. I've been running from things for years, even when I'm just sitting in this bath. But not anymore.*

'Yes, it is you, Astolf. I see you very clearly now, even through the steam. What's going on out there? I hear all sorts of strange noises.'

'Bad news. Dayraven –'

The emperor felt the water turn to ice around him. 'Dayraven? What's happened to him?'

'I hate to tell you, my lord, but he's a traitor. A killer working for the duke of Theodorica, it seems.'

'What?'

'He met the old Jaelite in the Octagonal Temple tonight. And killed him. I've seen the body myself.'

'Killed him? Dayraven?'

'I'm afraid so.'

'What about the intruder?'

'Intruder?'

'The one the guards were chasing earlier tonight.'

'A false alarm. There seems no doubt that Dayraven killed the Jaelite.'

94

'How can you be so sure?'

'Because he ran off like a murderer. The daughter of Ado of Metos is with him, dressed as one of your soldiers.'

'Sunniva? What's going on?'

The emperor's mind was struggling to rush on through a swamp of sluggishness. He realised how deeply his mind was buried under whatever Astolf had been feeding him. He knew he had to buy time to think. And to act.

'I'm shocked by what you're telling me, Astolf. But if you're so sure of this, why didn't you stop Dayraven?'

'We tried. But he and Sunniva had special help.'

'Not more traitors around me?'

'No, my lord – your elephant, Abul Ahaz.'

'My elephant?'

'They used him to break down the city gate and then rode away. Don't worry, my lord – I will get your elephant back for you. And I'll get Dayraven.'

'Do we know whether the Jaelite was carrying any secret or message? Perhaps Dayraven has taken it with him.'

'I don't think so – it looks as though Dayraven's job was just to kill the Jaelite. But we'll make him tell us the whole story when we catch him.'

'He is still the son of Urland. If you catch him, you will treat him well until we know the truth of all this.'

Astolf smiled his crooked smile. 'Of course, my lord.'

The emperor lifted himself out of the water. For a moment, the damp air gripped him in a cold embrace. Two servants came forward to help him.

'I will have to leave you to look after this, Astolf,' Calvo said as the servants dried him. 'I'm going away to rest. I will spend time at one of my hunting lodges.'

'So soon this year, my lord?'

'I'm older and more tired every day, Astolf.'

'I understand. If you will allow me, I will go and take this Dayraven business in hand.'

'Good. And let's hope the truth comes out.'

'Don't forget to take your medicine, my lord.'

'I'll remember.'

Astolf walked away, shrugging again to lift his habit from his sweaty back.

The emperor began dressing. *I'll leave as soon as I can. For a different kind of hunting.*

***

Dayraven steered the elephant into a clearing in the forest and brought it to a stop. The late morning sun was shielded by the huge trees. He could feel the elephant panting; they had been on the move for hours since breaking out of Axo.

'We'll get off here,' he said and jumped to the ground. 'The river's about two hundred paces down that way. Here, let me help you – it's trickier than dismounting from a horse.'

'Thanks.' Sunniva clambered down next to him, staggering a little. 'It's trickier, all right, and so high up! Are you going to let the elephant go now?'

'Yes. He's tired, which will make him harder to control. He wants to wander off on his own. We would be very easy to find if we keep him – we must be the only people around here riding an elephant. Give me a hand to unload him.'

Dayraven reached for a pack of food and laid it on the ground. The elephant waited to be freed of its burden.

96

'No one came after us, did they?' Sunniva heaved a pack of clothes to the ground.

'Not that we know of – someone will, though. The Riders never give up once they've taken on a job, and then there's Astolf.'

'So, we'd better make a good plan.'

'You know the area better than me – what do you think?'

'We let the elephant go here, as you said. It's going to be safer travelling at night, so we hide in the forest, eat, rest and prepare ourselves until dark. Then we go on foot until we find a boat to take us upriver to Metos.'

'Anyone who's chasing us would think of that, wouldn't they? They would probably expect us to go to your father's house in Metos or my estate up north near Liga. They will be guarding the river.'

'I think we can reach Metos by boat before anyone could put guards on the river. Then we find the missing bracelet in my father's house. And then – then we'll think of something else, depending on what the bracelets tell us.'

'Agreed.' Dayraven went up to the elephant and stroked its rough trunk. 'Thank you, Abul Ahaz – we couldn't have got out of there without you. Now you can go back to your sweet food.'

The elephant wandered off, brushing the trees aside as if they were nothing.

'Will he find his way back to Axo, do you think?' Sunniva asked.

'Oh, yes. He's got a better sense of direction and a better memory than we have. Now let's sort out the things we really need – we'll test our own sense of direction later.'

'Good. But first, I think you'll have to change clothes. Anyone coming after us will be looking for someone dressed like you are. That tunic was clearly made in Magia. And the trousers, the shoes. Everything.'

Dayraven felt the cloth of the tunic and thought of the baking hot day in Theodorica when he'd first worn it. He had hoped these clothes would help him blend in back in Faustia, but he had seen immediately how different the cloth and style were. Still, leaving them behind would be the final break with his old life.

'You're right,' he said. 'We've got some other clothes among those bags we carried on the elephant, haven't we?'

'Yes.'

'And I'll have to cut my beard and hair as well – that will help with the disguise. My tan has already faded a lot, so the paler skin underneath the beard won't stand out so much.'

'I'll do it for you.'

'With what?'

'This.' Sunniva lifted up her sword.

'That?'

'I was only joking.' Sunniva laughed. 'I'll use my knife – it's nice and sharp.'

Dayraven pulled off his shoes and trousers and stood in front of her. He thought he saw a glint of more than mere soldierly interest in her eyes. *Or maybe that's just my imagination.*

'If we're going in disguise and we're captured and searched, anyone could tell you're not from here by any of your clothes – even your underpants.'

Dayraven lifted his tunic over his head. 'This whole empire's crazy. In Magia, it was hot all the time and we went around fully dressed. Here, it's cold and everyone runs around in the nude.'

'Well, I'm not complaining.'

Dayraven turned his back and stepped out of his underpants. 'Why doesn't the emperor just go ahead and make this the national costume?'

'Stop making so much out of so little.'

Dayraven felt himself blushing. 'Well, is this my disguise, or do I get something else to wear?'

'Put these on.' Sunniva threw him a bundle of clothes that landed on his shoulder.

'These are priest's clothes.'

'Since I've been a soldier, I've made a habit of grabbing whatever might come in handy. Now that there are two of us, we can go in disguise as two of the emperor's travelling judges – they always travel in pairs. One is always a priest and the other is not.'

'You should be the priest.'

'Why me?'

'You've got the right look – pure, soft, unworldly.'

'Doesn't sound like any priest I've ever seen. But, all right – throw those back and take these.'

Dayraven caught the wad of ordinary clothes that Sunniva tossed to him and lobbed back the priest's clothes.

'I've just realised something,' Sunniva said. 'If I cut your hair and beard when you're dressed, bits of hair will stick to your clothes. Someone might expect you to shave and cut your hair as a disguise, so that's something they would be looking for So, you'll have to stay like that for a while.'

'You think of everything, don't you?'

'Some things I try not to think about.'

Dayraven thought he saw the hint of a smile on her face. It seemed strange to be playing this sort of game when they were in danger, but after the tension in the Octagonal Temple and the escape from Axo, it was too tempting to slow down and enjoy themselves.

'Well, let's get on with this haircut,' he said. 'By now, I'm used to being naked in Faustia, so another little while won't matter.'

'And if you can survive a day nude in a Faustian forest at this time of the year, you can survive anything.'

'Ah, so that's the secret of the empire's strength.'

'Shhh – don't tell anyone. Now kneel down.'

Dayraven turned around and knelt. He could feel the coolness of the earth under his knees and feet, and shivered in the fresh air. It struck him for the first time that he was not only naked but alone in a great forest with Sunniva. *We're just comrades. Just comrades.*

He heard Sunniva come up behind him and was suddenly aware how alert all of his senses were. He heard her take off her helmet and place it on the ground. Sunniva knelt behind him and her long hair caressed his shoulders. He trembled and a warm glow spread through his body. Scenes flashed into his mind of him taking her in his arms, but he shoved them away. They were on the mission that Halakh had given them. And Sunniva's father, wherever he was now.

He heard Sunniva draw her knife with a sliding scrape.

'Don't forget I'm armed now,' she whispered in his ear.

Sunniva reached out for Dayraven's hair with one hand, holding her knife ready in the other. Her own hair trailed across his shoulders, and Sunniva's eyes drifted down over the tight, hard muscles of his neck, upper back and arms. His skin was fairly tanned from years under the Magian sun, and the contrast made his blue eyes and dark blond hair shine even more. And her own blond hair looked so nice draped over those muscles.

Sunniva blinked hard to try and clear her thoughts. *I shouldn't be thinking like this now. I'm on a mission. It's his fault for distracting me.*

She reached out, seized his hair and yanked a lock of it back towards her. Sunniva grabbed another clump of hair and sniffed at the warm smell that rose off his skin. It reminded her of freshly baked loaves, with a hint of the smouldering ashes underneath. *No wonder he can stay naked in the cold, when he has so much heat in him.*

Sunniva gritted her teeth against these thoughts and sliced the hair through. She followed its fall with her eyes, down his broad back, over his tight buttocks and out of sight. Her eyes were drawn to the shaggy but light-coloured hair that covered the big, knotty muscles. How nice it would be to snuggle into, safe from everything. Perhaps he might push her knife away now, turn around and take hold of her with those big arms. He could lift this heavy armour off her, set her body free. *No. enough of that.*

Sunniva reached around for the hair that hung over his forehead and pulled his head back, watching the tendons in his neck tighten. *Just like the way his backside tightens when he walks. This is hopeless. I need something to keep my mind off all these thoughts.*

'Why don't you think about something useful while we're sitting here?' she said.

101

'How do you know I'm not?'

Sunniva cut through the hair. 'Well, let's hear it, then.'

'I was trying to put together what we know.'

'There's not much of that.'

'No, but let's see. Halakh, your father –'

'One dead, one missing.'

'Al-Suli is missing as well. Ow – watch what you're doing!'

'Keep still.'

'Let's assume there's some connection between all three missing men.'

'Halakh comes all the way to Axo to find you –'

'Us.'

'Us. Whatever secret he was carrying, it must be very big. Someone gets to him first, but we don't think they've picked up the trail.'

'But we think that we have.'

Sunniva sliced through the last long bit of hair. 'Done. I've seen worse. Now for the shave – turn around.'

Dayraven turned around, still on his knees. Sunniva couldn't help glancing down at the layers of bunched muscles on his belly. She felt herself blushing red and hot. She saw a thin lock of Dayraven's hair that had landed on his chest, just near the left nipple. Her fingers itched to reach out and pluck it away, running themselves through the thick hair, feeling the power that lay sleeping underneath.

Dayraven glanced down at the lock, picked it out gently with his fingers and let it fall while he smiled at her. Sunniva clenched her lips together and looked away.

Dayraven tilted his head back, very aware of the pulsing veins in his neck, just under Sunniva's fingers. Dayraven's whole body thrilled again at the thought of her hair cascading on his shoulders and of her breath on his neck. He tried to find something to think about, anything. He was on a mission for Halakh, his dead old friend and teacher. Halakh had trusted him with something extremely important – so important that he had died for it. What would Halakh have said if Dayraven made a fool of himself with Sunniva, when they were supposed to solve this mystery together?

The cold blade scraped along his throat, slicing off his beard with a rasping sound. Dayraven felt his heart racing.

'Hmm, not too much blood,' Sunniva murmured, lifting the blade away.

'Very funny. Why don't you keep talking about what we've found out so far? That'll keep my mind off that knife of yours – as long as you can keep your mind on what you're doing.'

'I'll try.' Dayraven held himself rigid as the blade met his skin. 'So, we think we are on the trail that Halakh left for us, and we think it leads to Metos and the bracelet. Someone will be after us, like they were after Halakh. Death the Rider we know about, but it wasn't one of the Riders that we fought in the Octagonal Temple earlier. So, it looks like two different groups are searching for the same thing. But we don't know what that thing is yet, and we don't know who these groups are.'

Sunniva made the last stroke on his neck and their eyes met. *She must see in my eyes what I've been thinking about her.*

103

'Then there's the gold bee we found in the Octagonal Temple,' Dayraven said. 'The Clovians must be involved somewhere.'

Sunniva bent over to shave his cheek and he felt her warmth. 'Except that they're supposed to have all died out long ago.'

Dayraven let his mind drift off in search of a thought that had been bothering him for a while now. The scrape of the blade on his cheek faded away until he hardly noticed it. A memory floated up out of his mind.

Dayraven must have been only five or six. He watched every move of his father as Urland got ready to leave. Dayraven strained his neck back to look up at his father towering above him. The last thing Urland did was take down his sword in its scabbard while Dayraven watched open-mouthed. A horn sounded.

'I have to go now, Dayraven, but I want to tell you the secret of this sword's power.'

'Here,' Dayraven said, pointing at the long, sharp edge.

'No.' Urland tapped the sword's hilt. *'Here. This is where the man joins with the sword.'*

The horn sounded again.

Dayraven came back to himself and the sound of the horn faded in his ears. That was the last time he had ever seen his father.

'Durendal,' he murmured.

'What?' Sunniva lifted the blade.

'The sword.'

Sunniva stared at him and he could tell she was trying to find the meaning in his eyes. Dayraven jumped up and fetched the sword from the pile. It felt heavy with meaning now, not just metal. The hilt was made of metal covered with wood, and the pommel on top was made of steel inlaid with silver and gold. On either side, worked in silver, was a warrior figure.

'The last thing my father ever told me was the secret of his sword's power – the handle.' Dayraven pulled at the pommel but it wouldn't budge. 'There must be a reason a message was left for us in the Octagonal Temple to take the sword, and not just because it's a good weapon.'

'You think there's something in there?'

'I don't know – I can't even open it.' He tugged again at the pommel.

Sunniva reached over and pressed one of the figures. Her fingers lightly touched Dayraven's and a ripple ran through him. The top of the pommel snapped open with a click.

Dayraven tipped the hilt of the sword downwards with his other hand underneath. A metal key fell into his palm.

***

The Twister crouched behind some sacks of grain in the market at Axo. All around him, wagons were being loaded to leave the city. The dawn light threw long shadows. The air was full of noise and the smell of different foods and he realised he was hungry. He waited for his chance and grabbed a loaf of bread and thrust it inside his cloak.

Everyone was speaking about the elephant and how it had broken down the nearby city gate and run off, carrying two people. He had seen it all from on top of a wall near the Octagonal Temple: the Rider, the battle, the elephant.

The Twister smiled to himself; everyone around him talked, but they didn't know the important things. None of them knew that the elephant had carried away the scroll and that the scroll was somehow the key to everything.

Above all, none of them knew the truth about the elephant. He hadn't understood it himself before, but now it was clear. It had all started with the lion. He realised now that the lion was really the evil spirit that had destroyed him before and put him in the hermitage. And it was still pursuing him. This shapeshifting spirit had taken the form of a lion and come down from the temple ceiling to get him, but he had escaped. Now it had taken the form of an elephant. Who knew what other form it might take in the future?

Astolf must have sent the Rider after Dayraven. Against him, the Twister, he had sent this spirit – and still he had escaped! Astolf had controlled the creature to begin with, when it appeared as a lion, but it had got away from him as an elephant. Now Dayraven was master of the evil spirit; he had ridden off on it, so he must have power over the creature somehow. Maybe it would soon escape from his control, and then it would come after him – the Twister – again. But he would be ready; it would not take him by surprise next time.

With a start, the Twister looked around. The wagons were starting to roll out of the city gate that the elephant had damaged. He scurried across and jumped on the back of one that was loaded with sacks of cloth and furs. He wedged himself in the middle of the sacks and spread a thick fur over himself. The wagon rumbled out through the gate and he heard the sounds of the city fade away behind. He quickly got used to the lurching movement of the wagon.

After a while, the Twister pulled the fur off his face and stared up at the lightening sky. He took out the bread, tore off a piece and chewed while he thought.

Only he knew the truth about the creature. It was a deadly enemy, but it could be beaten. Its true form must be neither lion nor elephant, but maybe something smaller and weaker. Perhaps it had to return to that form sometimes in order to rest and recover its power. One day, he would find the creature in that form and kill it – it was just a matter of waiting. Then he would be free of the spirit that had ruined him, and he and his hump could take up their rightful places again. He had to follow the scroll, which meant following Dayraven and the elephant creature. The wagon was taking him down the road they had followed. As time passed, the drivers of the wagon would ask for and hear news of the elephant, and then he would know where it had gone.

For now, he was comfortable and warm enough among these sacks on the back of the wagon, and he had a sword that he had stolen in the confusion over the elephant. This wagon was a much more comfortable bed than they'd given him in the hermitage. The hermitage! The bread turned bitter in his mouth and he spat it out; he must never think of that again. He ripped off another hunk of bread and chewed while the wagon lumbered on. *Never again.* He had got out of there and would never go back.

The Twister had been lugging a heavy bag of salt from the hermitage's workshop on the river to the storage room when Astolf had arrived to take him away.

'This is who you'll pretend to be working for.'

The Twister leant forward to look at the priest's smooth hand, so different from his own that was covered with calluses. Astolf was holding a gold bee, inlaid with gemstones.

'But that's – no, I can't!' the Twister said.

'Shall I tear up your signed release, then? You must really like it here.'

'No! I was just surprised. My father –'

'Your father knows nothing about this. Come with me and you'll never see or hear from him. Do exactly as I tell you, or you'll be back in here forever.'

Months later, the Twister woke from his daydream and lay back in the bumpy wagon, looking up at the sky. Hours must have passed. He felt good; he had a sword at his side, the bread had taken away his hunger and his hump was wedged comfortably among the bundles. Above all, the wagon was taking him closer to the scroll.

The driver of the wagon gave a shout of surprise and stopped suddenly. The Twister jumped up and looked around. The elephant creature was lumbering out of the forest. Fear shot through him. *The creature must know I'm here*. The Twister reached for his sword but then stopped. There was no point trying to fight the creature in this form; he would have to hope that it would later change into something much smaller.

The elephant crossed the road just twenty paces in front of the wagon. The Twister lay back down, sweating, but his hump sensed no danger. Was it possible that the creature did not know he was there? His mind raced. Perhaps Dayraven had really been the creature's greatest enemy and now it had killed him and was going away. But Dayraven had ridden off from Axo on the creature. By following the creature's path through the forest back to its beginning, he would find Dayraven, dead or alive. And the scroll. Was it luck or destiny? Either way, he was close now.

The Twister heard some crunching and swishing sounds up ahead to the left and looked around the side of the wagon. The elephant had crossed the road and was disappearing into the forest. The Twister scrambled off the back of the wagon and jumped into the grass at the side of the road, his chest heaving. The wagon rumbled off. He looked across the road to where the elephant had gone; the bent trees and broken branches showed the path it had made. Even after the wagon was out of sight, the Twister lay listening for the elephant to come back, but it was gone.

He stood up and walked to the break in the forest on his side of the road where the elephant had made a tunnel as it passed through. He touched some branches that had been wrenched out of shape. *And out of place, just like me. But those who did it will suffer once I have power again.*

He stepped into the tunnel and started following it. The smell of the trees was strong. The elephant's footprints stretched ahead like wells dug in the soft ground, and the Twister stepped in each one as he went, imagining that he was a giant. *I will be a giant when I have power, and my hump will be as big as a mountain.*

***

Sunniva stared at the key in Dayraven's hand, then looked at his face and saw that he was as surprised as she was.

'Is that all that's in there?' she asked.

Dayraven shook the sword hilt and upended it. Nothing else came out.

'That's it,' he said.

109

'A key – a key to what?'

'Could be to anything. A door? A chest?'

'You don't remember Urland ever talking about a special key?'

She saw that Dayraven was casting his mind back many years before.

'No,' he said eventually. 'Nothing at all.'

'We are collecting a lot of things that don't seem to make sense.'

'Let's just hope they start making sense when we get to Metos. Maybe together with the second bracelet we'll find a box or something that we can open with this key.'

Dayraven put the key inside his robe.

Sunniva looked up through the dense covering of trees. 'It will start getting dark before too long. We had better get ready, eat and then start walking by night. I'll change into these priest clothes, but first, I'm going to have a bath in the river. You stay right here.'

'If you say so – I'll sort out the things we'll have to carry.'

Sunniva walked off, carrying the clothes. The sun was low in the sky and shone in her eyes through the trees. She realised how much she was looking forward to this bath. She could feel cuts and bruises all over, and her arms and shoulders ached from carrying the sword and shield. She wished she had lighter weapons like a bow and arrow, but the sword, shield and mail coat were necessary. It felt like weeks since the last time she had properly washed, although she knew it had only been yesterday. So much had happened since that last bath: meeting Dayraven, Halakh's death, the fight in the Octagonal Temple, the elephant. *And surely this is just the beginning.*

110

The Twister hurried along the elephant path. It would be getting dark soon, and then the trail would be lost. He felt the cold of the forest falling around him like a wet blanket. It was going to be very tough out there at night, but no tougher than the hermitage had been, and he had survived that for years. But he would never go back there again. *Never.*

He stopped and listened. Someone was walking off to the right, among the dense trees; it sounded like one person cutting a new trail. The Twister waited a moment and then changed direction to follow the footsteps.

Sunniva chopped with her sword to clear a path. The rushing sound of the river grew louder until Sunniva pushed through the last bushes and saw the smooth-running water curving away to both left and right. The bend in the river meant that anyone sailing from either side would not be able to see her from far away, so she would have time to get out of sight.

The sun was vanishing below the tops of the trees on the far side of the river, but there was still enough light and time for a good bath. Sunniva couldn't wait to get in the soothing water; it was going to be cold in there, but she needed this.

She lay the bundle of priest's clothes on a rock, put her sword on top, took off her helmet, shook out her hair and then sat on another rock to take off her shoes and trousers. Piece by piece, she was leaving her male disguise behind and becoming a woman again.

A wolf howled. Sunniva reached for her sword but then realised there was no danger; the sound came from the other side of the river. She stood up and took off her chain mail and sighed as the heavy weight was lifted; it felt as if she had been trapped for years under there. Sunniva picked up her helmet and shined it on the priest's cloak. The metal was bent in places and the light was not good, but she saw a dull reflection. *Hmm, not so bad.*

She took off her arming coat and underclothes, walked to the edge of the water and put a toe in. It was very cold and she shivered, but she wanted to go in.

The Twister heard a wolf howl but wasn't afraid; he had far worse enemies than that. He reached the river, looked across to the left and froze in shock. A female water spirit was standing on the riverbank and he had never seen anything so beautiful. His mind ran on in confusion. This spirit must have been travelling with Dayraven – it was she who had driven the evil elephant creature away. Was she a good spirit sent to help him? The Twister was sure of it.

Dayraven tested the two bundles he had made. They were fairly heavy, but between them, they contained the essential things they needed. As soon as Sunniva came back, they would eat and then start by dark for Metos.

A wolf howled somewhere. Dayraven stood still, listening. Sunniva had insisted on going to the river alone, but what if she were in danger? He should not have let her go off on her own. He grabbed his sword and started through the forest.

Sunniva stepped out into the river and gasped at the cold. The water numbed her skin so that soon, she didn't feel it.

Sunniva went out until the water reached her neck and her hair floated behind her like a giant lily. Now she felt free of everything, at least for a few moments. Not just her armour and her male disguise, but free of worries.

The Twister watched as the water spirit vanished into the river. Was she going to swim away to where she came from, or was she still there? He looked around, saw a tree overhanging the river and climbed it, his breath gasping.

The Twister lay on a thick branch and looked down. The spirit was still there, almost covered by the water. His hump glowed as he looked at her.

Dayraven pushed through the last bushes and reached the riverbank. The sun was behind the trees on the opposite side. He had lost the trail Sunniva had made through the forest and didn't know at what point she had reached the river. He looked to the left and saw only the river curving away in front of him, then to the right and saw Sunniva in the water fifty paces way. She was perfectly safe – there were no wolves and no danger at all.

Sunniva stood up with water flowing off her. Dayraven felt his heart racing and couldn't move.

The Twister watched as the water spirit rose out of the river, glorious and shimmering. She had come back – she must know he was there. She loved him. She was his. He loved her like he had never loved anything.

Dayraven gulped; Sunniva was more beautiful than he could ever have imagined. How could he have ever believed she was a man, even for a second? He knew he should leave, but if he made a sound now she might discover he was there. If he waited until she went away, he could go back to their camp and say he had been out exploring the area.

Sunniva stepped out of the river and dried herself on her old clothes. Her wounds and bruises were not as bad as she had thought and would pass quickly. She looked at herself again in the shining helmet. *Much better.* She dried her hair and tied it up. Now it was time to go back to playing at being a man; she put on the priest robes and pulled the hood over her head.

Dayraven could feel his heartbeat slowing so that he could think clearly again. He turned to walk back to camp. Memories of what he had just seen floated into his mind, and he lost his footing and stumbled against a rock.

Sunniva wrapped her chain mail coat inside her old clothes and prepared to leave. She heard a crash on the riverbank to the right, dropped the bundle and drew her sword, but the sound did not come again. She walked forward, listening.

The Twister clambered through the branches of the tree to see better and looked down again. The water spirit was gone and now a priest was there. These creatures could change their shape anytime they liked, but that didn't matter; he had seen the spirit's true form and would never forget it.

He saw the priest suddenly drop his bundle of clothes and walk off with sword drawn, out of sight. He would have to change branches again. The Twister reached for the branch above him.

Dayraven stayed still. The sun was very low and throwing dark red light over the forest, but he could clearly see Sunniva approaching. She stopped twenty paces away.

'Who's there?' she said.

Now there was no doubt she knew someone was there. Dayraven stepped out.

'It's me, Dayraven.'

Sunniva walked up to him, frowning. 'I thought you were supposed to be back at the camp getting things ready?'

'I was. But I heard a wolf –'

'The only wolf here is you. Well, did you have a good look? I hope the light was bright enough for you.'

Dayraven felt himself turning red. 'I didn't mean to – I'm sorry –'

Her face softened. 'Well, I've seen a lot of you already, so it's only fair. Maybe now you really believe my story about being a woman.'

'We are still just comrades.'

'Oh, yes, just comrades.'

She came closer still and pushed back her hood. There was that face, those blue eyes and those full lips. Dayraven felt lost in a cloud. Whether it was right or wrong, he had to kiss those lips. *Now.* He bent forward and Sunniva's face rose to meet him.

The Twister swung around on the branch. What was going on down there?

He had to see what happened. He moved farther out on the branch. It snapped under his weight and he fell, feeling the leaves brushing past his face. He turned in the air so that he would land safely on his hump.

Sunniva closed her eyes, waiting for Dayraven's lips. *It's a crazy world. Be crazy with it.*

She heard a cracking sound, a kind of groan, a rustle of leaves and then a heavy thump somewhere behind her. She jumped back.

'Come on!' she said, and ran towards the sound, drawing her sword.

She could hear Dayraven running behind her. Sunniva ran past her bundle of old clothes. Up ahead she could hear something crashing through the forest. She ran on and then stopped. Whatever it was had vanished.

Dayraven ran up beside her. She could hear their breath rasping in the silence.

'We'd better get back to camp,' she said. 'We have to keep moving.'

And we have to just be comrades.

***

Death looked up at the moon as he rode. It hung perfect and round, gleaming white in the darkening sky, and the moonlight glinted on the double-bladed axe he carried. Anyone would be able to see him from far off under that light, but he would be able to see them as well.

He heard rushing water up ahead and knew the river was very close.

Death felt the pain of his broken ankle somewhere in the back of his mind. He knew it was there, but he'd pushed it deep, like a slug crushed under a rock. The anger he felt about the elephant and Axo still ran through him. There flashed into his mind the Octagonal Temple and the charging elephant smashing his foot and scaring off his horse. Death remembered how he'd hobbled out of the city

117

in the confusion, finally found his panicked horse and strapped up his ankle as best he could. He had never been made to stumble about like that before, and he had never failed to kill anything in his life. The other three Riders would hear of it; his reputation and theirs would be affected and so would the price they could command. It had to be put right. Death gripped his axe more tightly. He wouldn't fail again – Dayraven would die. Death thought again of the various ways he might kill Dayraven. A throwing axe in the throat. One giant downward slice with a huge double blade that would split him in two. Alternating swipes with single hand axes: one to cut off his sword hand, the other his head.

Something gleamed white in the darkness far on the other side of the river. Death tensed and sniffed the air, but the distance was still too great. He rode on.

Before long, Death could see the old stone bridge over the river. And now he saw that the gleaming white thing was Malombra's canopy standing on the far side. By the light of the long torches planted in the ground around it, he could see the carriers standing in dark clothes. Death felt a rush of excitement as he thought of Malombra so close by, but that was soon replaced by something else. *Revenge. Dayraven must die. It won't be long now.*

Death slowed his horse to a walk to cross the bridge. He could see that Malombra's men were waiting for him.

When they were twenty paces apart, Death stopped his horse and jumped to the ground. His weak ankle slipped under him and he had to steady himself against his horse's back.

He walked forward. Astolf was standing next to the canopy, looking pale and scared in the torchlight. Death ignored him and stopped in front of Malombra's thin white curtain. The torchlight threw strange shadows on its rippling surface. Death could smell the fear of the men standing around him, but there was no stink of fear under Malombra's perfume.

'Now we are all here,' Malombra said. 'Dayraven and Sunniva, daughter of Ado of Metos have escaped from Axo – what they have taken with them we must get back. They should never have been allowed out of the city.'

Death felt the rage soar inside him and lifted his axe.

'They won't always have an elephant to help them,' Malombra said. 'Astolf?'

'We think there are two likely places for Dayraven and Sunniva to go – his estate near Liga and her father's house in Metos. They might even split up, so we need to divide our forces and cover both places.'

'They have a head start,' Malombra said. 'We might not be able to get there before them, but as long as we stay close we'll get them in the end. So, Death – do you want to go to Metos or to Liga?'

Death pointed where he knew the human figures were spread across his chest.

'A man. Dayraven, so Liga. I thought so. Take some of my men with you – I will go to Metos.'

Death pointed to a headless corpse on his arm.

'Of course you can kill Dayraven. Now, let's get going – but remember that first, we must either get what they are carrying or find out what they know. Then you can enjoy the killing as much as you like.'

Death had never smiled in his life, but this must be what it felt like.

Malombra lay back on the cushions under her canopy. She could feel the slight rocking as the canopy was carried along. A light breeze fluttered the white curtains. *Like a spider web; I start it tingling and the whole empire responds.*

She lay on one side and picked up one of the mirrors that lay on the pillows. Running her fingers down the long, jewelled handle, she thought of who had given her this gift years before. *You'll be paid back before long.*

Malombra raised the mirror and looked at herself in the polished glass. She watched her eyes watching themselves and smiled. The face in the mirror smiled back.

She lay back further on the cushions with her hair spread out. The face in the mirror smiled even more broadly but with something savage around the mouth and a cruel gleam deep in the eyes.

So, you want me, do you? She giggled and stroked her face with a strand of hair. The eyes in the mirror followed the hair as it moved back and forth over the smooth skin. She saw the eyes narrow further and a hazy flush sweep over the tight cheekbones. *You do want me, don't you? I know you do.*

Malombra laughed and the face laughed with her, but underneath the laughter she could see the hardness, the coldness of the face's stare. The sharp edge of desire; there was no mistaking it.

She laid the mirror aside. The edge of desire was easy to spot, but once upon a time, it had been a new thing to her. Malombra had been not much more than ten. Her father was holding a great feast. For days, the house had been filled with preparations; the servants had rushed around, always fetching or carrying something. She lay in

120

bed, far from the feasting, which reached her as a dull, distant noise.

She heard a noise at the door and looked. Her old nurse was no longer sitting there, and one of the male guests was approaching her bed. Malombra felt very shy and hid under the covers.

'Don't,' he said, pulling the covers away. *'I gave your nurse a gift and a message from your father. I want you to have this.'*

Her fingers grasped the long, thin handle of a mirror and he gripped her wrist and wouldn't let go.

'Now you can see yourself like I see you now.'

Under her canopy many years later, Malombra lowered the mirror. *You'll be paid back for your gift before long.*

Raising the mirror, she watched the face again. It was smiling at her, but she knew the signs of the open lips, the pinched cheekbones and narrowed eyes.

'Maugris!' she called.

She lay back on the cushions, tossing aside the mirror. The canopy was still rocking. The curtain was pushed aside and the blind man clambered in. She watched him fumble around the bed, looking for her. He found her left foot and followed it up. Malombra felt herself smiling with pleasure. After the first time, no man saw her face. *No living man.* She felt yet again the thrill of knowing that this man couldn't see. He knew her – he *lived* her – only through his touch, smell, taste and hearing. As he reached her thighs, Malombra laughed. He ran his hands up her body and grunted with satisfaction.

Malombra reached up and tore off his tunic. She ran her fingers over the strong, hard muscles and admired his rugged face under the light blue cloth that covered his eyes.

He was almost perfect, but what he was missing made him perfect for her.

The blind man brought up his right hand and stroked her face, feeling every outline. Malombra shivered with delight.

'You're looking at me, aren't you?' he said. 'I can feel you looking at me.'

She took up the mirror and watched herself watching the blind man feeling her watching him.

'I'm looking at you,' she said, watching her lips quiver as she spoke.

'And I'm looking at you.'

He slipped his hands over her neck to grab her body.

***

Dayraven did not know how long they had been walking alongside the river. It must have been hours, and his feet were sore. He could hear Sunniva walking just behind him. The forest to their left was dark, but the moon was bright enough to light the way. It rippled on the water and was swallowed up by the forest on the other side of the river. The only sound was their tramping feet and breathing and the occasional howl of a wolf somewhere far off. He knew that a great tiredness was waiting to sweep over him after everything that had happened, but he couldn't give in to it. It would be so good to lie down and sleep, but he had to resist. They needed to travel as far as possible tonight. If they found a boat to take them down the river, there would be time to sleep then.

The events of the last day kept running through Dayraven's mind in random order. He tried to find a pattern in them, but there was only a confusing cloud.

Halakh – Astolf – Calvo – Death the bounty hunter – Sunniva – Ado of Metos – Al-Suli – the bracelets – the scroll – Urland's hunting horn and sword – the Clovians – Metos – the elephant – Axo – the Octagonal Temple. No form or shape to these thoughts appeared, no matter how many times they whirled through his mind. Halakh had taught him for many years about finding meaning and structure in symbols and events, but here, there was only confusion. He told himself yet again that it would become clear when they got to Metos. But would it? Maybe the bracelet would not be there or would not help them. Maybe they had made a mistake somewhere in solving the puzzles in the temple. The various thoughts swirled around in his head once more: *the temple – the bracelets – Metos – Axo – Halakh – the horn and sword – Sunniva – Astolf –*

He rounded a corner and stopped. There was a light up ahead by the riverbank. *It must be a river posting station.* Sunniva stopped behind him, and their rasping breath was the only sound apart from the gurgling river.

Dayraven walked closer. The light they had seen was a lamp hanging on a small wooden building on the very edge of the river. He could see boats tied alongside, and there was a smell of horses as well. It was one of the emperor's staging posts that provided boats, horses and lodging for those travelling on the empire's business.

He went up to the door and knocked. Sunniva stepped back a little into the shadows with her hood up and bowed her head. Dayraven heard some rustling inside the hut and knocked again.

The door was opened and a sleepy man looked out. 'Do you know what time it is?'

123

'We are judges on the emperor's business.' Dayraven showed the insignia he had used in the palace at Axo. 'We need to travel urgently upriver.'

The man's manner changed completely. 'Forgive me, sir – we get all kinds turning up here in the middle of the night. But if you wait until morning –'

'Our business can't wait. We need a boat and a horse to pull it upstream.'

Dayraven held out some coins. The man raised his lamp and glanced at Sunniva, then took the coins and came outside. Dayraven sighed with relief; now they could change horses and boats all the way down to Metos and no one would get there before them. He ran his fingers over his chin and heard the rasping sound; there, he could also shave more carefully than Sunniva had been able to in the forest. *The last bits of my old life are falling away.*

***

Dagon, head of the Clovian Dynasty, looked out over the moonlit hills and ran his twisted fingernails over the gold bees stitched into his robe, enjoying the scraping sound. Real bees buzzed nearby, and Dagon smiled a little at the sound while a light breeze ruffled his long hair. His hand rested on a golden bull's head standing on a table next to him. The world outside was peaceful for now. One day, there would be war again, before a long-lasting peace: the peace of the Second Clovian Empire. He looked to the north-west, towards the distant kingdom of Seanor, where he had lived in exile, waiting for the moment to return. Now he was back in Faustia, and soon it would all be his.

The voices of his ancestors rang in his ears yet again. Always the same questions. *When? When? How much longer must we wait?* He recognised them all: oldest of all was Clovo, founder of the dynasty and king at the time of the Fourth Unmasking; then his son Merech, a mighty warrior who extended the empire; his son Cilder, the wise maker of alliances. On and on, generation after generation down to Dagon's own father. The oldest ancestors carried the most weight in the discussions. Every other king or emperor had advisers and ministers, but the Clovians did not need them, when they carried the best and most trustworthy counsellors in their heads.

The ancestors' tombs were out there in the Clovian heartland, all hidden and intact. The incisions on top of their heads allowed their souls out after death, when they joined the other ancestors. The ancestors' bodies still sat on their thrones, mummified, dressed in their robes and surrounded by their weapons, jewels, magical objects and their favourite horse. Only the tomb of Merech had been discovered by enemies, but the desecrators had fled in terror, leaving everything as it was. The workmen had tried to return and steal from the tomb, but they had all been killed by the alerted guards. During the Clovians' long exile, they had had to trust to their few remaining secret followers to preserve the dynasty's tombs and villas. Now that Dagon was back in the homeland, bringing with him the accumulated memories and wisdom of the ancestors, their territory would be protected.

'It will not be long now,' Dagon said 'The power that was once yours will soon be ours again.'

So you always say. You told us that through all the years of exile. Yet still we wait. No one deserves the favour of the Akhen more than us.

'I know that. That is why the Face was sent to you all those centuries ago.'

*Because of our power, our knowledge, our magic –
the things we have lost since then. That is why the Akhen
allowed the empire to be taken from us. That is why we had
to stay so long away from the land that is ours.*

'The thief Calvo calls himself emperor, but he is old
and weak and enslaved to traitors. I still have the things
that made you great. Trust me.'

*Maybe we have slept too long in the darkness. The
world has changed and our time is over.*

'No! Our time will come again – you must believe in
me. I draw on your wisdom, memories and power, but I am
the one who must act.'

*The Face of the Akhen will not appear in our land
again. You know this.*

'We will find the Face, no matter where he or she may
be. The prophecy of the Hidden Face will soon be ours.
Then we will bring the Face back to Faustia to await the
Fifth Unmasking. After that, the empire will be ours again,
and no one will take it from us this time.'

*You always tell us these things. But at the last
Unmasking, we were many and strong. Now you are too
few to change the fate set by the Akhen. Too weak.*

'I have found people to help us. Once they have
served their purpose, they can be disposed of.'

Can you trust them? Perhaps they have betrayed you.

'They know what will happen to them if they fail us.
The name of the Clovians still terrifies everyone, even after
so many years.'

As it should.

The voices fell silent and Dagon sighed in relief, the
sweat on his face cold in the breeze. Speaking to the
ancestors was always exhausting. They were right, though;
the world had changed and grown treacherous since the

126

throne had been stolen from the Clovians. Calvo and his father had won victories in war since then, but they were thieves. Robbers who had stolen an empire from its rightful owners. The souls of thieves attracted other thieves. The whole empire was sick with robbery.

It would all be put right again once power was back where it belonged, but he had to know what these pawns he was using were doing. Why were they taking so long? The ancestors were right to be impatient. Dagon turned away from the window to give his orders.

***

Dayraven lay back in the small boat as it floated up the river. It was early morning now and the orange-gold sun was peeping above the forest that lined the water. On the left bank, the horse walked on, attached to the front of the boat by ropes. Going upstream like this, a horse was the only way to travel against the current, as the wind on the river usually blew the wrong way for sailing. He could feel the wind in his face now.

Dayraven brought out Halakh's copper bracelet yet again. He could read the Jael letters, but without the second bracelet that Sunniva thought was in Metos, he had only half the story and these letters made no sense. He put the bracelet away again. The regular clop of the horse's hooves and the swaying of the boat made his head droop, but Dayraven fought to stay awake. There should be no danger on the river, but he had decided that one of them should stay awake and had let Sunniva sleep first.

He turned to look at where she lay at the front of the boat, her head cushioned on a bag of clothes. She was still wearing the priest's robe, but the hood was pushed back, so that her blond hair streamed out and a few stray wisps fell over her face. Dayraven found himself staring at her face, following the line of her soft cheek down to her full lips. Those lips that he had almost kissed.

He forced himself to look away and think of something else, and a flood of other thoughts came into his mind: his journey back to Faustia, the meeting with the emperor, Halakh's dead body in the Octagonal Temple, the fight with the killer, the escape on the elephant. Through a lot of those adventures, Sunniva had been with him. He looked back at her, noting the swell of her hips under the severe priest's robe and watching them sway with the movement of the boat. The vision of what he had seen in the river poured into his mind. *No! I mustn't think like that!* Dayraven tore his eyes away again. *Sunniva is a comrade, nothing more.* She had shared danger with him and would go on sharing it until it was over, but when would that be? Metos would probably not be the end of it; if they found the second bracelet, that might just send them off on more dangers.

Still, one day it would all be over. He looked again at the full lips under the long blond hair. Maybe when it was all over... Dayraven stopped himself. How long had he known her for? Hardly any time at all, but it seemed so much more because they had lived through such a lot.

Dayraven sat back and looked at and listened to the scene that floated past: the clopping hooves of the horse, the buzzing of insects, the broad sweep of the river and the dense trees.

'What time is it?'

Dayraven jumped and looked at the other end of the boat. Sunniva was awake and leaning on one elbow, looking at him, her hair draped across her face.

'About three hours after sunrise.'

Sunniva sat up and drank some water. 'You should have woken me earlier. Now you get some sleep and I'll stay on guard.'

Dayraven realised how tired he was. It would be wonderful to drift off to sleep while the boat swayed underneath him.

'Did anything happen while I was asleep?'

'No. The horse is going well. Just one trading ship passed us going the other way, and I haven't seen any other boats. I was just sitting here thinking.'

'About what?'

'About what might happen when we get to Metos. And after.'

'There's no way of knowing that until we see the second bracelet.'

'True. Well, I think I'll get some sleep.'

'Now it's my turn to sit and think.'

'About what?'

'Something will come to mind.'

'I'll leave you to think, then.'

Dayraven lay down and made a pillow out of the bag of his old clothes. He looked up at the sky, a nice blue with wispy clouds drifting. His eyes closed and he fell asleep almost straight away.

Sunniva sat in the boat and looked around; as Dayraven had said, everything was peaceful. The horse walked on, flapping its tail, while the sun rose higher above the trees. It was good to have this time to rest and think.

Sunniva looked over the side into the water, where the wash of the boat drove up white froth. She could not see her reflection. *Just as well, probably.* She thought of looking in her shined helmet but didn't want to disturb Dayraven by unpacking her bag. She scooped up some water in her hands and splashed it on her face. The water was cold and fresh and she caught her breath. She waited a few seconds and then did it again. Sunniva dried her face on her priest's robe and sat back. *That's better.* The world seemed a bit brighter now and her mind was clearer but still full of thoughts. So much had happened in the last days. She still didn't know what had happened to her father, but many other mysteries had been added to that one.

Dayraven was one of those mysteries. Sunniva looked at where he lay. Was he asleep yet? Or was he just pretending and waiting to see what she would do? He had probably been watching when she washed her face. *Well, let him. There's no harm in that.* Then Sunniva thought of how he had been watching when she bathed in the river and felt herself going red. She turned her face away and pulled down the hood to cover her blushes. *If he sees that, he'll know what I'm thinking about. But then, I was angry with him only at first when I realised he had been watching. Only at first.* She remembered how Dayraven had moved to kiss her; she hadn't moved away.

But that was just a moment of madness, she told herself. They had been thrown together back in Axo and they had shared adventures and danger, so it was natural that some feeling would grow up quickly between them. But what feeling? She didn't want to think about that. Whatever feeling it might be, there was no room for it in her life until she followed these clues to the end and found her father. Then she would take off her armour and think about other things. What kind of man would she want to share her life with, anyway? Someone like Dayraven? How could she know? There had only been one man in her life so far, and that had been a mistake. She had thought it was love, but it had led only to betrayal. The hurt from that was far in the past, and she had been pleased to think only of practising fighting, helping her father and then searching for him. Now different kinds of thoughts were returning her mind.

When she had been a girl, Sunniva thought a lot about the kind of man who would one day be her husband. Probably every girl did, she imagined. Her wooden soldiers had represented different types of men. One was the Faustian warrior; tall, blond, with weapons and clothes that were familiar to her. The other was the Magian; shorter, darker, with exotic clothes and weapons. When she had been very young, they had fought battles against each other in different landscapes. Both were brave and courteous; sometimes one of them won, sometimes the other.

As she grew older, she began to wonder what it would be like to ride off with those soldiers. The Magian might whisk her away to his castle somewhere in the far-off deserts she had seen in books and tapestries. There she would eat strange foods and look out over the endless expanse of sand, surrounded by the Magian's servants. She would wear soft, rich clothes and walk through long corridors filled with treasure. There would be the Magian himself, handsome and shining with his gleaming black hair and beard. He would love her forever in the long desert nights. Back then, she didn't know exactly what 'loving

131

her' would mean, but she knew that it would be wonderful and passionate.

And the Faustian soldier? He would carry her off on his thundering warhorse to a big house much like her father's. There she would have as much of everything as she could want but all the same things that she had at home. The view from her window would be similar to what she had seen all her life; there would be mist and rain like there often were in Faustia. The feasts in the great hall would be like those she had seen before; the same foods, the same music. But would that be so bad, she used to ask herself? If her Faustian husband were as clever and wise as her father, she would be proud of him. But then she would think of the different life the Magian soldier could give her, and her thoughts would start all over again.

Sunniva looked at Dayraven. She was sure he was asleep now. He was a Faustian, but he had lived for years with Magians and learned much from them, so he was neither one nor the other. Even after she had cut his hair and shaved his beard and he had changed his clothes, there was something different about him; his manner, his accent. Maybe he had the best of what she had dreamed of in both her soldiers so long before: familiarity but also difference.

Sunniva didn't want to follow her thoughts any further. She turned back to look at where the boat was heading.

Dayraven woke up and sensed that the movement of the boat was changing, slowing down. He looked forwards, where Sunniva was sitting with her hood up. She seemed calm. Dayraven squinted up into the sun; it was almost

132

overhead, so it must be early afternoon. He had been asleep for four hours or so.

'What's going on?'

'We're approaching a changing station. We can change the horse and eat something.'

Dayraven sat up. Just a few hundred paces ahead on the left side of the river he could see the wooden building. It seemed calm enough, but Dayraven still tensed. *But no. No one could have got here before us. There is no faster way of travelling along the river.*

'Have you seen anything along the way?'

'Just trading ships and fishing boats.'

Dayraven took the rudder and steered the boat very close to the shore, while Sunniva seized the reins and brought the horse to a stop. Dayraven saw that a man had come out of the posting station. This was the station master, so nothing to worry about.

Dayraven stepped ashore, carrying his bag, and showed his insignia.

'We are judges on the emperor's business. We want to eat and change horses and go straight on.'

The station master rubbed his hands together. 'Very good, sir. Follow me, and while you have your meal, the horse will be changed. Any news from the towns you've been through?'

'Nothing much.'

Dayraven looked back at the boat, where Sunniva was stepping on to the riverbank. She had her hood covering her face and was trying to copy the priestly style of walking. *By daylight, she's not that convincing.* Still, they would be there only a short time and he would do all the talking.

133

Dayraven followed the station master towards the building and Sunniva walked behind. *One more change of horses after this and we should reach Metos tonight.* Then the adventure would begin again. Where were their enemies? What were they doing? There was no way of knowing, so all they could do was keep moving as quickly as they could.

***

Astolf stamped his feet and flapped his arms against the cold. He had been standing at these desolate crossroads for nearly an hour. The night was dark and quiet, and he felt the trees closing in on him. He felt again for the message inside his cloak. There could be no mistake; this was the place and the time. He had found the message wrapped around a tiny gold bee. It was from Him – Dagon, so there was no choice but to obey.

Astolf shivered even more as he thought about the double game he was playing. Dagon had got him involved in all of this to begin with and had offered untold wealth and power, and it was Dagon who had told him to bring the Twister out of the hermitage. But then Malombra had appeared. *It's worth the risk.* If Dagon accused him of treachery, Astolf would say he was only using Malombra to obtain what Dagon wanted. He knew how difficult it was to lie to Dagon, though. Astolf shivered again.

He heard the sound of heavy, slow feet and looked around. At first he saw nothing, but then a pale gleam appeared that grew into a rough wooden wagon drawn by eight oxen. There were a driver and one other armed man sitting at the front. The Clovians had kept all their characteristics down the centuries; their kings were considered too sacred to ride in horse-drawn carriages. At the time their dynasty was thought to have died out and power passed to Emperor Calvo's family, these wagons drawn by oxen already seemed things of the past. Here it was, though, very real and smelling of cattle and wood.

'Don't just stand there looking,' the driver said. 'He's waiting.'

Just like I've been waiting in the cold. Astolf climbed in the back and wrapped himself in a heavy blanket lying there. The wagon set off and Astolf sat looking up at the stars. After a while, the oxen started to go up a hill, and Astolf slid backwards with the incline and steadied himself. Riding in one of these was like journeying into the past, Astolf thought, only it was happening now. And maybe this was the future of Faustia. If it were, he wanted to be on the winning side. Then everything that he wanted could be his. Wealth, power, Malombra, revenge on Dayraven. He would complete the great plans his father had made all those years before.

The wagon turned a corner and jolted Astolf out of his daydreaming. Through the veil of the oxen's frozen breath, some lights were shining in an old-fashioned villa on a hill. Astolf gulped; every visit there was traumatic, but this time would be even worse.

Servants holding torches were waiting in the courtyard. Astolf stepped down from the wagon, his legs unsteady, and followed them inside. The corridors were gloomy and lit by occasional hanging torches.

The servants opened a heavy double door and Astolf entered the room alone. His legs were stiff after the ride in the wagon. Everything was just as he remembered it from the last time: the big room with charts of planets on the walls; the distant buzzing hum; Dagon standing like a statue in his long white robe covered with golden bees, looking out into the night, long dark hair and beard waving a little in the cool air, hand resting on the golden head of a bull and lips moving as if he were talking to someone. But no one else was there; just Dagon, head of the Clovian Dynasty. He looked at Dagon's fingernails, as long and curved as cruel winter branches. Astolf felt himself tremble all over and fought to stay calm.

Dagon took his hand from the bull's head and turned around, and his eyes locked onto Astolf's. Astolf felt drawn forwards and unable to escape from Dagon's grip. He could feel those dark eyes digging deep into his mind, searching every corner. There was nothing he could do; it was pointless to try and resist. Then there was nothing he wanted to do; he didn't want to block those eyes and this searching. He wanted Dagon to have control of his mind and wanted to obey.

Astolf felt the grip on his mind removed. He staggered and recovered himself; Dagon was standing as before, staring at him.

'So, the ancestors were right,' Dagon said. 'You are betraying us.'

'Lord Dagon – I can explain –'

'We know your mind better than you know it yourself, Astolf. When you left here last time, the ancestors had doubts about you. They thought you were too weak to be of use to us, and now it is clear – our control over you has been lessened by the woman known as Malombra.'

'I am using Malombra in order to get what you want, my lord.'

'Don't play the fool with us – you desire Malombra and she controls you through this desire. You are so small, so weak, Astolf. You cannot understand what is at stake

136

here. When we take back the throne, you could do what you wanted with Malombra – keep her as a slave, if you wanted to. Have any woman you wanted, all the wealth you wanted.'

'I know, Lord Dagon. That is why I am loyal to you.'

'Enough! Lie to us once more and you die. The ancestors wanted to kill you already, but I convinced them to leave you alive because you are useful – you are close to Calvo.'

'And I know Dayraven, son of Urland. He and Sunniva, Ado of Metos's daughter, got in our way at Axo – they have the secret now.'

'We know all this, Astolf – your mind is ours – but Malombra steals your mind when you are near her.'

'I will be stronger from now on, Lord Dagon, I promise.'

'Here.'

Dagon crossed to a door on the far side of the room and pushed it open. Astolf heard a deep buzzing sound. He went to the door and looked in; the room was filled with beehives made of wood. Dagon walked into the centre of the room and the bees buzzed more loudly. *They recognise their master.*

'Do you remember the last time you were here, Astolf? We told you that you must never show fear. Fear shows weakness and weakness brings death.'

'I remember, Lord Dagon.'

'Yet your mind is filled with fear – you are afraid because you have betrayed us.'

Dagon opened the big hive standing in the middle of the room, thrust both hands in and brought them out again covered in bees. Their buzzing grew louder as the bees swarmed up Dagon's arms like rising mud.

137

'Could you do this, Astolf? Or do you think the stench of your fear would drive the bees mad?'

Astolf couldn't take his eyes off the living flood of bees and felt sweat break out on his forehead.

Dagon came closer, holding his arms out, and Astolf shrank back, trembling.

'When they sense fear, the bees think that their king is in danger and they sting to save him,' Dagon said. 'Thousands of them ready to give their life for their leader – that is the kind of army my ancestors had and the kind we will have again. Unstoppable.'

'Lord Dagon –'

Dagon crossed back to the hive and gently pushed the bees off his arms and back inside. Their buzzing became quieter and Astolf sighed in relief.

Dagon opened a door at the far side. 'Bring in the prisoner!'

Two guards brought in an old man with his hands tied behind his back. Astolf felt his heart pounding; he knew who this was and could see that the man recognised him.

'This man deserves to die,' Dagon said. 'He says he is not afraid of us – not afraid to die. Let's see.'

Dagon opened a long, flat hive filled with bees, and their buzzing became a roar.

'Bring him forward,' Dagon said.

The guards brought the man to stand in front of the hive.

'Are you afraid now?' Dagon asked the prisoner.

The old man shook his head.

'Good,' Dagon said. 'If you are not afraid, nothing will happen to you, but if the bees smell even the slightest bit of fear, it spreads among them like an alarm. In a moment, they are driven into a frenzy and they have to kill – nothing can stop them then.'

'Lord Dagon,' Astolf said, hearing his own voice choked and strangled. 'There's no need –'

'Just watch and learn.'

Dagon grabbed the old man by the neck and thrust his head down towards the heaving mass of bees. The buzzing became louder.

'Afraid now?'

The man shook his head again.

'Yes, you are. I can smell it – do you think they can't smell it?'

The man spat at Dagon.

'Now let's see how brave you really are.'

Dagon plunged the man's head deep into the hive. The buzzing came like angry thunder and then the man screamed and thrashed around with his legs. Dagon let go and the body fell back on the floor, its face covered with a thick cluster of bees.

Astolf felt the blood thumping in his head as though it were about to burst. Dagon looked at him.

'If you devote yourself to us, Astolf, you have nothing to fear.'

Astolf opened his mind and heart and let Dagon's dark eyes fill them completely.

***

Sunniva stood up in the boat to watch the lights of Metos approach in the darkness. The moon was covered. She could never have imagined coming home in this way. And where was her father? Was he even alive?

139

Dayraven came and stood next to her. She felt his presence very strongly and remembered some of the thoughts she had had about Dayraven during the journey along the river. Then she recalled the scene by the riverbank when she had been bathing. That seemed years earlier, but she knew that only a day and a night had passed. She pushed that scene out of her mind. There was still much to do; this time on the river together had been an interlude, nothing more. Now they had to go on. Sunniva pulled up her hood and bowed her head.

The boat pulled up to the posting station. Some men approached, carrying torches. Sunniva tensed. Could anyone who was chasing them have reached Metos first? *Surely not.*

'We are judges on imperial business,' Dayraven said, showing his insignia.

'Very good, sir,' one of the men said. 'Welcome to Metos. Do you need lodgings?'

'No. We have our own.'

Dayraven stepped ashore carrying his bundle and Sunniva followed.

'Where are your servants?'

'They're following behind with our baggage.'

Sunniva passed in front of Dayraven and led the way. She felt a great wash of relief flood over her, but what would they find at her father's house?

The moon showed itself a little as they walked. The city seemed different to Sunniva seen like this, so silent and dark. She strained her ears but there was no one about. Sunniva relaxed when she saw the familiar central square up ahead. She glanced at Dayraven and he smiled back.

Sunniva went up to her father's house on the square. The familiar stone outline stood in shadow and there was no sound or light. *But there never would be at this time of night. I mustn't be nervous.*

Dayraven hung back, checking the square and streets, while Sunniva knocked at the door. Time passed. She knocked again and heard footsteps.

'Who's there?' an old man's voice said finally.

'Einhard – it's me, Sunniva.'

She heard some whispering and then the door was opened. Sunniva pushed back her hood and let her hair down. An old man and woman stood inside, both holding torches.

'Miss Sunniva!' the old woman said, close to tears. 'And at this time of night! Come in, come in!'

'I'm sorry to get here so late, Rotruda.'

Sunniva went in and Dayraven followed.

'Any news of your father, Miss Sunniva?'

'No. I came back here hoping to find some clues to help me.'

'But we've heard nothing here. When I saw you, I thought –'

'We have to stay hopeful. And what about my brother?'

'We haven't heard anything since he left with the army.'

She noticed that the servants kept glancing at the man standing behind her.

'This is Dayraven, son of Urland,' she said.

Sunniva saw the two old people smile with pleasure at the great warrior's name.

'There's just the two of us living here now,' Rotruda said. 'We don't have anything ready at all for you, but we'll prepare the rooms and some food now.'

141

'Thank you, but what we most need right now is as much light as possible in my father's study.'

'Right now?'

'Yes. I know it seems strange, but it's important.'

Sunniva followed the old couple up the stairs. Everything was just as she remembered it but also so different. Sunniva smiled at how curious the old servants looked about her priest's robe and the man she was travelling with. That was understandable, she thought, but explanations would have to wait. If they were being followed, there was no telling how much time they had. Maybe very little, so they had to use whatever time they had.

They reached the door to the study.

'Everything is just as your father left it,' Rotruda said.

She opened the door and Sunniva felt a flood of cold, musty air on her face. *Like a tomb. No, I mustn't think like that.*

Dayraven looked into the study. In the flickering torchlight he could see shelves of scrolls and a table covered with scientific instruments. Perhaps things would become clearer now.

The old people rushed around, fetching lamps and torches and lighting a fire. Dayraven took one of the torches out of its bracket on the wall and went over to the shelves. Sunniva's father had a fine library, as he had expected, but there was nothing there that seemed likely to help them solve the puzzles they had brought from Axo.

Dayraven crossed over to look at the instruments on the table. He had seen more modern versions of many of them in Theodorica, and these were covered in a thin layer of dust.

Sunniva opened the window to let in some fresh air. The door closed and Dayraven looked around. The old couple had left and there was plenty of light and warmth in the room now. Sunniva was standing at the bookshelves, reaching behind some scrolls at the very top.

'My father used to keep the second bracelet hidden in a box behind a panel in the wall –'

'Maybe I can help you.'

'I've got it. But –' Sunniva brought back down a long, flat metal box with jade inlay. 'But this isn't the box he used to keep it in.'

'There's nothing else hidden up there?'

'No.'

'Then let's try and open this one.'

Dayraven took the box and turned it around. It was beautifully made and seamless.

'There doesn't seem to be a lock on it,' he said.

'There must be. Or else we'll have to smash it to get it open, and that wouldn't be easy. We might even damage whatever's inside.'

'Just a moment. Halakh used to have something similar.'

Dayraven took out his knife and dug at some of the ornaments on the box. Finally, one of them lifted up and revealed a lock underneath. He looked up and saw Sunniva's face glowing with excitement.

'Try the key we found in Urland's sword,' she said.

Dayraven took out the key and fitted it in the lock. It slotted in perfectly. He turned the key and heard a slight click. Dayraven's breath caught in his throat and his eyes met Sunniva's. Hers were shining. *Like mine must be.* He

143

lifted the lid and saw the second bracelet resting on a thick pile of parchment.

Dayraven picked up the bracelet. 'This is an exact match for the one Halakh was wearing. I'll start trying to decipher the writing on them.'

'Let's see what's written on the parchment first. It might explain things.'

She took out the pile of parchment and opened it. There were many pages. Dayraven could see a look of surprise on Sunniva's face and moved to glance at the first page. It was covered with strange symbols.

'It's from my father,' Sunniva said. 'He's written it in a code that we used to use when I was a child. It's based on substituting letters with invented symbols.'

'Can you still read it?'

'Yes, but it will take me a little while to get used to it again. I'll read it aloud. "Dearest Sunniva. If you are reading this, I am probably dead."'

She closed her eyes for a long moment and then looked at Dayraven. He felt a stab of sadness run through him, and put his hand on her shoulder.

'We don't know what's happened to him yet, Sunniva. Try to read on.'

'"And if you are reading this, then Dayraven, son of Urland, should be with you."'

'Remember how the clues in the Octagonal Temple at Axo referred to both of us? Obviously, your father knew about that.'

'"We need you and Dayraven to work together. As you know, I have never trusted your brother for my work as I have trusted you, Sunniva. You and Dayraven have both been trained for many years for what you must do.

144

The risks are great, but we had no choice but to involve you.'"

'Who's the "we" he talks about?'

'I don't know. I'm sure it will be explained – ah, here it is. "For most of my life, I have been one of three Guardians of a great secret. The other Guardians and I inherited this task from those before us, as they inherited it from those before them. There have been many generations of Guardians. The secret we guard is so great that all the regions of the world where the Face of the Akhen has appeared were involved in protecting it. In my time, one Guardian was a Faustian, one a Magian and one a Jael.'"

Dayraven was trembling with anticipation. He knew what was going to come next.

"'I was the Faustian Guardian. The Magian Guardian was Al-Suli of Theodorica. The Jaelite Guardian was Halakh, whom you knew as the Jaelite Uncle.'"

'It all makes perfect sense. You and I are the links to all three Guardians, Sunniva.'

'Yes. "We hoped to hand over the secret to you, Dayraven and another younger person at some future time, but events forced us to act much more quickly. You know the rumours that the Clovian Dynasty is still alive. We came to know for certain that this was true, and we also knew that the Clovians were on the track of our secret.'"

'The golden bee in the temple.'

"'You have heard of Malombra – she is also after the secret for reasons of her own. The safety of the entire empire and the rest of the world is threatened. When Al-Suli disappeared, we knew it was time to act urgently. Dayraven had already returned to Axo, so Halakh went to find him. We both knew that the enemy was close behind us. We Guardians had sworn to protect the secret with our

145

lives, so that the threat of death would never make any of us reveal it, but the enemy could still find the secret. Now it is up to you both to stop them."'

'Halakh left the clues in the Octagonal Temple for us – he must have known the Clovians were close behind.'

'So did my father. "Halakh and I knew the risks when we took our places as Guardians. I am sorry to ask you to take our places in this sudden way, but there was no choice. You will understand when I tell you that we are guarding the Hidden Face."'

Dayraven jumped in shock. He could see that Sunniva was just as surprised.

'Go on,' he said.

'"You have heard about the Hidden Face all your life, Sunniva, but it really exists. All the signs are that the time has come; the Face of the Akhen is alive on Earth now and the Fifth Unmasking is close. Remember everything I told you about the Hidden Face and you will understand the danger we are all in if the Clovians find it. I have tried in this letter to tell you what you need to know about your task. I cannot put anything more in writing in case this falls into the wrong hands. You should have brought with you an object that Halakh was wearing. It is identical to the one you remember from years ago that should be with this letter." That must be Halakh's bracelet and this matching one.'

'Yes.'

'"You should have also brought with you two objects belonging to Dayraven's father. One of them gave you the key to open the box containing this letter. The other will blow its secret from the deep."'

'We found the key in the hilt of Urland's sword. The other object must be Urland's horn. But what does he mean, "blow its secret from the deep"?'

'I don't know. We'll have to think about it later. "These are the only things I can leave you to carry on your task. They will lead you to a tomb you saw as a child. You cried in the mud out of terror. Now you must go back there. You are the only one I can trust. Pray for me as I pray for you now."'

Sunniva folded the parchment and looked up.

'You'll have to explain to me,' Dayraven said. 'What tomb?'

'The tomb of the Clovian king Merech the First, in an abandoned temple near their old capital up north. The king is sitting there, embalmed. My father took me there when I was a child. I thought the king was coming alive again, and I've had nightmares about it ever since. Now my father's sending me back there.'

'We're together now, so we'll both go there – that's what your father wanted, and Halakh and Al-Suli wanted it as well. We'll fight together. Halakh talked to me about the Hidden Face, but tell me what you know about it. The Guardians wanted us to work together, so let's try.'

Sunniva added some wood to the fire; this was going to take some time, and the night was cold. She kept walking up and down while Dayraven sat at the table. Thoughts of her father rose in her mind, but she knew that she had to go on and that there might not be much time.

'The Hidden Face is the identity of the Face of the Akhen,' she said. 'My father used to tell me about this – he researched this and other mysteries all his life. As my father said in his letter, the signs show that the Face is alive now somewhere.'

'That's what Halakh told me as well. He used to say that Jaelites once had the knowledge of when the Face would come and exactly who he or she would be. If anyone found the prophecy, used it to locate the Face and could somehow control him, they would be unstoppable.'

'That's why the Clovians want to find the Face. The last Unmasking gave them power, and they want it again. If the Face is alive somewhere now but has not reached the age of thirty, he is probably living somewhere in seclusion, not even knowing his own real identity. If the Clovians get control of him before then, they – Well, we can't let them gain power again.'

'But the Akhen would not plan on sending the Face back to Faustia again, would it? That has never happened before.'

'No. The Clovians are powerful magicians, though, and the accumulated wisdom of their ancestors that the leader can call on makes them very strong. Maybe they hope that, if they can find the Face, they can alter even the plans of the Akhen.'

'Can anyone do that?'

'I don't know. If anyone can, it would be the Clovians. But you are right – the Face has never appeared in the same part of the world twice. Each Unmasking takes place in a new region, which is how the religion of the Akhen spreads.'

'So, if the Face is already alive somewhere, he or she is probably not in Faustia or anywhere else where he has Unmasked in the past. But where?'

'There's no way of knowing at the moment. As Halakh would have told you, the prophecy of the Hidden Face goes a long way back in history. To King Akhnan of Karna more than two thousand years ago, in the Sisan Era. The Hidden Face apparently contained the complete list of his ancestors going back many centuries, as well as the dates and places in which they lived. If the time has really come now and the Face is living somewhere on earth, the Hidden Face would describe him, identify him. At some stage, that information was placed on a gold tablet as part of the lost Treasure of Akhnan. Let me show you something.'

Sunniva moved to the bookcases and pulled out a very old scroll. Dayraven could see that it was made of a thick, yellowish material that was very different from the usual parchment. Sunniva walked back to where Dayraven was sitting. He moved up a chair and she sat next to him. She opened the scroll very carefully and spread it out on a clear space on the table. Dayraven helped her weigh down the corners with scientific instruments.

Sunniva moved a candle closer. 'This scroll has been precious to me as long as I can remember. It is written in the Periclean language, and the letters are made in a very old style.'

Dayraven bent forward to look at the document. 'I can't really read it. How old is this?'

'Probably about nine hundred years, from the late Periclean Era. My father found it while researching a long time ago. But see the material it's made from? That's papyrus. The scroll was made in Karna.'

'But what does it say? Read it.'

149

'I can probably remember the whole thing. When I was a little girl, it used to fascinate me, so I read it countless times.'

'Well, tell me.'

'It says at the top "Damo, daughter of Agathon the philosopher and Quintus Valerius Ligurius, Apollinian student –"'

'Who were they?'

'I don't know, although I've always wondered. But let's come back to that. It goes on: "- made this list of the Treasure of Akhnan."'

Dayraven jumped in his seat. *The Treasure of Akhnan!* Like many people, he had always heard vague stories about this fabulous collection of wealth and artefacts from the distant past, and here was a description of what it contained.

'Go on!' he said.

'It says "Countless jewels and riches. The Hidden Face."'

'There it is!'

'"The giant golden Akhen. The Sword of the Akhen. The Words of Power. The Tomb of Masks."'

Sunniva looked up at him.

'That's it?' he said.

'What do you mean, "that's it?"? That's an incredible list of treasures!'

'Yes, but doesn't it give any clue as to where to find them?'

'No – it seems to be just a simple catalogue of the Treasure of Akhnan. This is probably the last glimpse we get of the complete treasure before it was split up over the centuries.'

'So, the Hidden Face and these other things could be anywhere.'

'Yes.'

'But some of them sound amazing. "The Tomb of Masks." "The Sword of the Akhen."'

'My father collected legends and stories about them all – if they really exist and are what the legends say they are, they would be incredible prizes as well. But there's no time now to go into all of those – let's keep chasing the Hidden Face. We can't be sure when this list was made. And as for these two people whose names appear – Quintus and Damo – we have no way of knowing exactly what relationship they had to the treasure. If this papyrus was really written in the Periclean Era, as my father thought, then that's more than a thousand years after Akhnan's time. So, did Quintus and Damo make a copy of a list that came from Akhnan's time, or did they make the list themselves?'

'A thousand years later? How?'

'Maybe they rediscovered the treasure after it had been lost for centuries – that would fill in the long gap in the history of the treasure after Akhnan's time. Or maybe someone else found it, and Quintus and Damo saw the treasure and made the catalogue then.'

'And there's no other mention anywhere of Quintus and Damo?'

'Not that I know of. My father spent years looking. When I was a girl, I used to spend a lot of time wondering and inventing stories about them.'

'Stories?'

'Yes. All kinds of stories. I used to wonder if they were students together – they must have been, I think. And Damo's father Agathon the philosopher – did he search for

151

great mysteries from the past like my father did? Did Quintus and Damo have adventures? Did they find the Treasure of Akhnan after it was lost for centuries? Were they in danger from enemies who wanted the treasure for themselves? Did they fall in love? Did they marry?'

Sunniva lifted the instruments off the corners of the papyrus and stood up. She rolled up the papyrus and put it away in the bookshelves. It had been fun to relive her old stories about Quintus and Damo, the young lovers chasing a great treasure. She hoped that Dayraven hadn't thought she was trying to suggest any similarity to their own situation. *Well, there isn't, is there?*

Dayraven stood up and moved closer to the fire. He added some more wood and felt the flames glow hotter.

'If the Guardians knew how dangerous the Hidden Face was, why didn't they just destroy it?' he asked. 'No, of course they wouldn't – it's holy. I'm just getting desperate. Anyway, we still have to find the Hidden Face and stop the Clovians from getting it first. What have we got to go on?'

'Apart from my father's letter, the bracelets and a place – King Merech's tomb.'

'And my father's hunting horn, although we haven't understood yet how that will help us.'

'We have to look at the bracelets next. But what is written on them can't be the Hidden Face itself, can it?'

'I expect it's another part of the mystery the Guardians constructed to hide the Hidden Face.'

There came a knock at the door. The old woman looked in.

'I'm sorry to disturb you, Miss Sunniva, but the baths are hot now and there's food downstairs.'

'You've saved my life, Rotruda,' Sunniva said. 'We'll be down in just a minute.'

The door closed and Dayraven heard the old woman's footsteps retreating. He realised how hungry he was.

'Now that I think of it, food sounds wonderful,' he said. 'I don't feel up to trying to solve any more Jaelite puzzles until I've eaten.'

'And a hot bath! I can't wait to get into some fresh clothes. I'll put the bracelet back in the box where it was – it's sat there all this time, so it will be safer there.'

Dayraven watched as Sunniva put the box containing the bracelet and parchment back in its hiding place, and then followed her out of the room and closed the door behind him. They went downstairs towards the smell of hot food.

There was roast boar, bread and ale on the table. The two old people left Sunniva and Dayraven alone to talk. Dayraven sat down opposite her at the heavy wooden table. This old-fashioned Faustian food was very different from the refined dishes he had been used to in Theodorica, but right now it looked just perfect. He took some bread; it was hot. He bit off a chunk and the taste brought back lots of old memories. The boar was excellent as well.

'Remember what your father wrote about Malombra?' he said. 'She's also looking for the Hidden Face for some different reason. What could that be?'

'I don't know. What do you know about her?'

'The most beautiful woman in the world, so the stories say.'

'I bet you'd like to find out if the stories are true.'

153

'I've wondered about it.' Dayraven saw Sunniva look annoyed. 'But what does it matter to you if I daydream about Malombra or not?'

'You're absolutely right. It doesn't matter to me at all – you can think about her all day if you want.'

Sunniva looked even more annoyed.

They finished eating in silence. Dayraven bathed and then went to his room, where some clean clothes had been laid out for him. He felt fresh and awake after his hot bath and lots of hearty food, but his head was filled with the mystery of the Hidden Face. It all seemed unreal, but after what he had seen in the last few days, he had to believe in it.

There was something else as well, he realised. The prize they had to find was so great that the danger they were in would only increase the closer they got to the secret; their enemies would stop at nothing. He felt ready. His whole life had prepared him for this, and the same applied to Sunniva, he knew. But when he thought of her in danger, other thoughts flooded in as well. This was not the time to say anything to her, though, or even to think those thoughts. The Hidden Face was too important, and the Guardians had trusted them with it.

Dayraven finished dressing and sat on a chair to put on his shoes. A knock came at the door.

'Come in,' he said.

Sunniva pushed open the door. She was dressed as a soldier again.

'My father's old clothes are a good fit for you,' Sunniva said.

'A little tight but good.' He stood up.

'I was very tempted to dress as a woman when I saw the clothes I'd left behind here – it feels as if I've been a

154

man forever, but I'm back to being a soldier again. A priest wearing weapons and chain mail would not be very convincing, and from now on, we have to be ready for anything.'

'Yes. I've been thinking – whatever happens, we have to keep going until we find the Hidden Face. So, if somehow we are separated along the way, we must each go on alone.'

'I was thinking that as well. We need a place to meet up again, but not here.'

'No. We might be followed.'

'Well, we can't go back to Axo.'

'No, so it will have to be my father's estate near Liga up north. I haven't been back there yet to see what condition it's in, but it should be good enough for us to hide out for a while if we need to.'

'Urland's estate near Liga – should be easy to find. And not that far from the old Clovian capital where we have to go now.'

Dayraven saw a cloud pass over her face.

'Sunniva, you were just a child when you saw King Merech's tomb last time. He's been dead for centuries – there's nothing to be afraid of.'

'You weren't there.'

'Well, I will be this time. Now, we'd better go upstairs and try and find out what's written on the bracelets. I feel ready now.' Dayraven slung Urland's hunting horn over his shoulder. 'I hope we can understand what this horn has to tell us as well.'

Sunniva left the room and Dayraven followed, closing the door behind him.

Sunniva walked up the stairs, hearing Dayraven behind her. She felt for Halakh's bracelet that she was carrying inside her cloak.

She pushed open the door of the study and caught her breath in shock. The man they had fought in the Octagonal Temple was standing at the table, taking the other bracelet out of its box. The box had been levered apart by his knife. The man's hood was pushed back. He looked up, and Sunniva gasped and stood frozen to the spot.

'Perin!'

The man rushed to the window, carrying the bracelet, and looked back at her for an instant while Dayraven ran forward with his sword drawn. He chopped at the man at the window, who blocked with his own sword and lashed out with his foot, striking Dayraven in the chest. Dayraven staggered back and the hunting horn slipped onto the floor. The man slid out the window and vanished. *It's like seeing a ghost.*

Dayraven ran to the door. Sunniva picked up the horn and followed.

'You recognised him?' Dayraven called back to her.

'He's Emperor Calvo's illegitimate son, Perin the hunchback.'

Dayraven started down the stairs.

'Miss Sunniva? What's happening?'

She turned and saw Einhard the old servant holding a candle.

'I don't know, Einhard, but you and Rotruda should get away from here.'

Sunniva took a deep breath and started down the stairs. She hoped the old people would be all right – they knew nothing about all this. She heard Dayraven fling open the front door. His footsteps ran into the darkness and turned to the left.

She reached the bottom of the stairs and opened the door, drawing her sword at the same time. Yells and the sounds of fighting came from the left, and Sunniva ran that way.

She turned the corner and stopped in shock. Dayraven was surrounded by armed men, and behind them stood a white canopy. Sunniva started forward.

'No!' Dayraven shouted. 'They've got me – go on alone!'

Sunniva stopped, her mind racing. Dayraven was right; there were too many of them. If they were both captured or killed, no one else could protect the Hidden Face. Two men advanced from around the canopy with drawn swords and there was no more time to think. Sunniva blocked the first attack and stepped out of the way of the second, kicking the man to the ground as he passed.

'Go!' Dayraven yelled.

'I'll find you!' Sunniva shouted back.

She turned and ran back past her father's house. Fast footsteps followed her, and Sunniva ran on, her heart racing.

'Here,' a voice whispered from the shadows near the house.

Sunniva ran towards the voice and a low doorway opened. *The passage to the cellar! There's a way out from there.*

She ducked under the door and it was closed behind her. Sunniva heard her heart pounding. There was a soft scratching sound and then a candle flared and she saw Rotruda.

'We'll leave once I've seen you safe, Miss Sunniva,' Rotruda said softly and then led the way.

From the roof above, the Twister watched Sunniva run. He looked back and saw Dayraven being disarmed and led away after the white canopy. So, Malombra had captured him; she would have captured the water spirit as well if she could. The Twister felt anger boil inside him. Malombra was his enemy, like Astolf. It was all lies and treachery, but he had what they wanted.

He brought out the bracelet and it gleamed in the moonlight. He didn't know why it was so important, but this must be what Malombra was looking for. He had been outside the window just long enough to see and hear it being hidden in the box. The Twister put the bracelet away. With this, he could somehow save the water spirit and get his power back. His hump tingled at the thought. *Yes, both of us will get our power back,* it said. *Of course, hump – where I go, you go.*

He thought of how the spirit had called him by a different name. *Perin. Perin. Yes.* Once, he had been Perin. But that was before the hermitage, before he had been thrown out into the darkness. As Perin, he had been happy, but Perin was dead. Now he was the Twister. That was what they had made him. *Not Perin. The Twister.*

PART THREE

The forest near Metos.

Sunniva stepped off the road into the darkness under the trees. The chasing footsteps had stopped long since. She looked back at the town in the distance, where a few lights shone, and leant against the trunk of a tree. Her breath came in gasps and her heart was thumping.

She needed to think; there had been no time before. Had it been right to leave Dayraven? But he had told her to go, and there had been too many enemies. It looked as though they wanted to take Dayraven alive, not kill him, so there was still hope.

But that white canopy? They said that Malombra travelled around like that. Her father's letter had warned them about Malombra, so it must be her, and now she had captured Dayraven. And what about the old servants, Rotruda and Einhard? She hoped they had escaped.

Sunniva heard horses approaching from the direction of the town and drew farther back into the shadows. The sound became louder and then she saw a large group of armed riders. Sunniva reached for her sword but then stopped; this was not Malombra's group. They were heavily armed cavalry soldiers but dressed in dark colours without any distinctive markings, so there was no telling who they were or where they came from. The soldiers passed by just twenty paces in front of her. The smell of horses was strong, and the clinking of metal and the drum of hooves were loud. Sunniva tried to see the face of their leader under his helmet, but it was too dark for that.

The horses went on and Sunniva breathed more freely and thought. *Perin the hunchback!* It was definitely him.

159

She had seen his face and there was no doubt; she had even seen his hump clearly. He was supposed to have died of fever years earlier, but here he was, alive. Everything about the last few days had been surprising, so why not that?

Perin had taken the bracelet. He must have been hidden at the window and overheard them talking about it. He was agile enough to have climbed up there; she had seen that in the Octagonal Temple. It had clearly been him in the temple. The same clothes, the same stature. But why had Perin taken the bracelet? Was he working for Malombra? He had not been among Malombra's group when Dayraven was captured. *But wait!* In the Octagonal Temple, he had left the golden bee, so he was working for the Clovians. But was that possible? The Clovians were the enemies of Perin's dynasty.

Sunniva's mind was whirling. She pushed all these thoughts aside; there were too many of them and she knew too little to be sure of anything. *Was it right that I left Dayraven behind? But that was what he told me to do.* Sunniva felt the weight of the hunting horn on her shoulder and half the bracelet inside her cloak. Dayraven had sent her away not just to save her but to save those objects; if she went back now and was caught, Malombra would get hold of them.

No, she had to go on as her father had wanted, back to the tomb of Merech. Sunniva gulped as she thought of the mummified king still sitting on his throne after centuries, but there was no other way; she had to face him again. What was she going to do there? There was no way of knowing, but there was no choice either.

Sunniva looked left and right. The road was clear, so she stepped out and turned away from the town, north

160

towards the homeland of the Clovians. She had to get as far away as possible by the time daylight came.

One step after another, Sunniva lulled herself into a walking trance. The only thing that mattered for now was to keep moving. She let her mind wander where it wanted, while her body went on. Thoughts floated up, showed themselves for a while and then disappeared, to be replaced by others. *Father – Dayraven – Perin – bracelets – Halakh – Octagonal Temple – Death – elephant — so tired – Malombra – river – Father – Dayraven – Metos – Axo – king Merech in his tomb – feet hurt – Urland's hunting horn – lion on the ceiling – thirsty – Clovians – Dayraven – hungry – bracelets – Hidden Face – guardians – can't go on must go on – Perin – Merech's tomb – the Face of the Akhen – the Fifth Unmasking –*

Light. Dawn was rising to the right. Sunniva saw a clearing in the forest along the road and went in so that she would not be seen from the road. She sat down on a fallen tree trunk and realised how tired she was, and how hungry. Her feet were aching. She had walked all night. That had kept her warm, but now she needed to rest, sleep even. And to eat and drink – but eat what? She had left the house in a rush without taking any food or wine. Even if she had food, it would be too dangerous to light a fire for cooking or for warmth. And what about a horse? During the night, the important thing had been to get as far away as possible, but now she had to think of these things.

Together with these thoughts, worries about Dayraven pushed their way in, although there was nothing she could do for him now. Sunniva took off the hunting horn and her sword and rested them against the tree trunk. She took off her cloak, then lifted off her chain mail coat and stretched her shoulders and neck; it felt good without that weight. She took off her helmet and put it down next to her.

Sunniva loosened her hair and shook it out. Keeping her hair tied up for so long always gave her a slight headache. She looked around; the forest was thick, dark and very quiet. The early-morning sun struggled to fight its way through this dense growth. Now it was time to think of the things she needed and how to get them.

Something landed at her feet with a thud. Sunniva jumped and drew her sword. She heard a rustling sound in the branches and looked up, but there were only leaves and branches above her. She glanced down and jumped in surprise; a loaf of bread was lying there. Sunniva looked around her. Everything was still. Keeping her sword in one hand, she picked up the bread. It was warm and smelt good.

There came another thud behind her. Sunniva spun around and saw a small wooden cask of wine rolling on the ground. She heard more rustling in the trees above her and looked up but couldn't see anyone.

'Who's there?'

'I am the Twister now,' a voice said somewhere above her.

'Twister? Perin, is that you?'

'I was Perin, but Perin is dead. Now I am the Twister.'

'Do you remember me, Perin? I'm Sunniva, Ado's daughter – we knew each other when we were children.'

'I know you. You are the water spirit. You can change your shape, but I always recognise you.'

Sunniva felt a spasm of surprise run through her. *Water spirit?* What was he talking about? Perhaps an illness had driven him mad.

'Perin, I thought you were dead. Really dead.'

'That's what Astolf told everyone when they shut me in the hermitage, but I didn't die. I changed into the Twister.'

'Astolf? You can't trust him, Perin.'

'I know. He sent the creature to kill me, but now I have you to protect me. And I will protect you.'

Sunniva's mind was hurrying ahead. *What creature?*

'Listen, Perin. I know how you must feel about your father the emperor.'

'Nobody could understand. He threw me out and gave my name to someone else.'

It was true, Sunniva knew. Calvo had been desperate to make his dynasty secure. Perin had been illegitimate and a hunchback, but while the emperor had no other son old enough, Perin had been named crown prince. When the emperor's eldest legitimate son grew up, Perin the hunchback had been disinherited and his name had been given to that other son. Perin was the name of the emperor's own father and a traditional name in the family.

'But, Perin, you can't hate your father enough to want the Clovians back, can you? Why are you working for them? They hate all of the emperor's family, including you.'

'I'm not working for them – Astolf had me dress as a Clovian to scare everyone. I am working for myself.'

'What do you mean?'

'I should be the next emperor, not my half-brother. Malombra will help me get my position back. So will Astolf, before I kill him.'

'No, Perin – they are all just using you. Behind all this, there are really the Clovians. Once they get what they want, they won't need you anymore.'

Sunniva heard more rustling and then silence. She looked around the trees above, but it was still too dark to see anything.

'Perin? Perin? You must believe me.'

'I want to believe you. You are my good spirit.'

The voice came from a different place above her. Sunniva turned around, looking up, but couldn't see anyone.

'You must believe me, Perin. If the Clovians come back, they will kill us all.'

'Yes, I see now. The evil creature is a bee – that is its true form. It can change into a lion or an elephant, but in the end, it must turn into a bee again, and then I can destroy it.'

'Listen, Perin. You took something from us back in the town – a bracelet. It is very important.'

'I know; that is why I took it.'

'But you must give it back to me.'

'I cannot; it is the key to everything. I can use it to defeat our enemies and save you.'

'Don't worry about saving me. If Dagon or Malombra get that bracelet, it will be disaster for all of us.'

There was only silence above. Sunniva sheathed her sword.

'Perin? Are you still there? You must listen to me!'

'Eat and drink now, then rest – sleep. I will come back later. I will always be near you. You are mine.'

The branches above rustled and then there was silence again.

'Perin! Come back! Perin!'

Sunniva stood listening, but the only sound was a slight breeze running over the leaves.

***

The dawn light was touching the tops of the forest, and Astolf felt tired and stiff from riding. He had passed the town of Liga some way back, so this must be the place. *A crossroads with a disused road heading off to the right.* Malombra had arranged this meeting place so that information could be exchanged. He was going to use it for something else, though. Astolf knew that he would be unable to find the person he was looking for, so the only way was to show himself like this and wait for the person to find him.

Astolf stopped his horse, climbed down and stretched his legs and back. The mist was lifting around him, and the first day birds were singing. Astolf took a bottle of wine from his saddlebag and drank. That warmed him. He thought of how different his dreams of power and wealth had been from the reality. He had hoped to sit around in luxury while other people took the risks; instead, he found himself riding from one scary person to another, hoping to somehow stay alive. He drank again and tried to cancel these thoughts. Ever since last time at the villa of the bees, he had felt Dagon inside his mind; not openly at the front but hidden in the back, watching. He shivered.

Astolf put the bottle back in his saddlebag and then froze; an axe blade had appeared at his throat.

'It's me, Death,' he managed to say. 'Astolf.'

The blade withdrew a little, and Astolf slowly turned around. Death the bounty hunter was watching him from behind a long-handled axe, his nostrils quivering. Astolf shivered. *He could have been camped just ten paces away and I would never have known.*

165

'I came to find you, Death. The game has changed. You can still kill Dayraven, but now you're working for someone else. I have something for you.'

Astolf reached inside his tunic and the axe blade moved a little closer.

'Here.'

Astolf held out a small golden bee, noticing how much his hand shook.

'Malombra is not employing you anymore. It's the Clovians. Yes, they are really back and will win the empire. You'll be paid even better – I have money here for you now.'

Astolf reached for his saddlebag and brought out a small bag of gold. He held it out in front of him.

'There'll be much more for you later. When the Clovians are emperors again, there will be no limit to what they can give you.'

Death shook his head.

'I know you don't like to change sides, but you want to kill Dayraven, don't you? There's a better chance of doing that with the Clovians helping.'

Death took the gold.

'Now come with me.'

The axe was withdrawn and Astolf climbed onto his horse. His legs were unsteady, and his throat was so constricted, he could hardly breathe. *This will all be over soon. Soon. Please let it be soon.*

***

Malombra stepped out into her garden and breathed in the scent of the hundreds of different plants that grew there. Early morning was the best time to be there, she

166

thought again. Malombra had rushed in a carriage, ahead of the white canopy and her prisoner, to make it back by dawn.

The sun peeped over the high stone wall around the garden, bathing the trees and the rows of flowers and shrubs a pinkish red. The little birds chattered as the light flooded in, and the rare white peacock that sat on top of the wall honked. *Yes, all of nature loves the dawn.*

Malombra walked over the cool grass, wearing a simple white dress and sandals; she loved the feel of the dew on her ankles and toes. This was the time of day when everything was freshest. Most of the flowers were opening out for the day, showing their beauty to the light, and so did she. Malombra wore no veils or any kind of mask there in her garden, showing her face to the plants just as they showed themselves to her.

She brought out a slender knife from the folds of her dress. Dawn was also the best time to select and cut the herbs she needed, as they were freshest then. It was a constant delight to her to see fronds, flowers or leaves that had been short of perfect the night before turn out to be just right early the next morning; that extra night's rest often completed nature's work.

Malombra stopped a moment to breathe in deeply once more. The scent of the garden was as rich as anything could be, but delicate at the same time. Business had called her away from this villa and from her garden for some days, and it was blissful to be back there again. Every individual scent in the air and every single plant had a use and a story. She walked along the lanes of plants, running her fingers over some of them. There couldn't be a garden like it anywhere, Malombra thought again. All of her pleasure herbs, poisons and drugs grew there. Her garden children, she called them. The garden was the result of years of work in finding and sending for plants from all over the world, and of her own skill in caring for them.

Men obsessed about her beauty, but the garden was the real secret of her power, and partly the secret of her beauty, as well. Malombra gathered particular roots to crush, flowers to press for their juices, fruits to squeeze and herbs to pound, and from them made creams, pastes, drops and powders for her skin. Some kept her face youthful, bright and free of lines, her forehead clear, her cheeks glowing with youth and vitality, her lips full and succulent; some kept her eyes glistening; from other garden children she ground pomades and lotions that she mixed in her bath water or smeared over her body to keep her skin firm, her waist trim and her buttocks and thighs tight and smooth; others produced a juice that kept her voice sweet and irresistible to men.

Malombra reached the back wall and turned left. The beauty plants were her everyday friends that were like food and air to her, but this section of the garden she was walking in now contained special friends she called on when needed for precise tasks. This powder-blue flower on a long thin stalk was leopard paw, the core ingredient of an exquisite invisible poison that left no trace; this ugly brown root was stone bush, giver of excruciating pain in the tiniest amounts. She stopped in front of a shrub hung with flat, long fruit; this was today's special friend. Malombra reached out and gripped it with one hand, and used the knife to detach one of the fruits. This was succubus tongue, just right for today's guest.

She turned back towards the villa. The ancient marble pillars and arches glowed orange in the light, while the darker new stone around it seemed to soak up the light instead. Usually at this time, she would practise her two-sword fighting technique out there. The exercise helped keep her figure perfect and gave her another useful way of disposing of enemies, particularly when the sword blades were coated with a poison from her garden. She would not practise swords this morning, though; today, she had another appointment.

Malombra walked to a secluded corner up against a wall of the villa, where there stood a chair and an empty wooden cradle. Malombra sat in the chair and placed the knife and the succubus tongue fruit in the cradle, admiring yet again the cradle's ornate carving. There had not been a moment to admire the child she had given birth to years before; it had been taken from her immediately and she never saw it. Boy or girl, she had never learned, but soon she would have another child that the whole world would admire.

Malombra checked the sundial that hung on the wall of the villa in front of her; it was almost time. She shifted her chair closer to the wall and put her head against the opening there. This was connected by narrow tunnels with the basement and dungeons far belowground. By opening certain vents and closing others, Malombra could hear directly from any particular room in the large underground area. Today, there was just one room that she wanted to hear from, any second now.

Malombra rocked the cradle back and forth and sang a lullaby. Then came the sound she had been waiting for; a man's screams of agony. They grew stronger, faded, stopped, then started again. Malombra smiled and rocked the cradle a little faster; her chief torturer knew his trade well. The victim started to plead a long prayer for mercy, for death, for anything to stop the agony. Then the screams

169

returned, louder than before. Malombra closed her eyes, rocked the cradle and sang the lullaby. This would put her in just the right mood for Dayraven's visit.

***

Dayraven ached all over. The ropes he was tied with dug into his wrists and ankles. He had been lying in this covered wagon for hours. Exactly how long, he couldn't tell, but he had seen the light outside change from pitch black to the pink of dawn and had felt the wagon rattle over bridges and along roads, crawl up mountains and splosh through rivers. There was no way of telling where he was now, or even in which direction they had travelled.

And Sunniva? What had happened to her? Was she also a prisoner of Malombra? If she had escaped, where was she now? Had she decided to try and rescue him, or was she following the trail of the Hidden Face? Dayraven hoped that she was heading north as her father's letter had told them to. It was unlikely that Sunniva could rescue him alone, and by trying, she would risk being captured herself and giving her half of the bracelet to Malombra.

The man who had stolen the other half of the bracelet – Sunniva had said it was Perin, Emperor Calvo's illegitimate hunchback son. Dayraven thought back to when he had last seen Perin, before his own exile to Magia. Sunniva was probably right about him; Dayraven's own memories went back fifteen years or more, so he couldn't be sure, while Sunniva must have seen Perin more recently. He had heard that Perin the hunchback was dead, but now he was alive and working for the Clovians, it seemed. *Anything is possible in this world.*

Dayraven thought again of Sunniva and gritted his teeth at how powerless he felt. He couldn't help her now; all he could do was try to stay alive and understand why he was still alive. Malombra's men had searched him thoroughly, so she must know that he wasn't carrying any important objects. What was Malombra planning?

He heard gates open and close behind the wagon. After a very short time, the driver stopped the horses and got down. Dayraven heard many men crowding around the wagon. The cover was wrenched off, bright light poured over him and Dayraven closed his eyes against it. He was dragged upright and opened his eyes. Guards were unloading horses and other wagons; it was late morning, judging by the sky. The wagon had stopped in the courtyard of a huge villa. The two-story building enclosed the open space on all four sides. There were a lot of houses like that in the empire, so he still had no clue as to exactly where he was.

A guard clambered into the back of the wagon and cut the ropes with a knife, and Dayraven felt the blood burn back into his hands and feet. The guard and another man pulled him out of the wagon onto his feet. Dayraven staggered, and they held him upright until the feeling came back into his legs. He was surrounded by armed men. He walked unsteadily between two men up the stairs and into the house. They had given him no time to try and recognise the surrounding countryside.

The inside of the villa was clean and elegant but contained little furniture and few ornaments. There were many servants and guards in the corridors and rooms they passed through. Whoever lived there wanted to give little idea of who they were or where they came from, Dayraven thought. He felt the strength coming back into his arms and legs. They were taking him to the far side of the house, Dayraven could tell.

The two men on either side let go of his arms and Dayraven walked unaided. He saw a heavy, high door up ahead with guards on either side. Well before he reached the door, the guards pushed it open. Dayraven could see a gigantic bed covered by a white veil at the far end of the room; there was no shadow or any movement behind the veil. In front of the veil stood a large *shatranj* board, a chair and a small table. The table held silver plates of bread and fruit, a gold pitcher of wine and a cloth. The guards waved him forward, and Dayraven went and sat in the chair. Two men armed with spears stood on either side of the veil, and many others all around him.

The sight of the food made Dayraven realise how hungry he was, but he remembered that Malombra was as famous for her potions and poisons as she was for her beauty. He tried not to look at the food or even think about it, and turned his attention to the *shatranj* board. It was set up with a game in progress. Dayraven concentrated on the position of the pieces to block out the smell of the food. The pieces on his side of the board were badly placed; whoever had put them there had little idea of strategy. The other side's pieces had been handled very well. The opposing player had used an aggressive double-flank *tabla* known as the "pincer": both chariots had been brought up early into the middle of the board, pointing at the king on Dayraven's side. Al-Suli had never used this *tabla* and never taught it to Dayraven, because it was too risky, but he had taught him how to play against it. If only the defence hadn't been handled so badly from his side of the board.

'Interesting game, isn't it?' a female voice said.

172

Dayraven looked up and saw a faint shadow behind the veil. 'Interesting from your side of the board, Malombra – from this side, it looks difficult.'

Silver laughter came from behind the veil, and Dayraven felt a shiver of delight run through him. His thoughts immediately jumped to the other side of the veil, but he fought to control them.

'Yes,' Malombra said. 'My opponent has defended badly against my *tabla*. You know him – Astolf.'

Astolf? It was no surprise that Astolf was a traitor, but what exactly was his involvement with Malombra? Were they working with the Clovians? And what had happened to Sunniva? There were many questions to be answered. Escape seemed impossible, but as long as he was alive, there was hope, and anything he learned might be very important later.

'You've gone quiet, Dayraven.'

'I was thinking about the *shatranj* position.'

Again the silver laughter rang from behind the veil. It raced over his body like the thrill of wine.

'But you must be starving, Dayraven. Eat. Drink.'

'I can go without.'

'You think I would bring you all this way to poison you? If I wanted that, you'd be dead already.'

'What do you want, Malombra?'

'I want to finish this game.'

'Then bring Astolf here – it won't take you long to beat him from this position.'

'Astolf is a fool, as you have known for many years, and he plays *shatranj* like a fool. But you, Dayraven – you are a master of the game, and the best student of one of the supreme masters.'

173

'Al-Suli? You know Al-Suli? What happened to him?'

'Think of yourself, Dayraven. Could you win this game starting from this position? Do you want to try? I've waited a long time to test myself against a master like you.'

Dayraven looked again at the pieces. It would be hard to do, but his king could be defended, and then he could start taking advantage of Malombra's overextended position.

'What if I refuse to play?' he said.

'Then there was no point bringing you here. And no point keeping you alive.'

'And if I play and win, what's the prize?'

'The same prize that Astolf was playing for but was never going to win – you get to cross the veil and see me.'

'Every man who has that good luck ends very badly, I hear.'

'The only ones who say that are the envious ones who have never been on this side. The ones who have think it's worth any price. Look over to your left.'

Dayraven turned and saw a young man about his own age with a light blue cloth tied over his eyes. He was looking towards the sound of Dayraven's voice with an expression of hate, anger and jealousy all mixed together.

'Look at him, Dayraven,' Malombra said. 'He hates you now because I am giving you a chance to have what I give to him. He wouldn't want his eyesight back if it meant losing me.'

Memories flooded into Dayraven's mind. Where had he seen this man before? He was very changed. Then it came to him.

'Maugris!' Dayraven said. 'We knew each other as children. You went to Seanor for many years, but then I

174

met you once in Theodorica when the emperor sent you on a diplomatic mission there. Do you remember me?'

'I remember you,' the blind man said in a bitter tone.

Dayraven felt shocked. Maugris had been one of the most prominent young men in the empire. He was descended from the oldest, most important families and was as good a warrior as anyone, and now he was a blind slave obsessed with the pleasure Malombra gave him.

'Is that what I have to look forward to if I win?' Dayraven asked. 'To end up like Maugris?'

'If you lose, all you have to look forward to is death,' Malombra said. 'But beat me in this game and I promise you ecstasy like you never dreamt of. But enough talk – either play or die. It's your move.'

Dayraven's mind was racing. The only way to have any chance of finding Sunniva and saving the Hidden Face was to stay alive, and to do that, he had to play the game. He ate and drank a bit, then reached out and brought a horse into the centre of the board.

Dayraven watched the perfect hand emerge from the veil and pull back an elephant in retreat. He drank some more wine and thought of his next move. It was not comforting to be eating and drinking in Malombra's villa, but the food and drink were giving him the strength to play and win this game. Malombra had laughed at how cautious his first sip of wine had been, and nothing bad had happened. His mind was running quickly over the possible moves; Dayraven thought that he had never played better than this.

He pushed up a foot soldier in the centre and Malombra retreated with her vizier. Dayraven advanced another foot soldier, and the hand twitched and then vanished inside the veil.

Dayraven ate some more fruit and wiped his hands on a cloth laid over the table. The game was turning against Malombra; the position he had taken over from Astolf had been difficult, but Dayraven had managed to save it. As Al-Suli had taught him, the *tabla* used by Malombra was designed for a quick victory by smashing through the centre with the chariots to attack the enemy king, so Dayraven had fortified the centre and now he was starting to advance with his foot soldiers. Malombra's slowness in moving showed that she had realised the dangers in her position; the chariots were the most powerful pieces, but bringing them out so early in the game left them vulnerable to attack in the middle of the board.

Malombra's hand reappeared and dragged one of her chariots sideways, trying to find a way to get the chariot safely back behind her less valuable pieces, so he brought up an elephant to cover the retreat square. Malombra shoved the chariot sideways again and Dayraven advanced a foot soldier. Malombra brought her other chariot to the side of the board, so Dayraven moved up a foot soldier on that side. There was no escape for the chariots now; they were lumbering around like bulls trapped in a tiny room.

Malombra shifted her second chariot back towards the centre, and Dayraven advanced another foot soldier. In a few more moves, both chariots would be captured by his foot soldiers, and then he would have a huge advantage in pieces and could bring out his own chariots to attack Malombra's king; she would have no defence.

The perfect hand clenched and unclenched its fingers and then moved the first chariot to the side of the board. Dayraven advanced another foot soldier; now both chariots were immobilised and would soon be taken.

The hand disappeared inside the veil for a moment and then came out again to knock over Malombra's king. She had conceded the game; Dayraven felt a weight lift from his shoulders.

'Bring him,' Malombra said.

Men grabbed Dayraven from every side and dragged him away.

***

Sunniva woke with a start. She was slumped against a tree trunk and the sun was streaming through the branches. Her neck was sore from having slept awkwardly, so Sunniva stood up and flexed her shoulders. She looked at the half-eaten bread and the bottle of wine and smiled. So, it had really happened. *Perin up in the trees.*

But what woke me? She was sure there had been a particular noise. Then it came again – a horse! Sunniva took up her sword and walked towards the sound.

Behind a large tree stood a tall stallion wearing fine fittings, grazing. She went up to the horse, and it lifted its head and looked at her. This looked like a very good animal. The saddlebags looked full, so Sunniva opened them; they were loaded with food, drink, money, flints, torches and a change of female clothes, and a well-made spear hung by the horse's side. Sunniva laughed – Perin was a great thief. Somewhere, the owners of all these things must be furiously searching for them. She had to hope that the owner of the horse did not see her, but that was a risk she would have to take.

Sunniva untied the horse, led it back and tied it to another tree. She drank a little wine and ate some more bread, and then put the food into the horse's saddlebags.

177

Sunniva looked around the trees swaying above her. If Perin were up there, she could see him in this light, but there was no one in the trees and she heard no voice. *What is Perin doing? And Dayraven?* Sunniva felt a stab of worry for him, but she had made her choice and had to follow it through. She was still sure that Dayraven would have agreed with her choice.

Sunniva tucked up her hair and put on her armour and weapons. She would have loved to bathe, but that had to wait. At least she had had a hot bath at the house in Metos, although that already seemed a very long time ago. The horse stamped its foot.

Yes, it's time to move on. She untied the horse and stood on the tree trunk to mount, then walked the horse to the edge of the road and looked both ways. A merchant's wagon in the distance was approaching from the town, but otherwise there was no one. Sunniva trotted the horse onto the road and turned left, heading north.

Sunniva urged the horse into a canter; it was a pleasure to ride such a well-trained stallion. The wind rushing past her face was fresh and she wished her hair could be left flying free, but she still had to play the part of a soldier.

Her plan now was to travel by day and rest by night; not knowing this country well left no other choice. The horse was fresh and well fed, so she could go a long way before dark.

She saw two riders in the distance. It was difficult to be sure from so far away, but they looked like the soldiers she had seen the night before. *Probably scouts sent out by the main group.*

Sunniva saw that the road divided up ahead. The main road she was on now was faster but also gave a much greater chance of being seen, while the other road branching off to the left was narrow and overgrown with weeds, but she could probably travel unnoticed.

Sunniva swung the horse to the left on to the narrow road. Weeds brushed her legs as she rode, and the country became flat and swampy. Light drizzle started to fall, reminding her of that trip to Merech's tomb when she was a child; she recalled the wagon rolling through this type of landscape for what had seemed like weeks. Sunniva pushed those memories aside. She was no longer a child. The Guardians had trusted her with a great secret because they believed in her, and she had to be worthy of their trust.

Time passed in a grey blur. The horse began to tire, so Sunniva rode into a clearing and dismounted. The rain had stopped but the ground was still a little muddy. She tied the horse to a tree, took off the saddle and fittings, and rubbed it down as best she could. The horse started grazing, and Sunniva realised that she was hungry as well. She took off her armour and brought some food out of the saddlebags. Perin had stolen some beer as well, so she opened the small keg and tasted it; the beer was good and she felt better straight away. Sunniva walked up and down while she ate, trying to ease her tired muscles after hours of riding.

They had made good time. There were still two hours of daylight, judging from the sun, but every step was taking her closer to her old nightmare of King Merech in his tomb. *What's going to happen at the tomb? What do I have to go on? Half a bracelet that I can't understand and a hunting horn.* Sunniva thought again of what her father had written about the horn: '*It will blow its secret from the deep*'. What did that mean? Did she have to find a valley somewhere and play the horn to call someone? But which valley? And

179

how would that help? There must be something else, but what?

Sunniva put the food and drink back in the saddlebags and took up the horn, feeling the dents made in it during the fight in the Octagonal Temple. '*It will blow its secret from the deep':* her father had written that. He knew how she thought – he had taught her, so it must be a message that she could understand. It must be the seeing game again. The horn was not just a piece in the game but a real object; she was only seeing the outside, but the horn had an inside as well. '*It will blow its secret from the deep'. From deep inside.*

She grabbed her sword and sat on the ground with the horn held between her feet and the point stuck in the ground. It was a shame to ruin such a precious object, but she had to try. Sunniva hacked at the wide end of the horn; it was hard and just a few splinters broke off. She chopped again and saw a thin split appear. She hit the split and then again, harder. The horn was breaking open. She struck again; the split was over halfway down the length of the horn. She struck again and the horn fell apart in two pieces. Sunniva laid her sword down and picked up one of the pieces. There was something etched inside; the symbol of the Fifth Planet. She picked up the other piece. There was something etched in there as well; the symbol of the First Planet.

She scratched with her nails to see if there were anything else to find, but that was it; Fifth Planet and First Planet. Did it mean just the names of those planets, or was it some sort of code? She had to hope that their meaning would become clear at the tomb of Merech.

Sunniva looked up at the sun and calculated that she could travel for at least another hour before dark. That would bring her close to the tomb, where she would camp overnight and then reach king Merech early the next morning. And then? There was no way of knowing. *Fifth Planet and First Planet*. Would they help? *And Dayraven? Where is he now?* They had travelled so far and solved so many mysteries together, but she would have to solve this one alone.

She shivered at the thought of King Merech still sitting there on his throne, mummified. He had waited centuries for her to find him when she was a little girl, and now he was waiting for her again.

Sunniva forced herself not to think of these things. She was deep within the Clovians' traditional territory there, and every step meant greater danger. If she were caught, the fewer clues she were carrying, the better. Fifth Planet and First Planet were easy to remember, and the other things had already provided their clues and were of no further use. Just in case, she would mark the spot so that she could find it again if necessary.

Sunniva used her sword to dig a shallow hole in the spongy ground under a tall tree. She wrapped the pieces of horn, Dayraven's wax tablet and the scroll from Axo in a cloth and laid them in the hole, filled it in and covered it with leaves. The place was set back from the road and could not be found by anyone who was not looking for it. Sunniva used her sword to mark a cross on the side of the tree trunk facing away from the road.

She dried her sword on some grass, cleaned it with some oiled cloth and put it back in its scabbard. Now the clues lived only inside her head, so if someone wanted to know what they were... Could she stand torture? No one could, they said, so better not to think of it. She would

181

resist, no matter what they did; the secret of the Hidden Face was too important.

The horse looked rested and it was time to ride on. She mounted and walked the horse back onto the road. *Fifth Planet and First Planet. First and Fifth.*

***

Dayraven strained against the ropes that tied his wrists and ankles to the bed, but he knew it was no good. *Malombra's servants must have had a lot of experience in tying men up for her.* Six men had held him and tied him fully clothed to the four corners of the bed, and all he could do was lie there and look up at the white canopy above him, where hung various strong-smelling herbs. There was a small table holding two empty wine goblets and more herbs, but nothing else to see. He had won the game of *shatranj* to stay alive, but there was no escape in sight now.

And Sunniva? He tried to imagine her face but couldn't; his mind filled with Malombra's voice and perfect hand. *Is Malombra really as beautiful as they say?* But how could he even think about that? *Malombra is cruel and evil. If it suits her, she will kill me and Sunniva and anyone else without thinking about it.*

The canopy lifted up at one side and a woman came in and stood by the bed, carrying a big chalice of wine that she put on the table. Dayraven turned and stared; was this Malombra? The woman was dressed in loose white clothes that covered her completely, and wore a soft white hood with a veil that hid her face. *Her body looks superb. What's the matter with me? I shouldn't be thinking of Malombra like this. That wine must have been drugged somehow.*

182

'You look good like that,' the woman said in Malombra's voice. 'And much less dangerous.'

'That wine was drugged.'

'But of course, darling.' She knelt on the bed.

'I'm not your darling.'

'Not yet.'

'What have you done to me?'

She laughed, and boiling blades of desire ran over Dayraven's body.

'Nothing so far, darling – we haven't even started yet. The wine you drank before was just a beginning. You must have noticed some effect already.'

Yes. 'I think it made me play *shatranj* better.'

'Oh, darling, you played wonderfully, but that was just because you wanted me so badly.'

'Let's say I do. Why not untie me?'

'Darling, it's much too early for that. Look at those muscles – you might hurt me or try to escape.'

She ran her hands over his arm and chest, and Dayraven shivered with excitement. *I shouldn't be feeling like this, but I can't help it.*

Malombra poured wine into the two goblets and held one out towards Dayraven.

'No,' he said.

'Darling, this will make our pleasure greater.' She drank some. 'See? After you've been here with me for a while, you'll learn how delicious things can be.'

'And then you'll make me blind like Maugris, or kill me like you've killed other men.'

'Only because they've seen my face. They all became so obsessed with me that they insisted on seeing my face – no man is allowed to see that and keep both his sight and his life.'

'Then keep that veil on.'

'That's what you say now. Poor Maugris was just like you at the start, but now the only thing that keeps him alive is the memory of my face. Drink up – I've waited long enough for you already.'

She put the goblet up to his lips and Dayraven turned his head away.

'Now, darling – you're going to get me angry. I can call men in and have them force this down your throat.'

'Call them, then.'

'What a warrior you are, Dayraven! But I don't want to start out with violence.'

'No? I was expecting to be tortured by now.'

'For what you know about the Hidden Face? Torture would never make you talk, I know that, but soon you'll want to tell me everything. There'll be no secrets between us, darling.'

'No secrets? All right, then – tell me why you want to find the Hidden Face.'

'No secrets.' She drank some more. 'Have you heard of the Holy Graal?'

Dayraven's mind was getting more and more fuzzy. *It must be the wine and the smell of these herbs.* He tried to get his thoughts under control.

'Holy Graal?' he said. 'A hermit had a vision more than three hundred years ago of something he called the Holy Graal, didn't he?'

'Yes, but do you know what it is?'

'A container of some kind – some say it's the cup the Face drank from on the last day of the Fourth Unmasking, before he disappeared.'

'A container, yes, but not of that kind. Inside the Graal there's a child.'

184

'A child? You mean the Holy Graal is a woman?'

'Yes. Me.'

A bolt of shock lanced through Dayraven's dulled mind. 'You? I can't see you as a mother, somehow.'

'I use men for pleasure, yes, but the prophecy of the Hidden Face will lead me to the Face of the Akhen – and he will give me a child.'

'You think the Face could not resist you?'

'Before he is Unmasked, no. No man can – you know that.'

'You're mad.'

'Think of it. A whole dynasty starting with the Face's son – my child. I will almost be the mother of the Akhen. When the Face rules the world, I will be at his side, and when he is gone, the world will belong to my son and to me. Only you know my real plan. Telling you has made me want you even more.'

'What if the Face is female next time?'

'No. I can feel that is impossible. My beauty, my skills in lovemaking, everything has been leading up to this. It is my destiny.'

'You're mad, Malombra.'

'You've already said that, darling – don't be boring. Now, drink up your wine and we'll enjoy each other.'

'No.'

'I'll make it easy for you.'

Malombra put the goblets down and started taking off the top half of her clothes. Dayraven couldn't shift his eyes away; he realised he was losing control but couldn't stop himself. She pulled off the loose white garment and threw it on the bed. Her naked upper body was perfect in every way, and he felt himself fall over the edge into another world, seeing things as though the whole world were somehow slowed down but brighter; all his senses were heightened but as if he were outside himself, watching but unable to control his actions.

Malombra picked up the wine goblets and dipped her breasts into both of them at the same time, then straddled him on the bed and lowered her breasts onto his face.

'Drink, darling – that's it. Now the other one. Good. You're greedy. I like that. Again – here.'

Dayraven heard the words as if from far away; he was floating further and further into the distance.

'Now, darling – drink from my mouth. Mmmm. Now more. More.'

A voice somewhere was calling him back, but he had already drifted too far.

***

Malombra looked closely at Dayraven's backside. *Very nice.* She was kneeling on the bed fully clothed except for her veil that lay on the small table. Dayraven was lying naked, face down on the bed.

He would sleep for hours yet, Malombra knew. He had as much of her potions inside him as she had seen any man take in a single session. Once he lost control completely, she had fed him potent herbs that he gobbled down, especially the succubus tongue. The herbs had increased his pleasure as well as her power over him. Another session like that and he would be a slave to her; then he would tell her everything he knew about the Hidden Face and where the woman Sunniva was. At that point, it would be safe to untie him even when he was awake, Malombra thought and smiled to herself. She ran her fingers down the small of his back, over his firm rear

186

end and on to his hairy thighs. *So strong.* Already she had enjoyed him as much as any man ever. How good would it be when he was untied and totally under her power? *Wonderful but brief.* Dayraven's knowledge of the Hidden Face meant that he would have to die very soon after he had told her what she wanted. She stroked the hard muscles in his upper back. *A pity, but it will be very good while it lasts.*

Dayraven stirred in his sleep and turned his head to one side. Malombra took up a tiny bottle and opened it under his nose; the fumes rose into his nostrils and Dayraven sank deeper into sleep. She saw a flicker of a smile on his lips for an instant. *He's dreaming about me.* When he was half-awake in a few hours, she would feed him some more herbs and wine, and soon he would be dreaming about her both awake and asleep.

Now it was time to get to work; every one of her lovers had to wear her mark. She put the stopper back in the bottle and placed it on the table, then a tiny brush and some small pots containing coloured pastes that she made from the crushed leaves of plants in her garden.

Malombra traced a design on Dayraven's backside with the dry brush and smiled. *Perfect. Good of him to have such a tight rear end. That makes my job much easier. And enjoyable.* Malombra dipped the brush into the black pot, narrowed her eyes in concentration and traced a line on the firm skin, then lifted the brush and checked the result. *Good. Now some more.* The dye was quick-drying and almost permanent. The next time, she would prick the outline of the design into his skin with a tiny needle to make a sort of tattoo, then reapply the colour, and it would be permanent. Then he would be marked as hers forever. *Or for as long as he lives, at least.*

187

The curtain at the back was pushed aside.

'Maugris!' she said, without looking around.

'Yes, me. I can smell that paste you use.'

'I know.' She retouched the borders of the black square. 'That's why I always expect you at this time, although you are not supposed to be here now.'

'Dayraven, is it?'

'Of course.'

'Was he good?'

'You don't really want me to tell you that.'

'Why, Malombra? Why?'

'Why what?' She shaded in the inside of the square again. 'The sex, the painting or Dayraven? You already know the answers to all of those.'

'I'll kill him.'

Malombra turned at a rustling sound and saw Maugris holding a knife.

'Put that away, Maugris. These other men are just toys to me – you know that.'

Maugris's hand holding the knife clenched tighter. 'I heard you talking with Dayraven during the game of *shatranj*. There was something different about how you spoke with him. I can hear it in your voice now – you are more satisfied than ever before. I'll kill him now – he won't know a thing.'

'Stop, Maugris!' He had started forward, but halted. 'You're jealous? Of a man who will be dead soon anyway? What you and I have is forever.'

'I can't stand it anymore! Maybe I should kill you! Then the pain will stop.'

'Kill me? That would be worse than killing yourself. Much worse.'

'Why is he so important to you, this Dayraven?'

'I can't tell you that. Go now. I will find you later and make you forget everything.'

'Always the same. You know I need that memory of your face – you keep it alive in my mind.'

Tears rolled down Maugris's face from underneath the eye-cloth. Malombra took his hand and helped him sit next to her. Maugris buried his face in her shoulder while she stroked his hair.

***

Astolf rode on under the gentle rain. *I'm always riding alone in the cold from one place to another.* When this was all over and the Clovians controlled the empire again, things would be different, but none of that could happen until the Hidden Face was found, and that meant finding the woman Sunniva; she had the bracelets.

He knew that Malombra had captured Dayraven. A stab of envy ran through Astolf. Malombra might let Dayraven see her, but Dayraven wouldn't be alive for much longer. Astolf smiled. *It will be different for me.* When the Clovians took back the throne, Lord Dagon would give him Malombra as a personal slave; he would make her do what he wanted for a while and then have her killed. Until then, he had to go back and forth between Dagon and Malombra, reporting. He shivered at having to tell Dagon that the bracelets had not been found. *Where is Sunniva?*

Astolf stopped his horse and stood under a tree out of the rain. He drank some beer and looked out at the muddy road; the sky was very dark.

Something thudded against the tree trunk behind him and Astolf spun around; the forest was thick and almost black. Something whirred past his head and flashed onto the road – a branch! He peered into the murk of the forest, but couldn't see anyone.

'Who's there?'

'Just me.'

'Twister!' Astolf made a move towards his horse.

'Don't think you can outrun my throwing axes.'

Astolf stopped, his heart racing. 'Where are you?'

'You lied to me.'

'Lied? I was the one who got you out of the hermitage.'

'You told me you would help me get my power back.'

'And I will.'

'No. You are working for the Clovians – don't deny it.'

Astolf jumped. 'That was Dagon's idea. He liked using you to destroy your own father.'

'So, that is why you brought me out of the hermitage.'

'I agreed with the plan because I wanted to free you, help you.'

'You're lying again – always lies, but I need you alive. You will help me kill the evil creature. You will take me to it.'

Evil creature? Astolf's mind rushed back to Axo. The Twister had said something about an evil creature then. He had to play along or he would never escape alive.

'The creature, Twister? You still haven't found it yet?'

'I did not know its true form when it showed itself as a lion and an elephant. Now I know its true shape – a bee.'

'How do you know that?'

'You work for the master of the bees; I know that now. When the creature becomes a bee again, I can kill it. You can take me to the place.'

'Yes, let's arrange a meeting – the bee will be there.'

As well as a lot of armed men. Then I can be rid of this madman for good.

'Later. I will tell you when. Now I have to go and look after the water spirit.'

'Yes, of course. The water spirit.' *What is he talking about?*

'I know her true form since I saw her bathing in the river. Dayraven was with her.'

Sunniva! But did the Twister know where she had gone after Dayraven was captured? If he could have the Twister followed, he might lead them to Sunniva.

'But the water spirit is no longer travelling with Dayraven, is she?' Astolf said. 'She left him behind in Metos.'

'She is riding a horse I found for her, heading north toward the sea. That is her true home, not the river.'

North of Metos to the sea. She must have followed the main road out of the town. That will take her through the old Clovian territory. Now we have a real chance of finding her. He couldn't wait to rush and tell Dagon.

'Do you know which river she might be in now?' Astolf asked. 'Twister? Are you still there?'

But all he heard were the sighing of the wind and the patter of rain on the leaves.

***

Everything was a blur at first, a fog of memories. At the centre was something – someone. Himself, but who

191

was he? The fog lifted a little. A voice was speaking somewhere far away but getting closer. He remembered a voice speaking before the fog fell, a woman's voice. *But who am I?* The voice came closer. A man's voice. *My voice? No.*

'Dayraven,' the voice said.

Dayraven! That's me. Yes. He opened his eyes. A man was standing by the bed. *Maugris. But where is Malombra?* A rush of memories flooded through him. Delicious memories. He wanted her again, he had to see her.

'Dayraven. Get dressed.'

Dayraven's vision cleared even more and he saw that Maugris was holding a knife and had a bag slung over his shoulder.

'Where's Malombra?'

'Away. Now's your chance to leave. Get dressed – I'll lead you out of here.'

Dayraven sat up. *Leave?* When Malombra came back, he wanted her, had to have her. He couldn't leave. Ever.

Maugris thrust the knife forward. 'Get your clothes on and get out of here, Dayraven. I'm blind, but I'll kill you if you don't. Don't think I can't – I know this bed and this house very well, even though I can't see them anymore.'

Dayraven held his head in his hands. His mind was a whirling mess, but somewhere behind them, a thought was trying to force its way through. He didn't know why, but he had to leave. There was something he had to do, someone he had to find. But no – the only one who mattered was Malombra.

'I need more wine,' Dayraven said.

'No wine. Get out of here – Malombra is mine.'

192

The thought was coming closer through the mist. He had to leave. *Now.* He stood up and put on his clothes.

'This way.' Maugris placed his hand on Dayraven's shoulder from behind and steered him.

Dayraven looked back at the white veil hanging over the bed. Why was he letting himself be taken away from Malombra?

Maugris opened a door and they passed into a dark corridor. Dayraven noticed how quiet it was. Maugris had said Malombra was away. Yes, she was looking for someone as well.

Maugris opened a door leading into a large room. Dayraven started forward, but Maugris gripped his shoulder and closed the door. They stood still and Dayraven heard armed men pass by. *Guards.* Were they there to stop him getting away? But why? He would never leave Malombra. But he had to. But why?

Maugris opened the door, they crossed the room and Maugris led the way through a dark passage underground. Dayraven felt many different thoughts whizzing in his head now. Malombra was his enemy. He had to get away. *Sunniva. Must help her.*

They came out into the light, where a dense forest stretched away in front of them. The sunlight was cleared his thoughts a little.

'Go,' Maugris said. 'If you ever come back here, I'll kill you.'

Dayraven stood looking at him. *Maugris. Blind. Why was he blind?*

'Come with me, Maugris. Your blindness might be curable once you are away from Malombra's potions.'

'You wouldn't understand – I love her.'

'Love her? She's blinded you, and one day she'll kill you. Maybe Malombra's let you live longer than any of the others, but one day, she'll kill you.'

'She was the first and only love of my life. Still is, always will be. You remember that I stayed in Seanor for many years, don't you? I have family there, and I met Malombra in Seanor when I was very young – we were both just children. She was already beautiful then, but different. You couldn't believe how different, Dayraven. So sweet and gentle. We swore we would love each other forever. Then something happened to her, made her hate – I'd do anything to change her back to how she was.'

'I understand, but that was a long time ago.'

'So? I've never forgotten and neither has she.'

'You might still love her, but how can you believe –'

'How can I believe she still loves me when she has all these other men, you mean? Men like you? None of you mean anything to her – you are all just a way for her to get pleasure and revenge while expressing her hate. I am the only one she has ever loved, just as we promised each other so long ago. Malombra could have married anyone – anyone at all – but she never will, because of me.'

'Maugris –'

'I've told you more than I've ever told anyone before, as we knew each other as children and our fathers were friends. If not for that, I would have stabbed you to death already, like the others.'

'So, not all Malombra's lovers are killed by her or her poisons.'

Maugris held out the bag. 'Here are food and money. Go now, before I change my mind.'

Dayraven took the bag. *I could kill him and then Malombra would be mine.* But that was wrong. Why? He didn't know, but it just was. Dayraven walked into the forest, and damp leaves brushed past his face like old memories.

Dayraven staggered into a small clearing in the forest, his body trembling and his head aching. How long had he been wandering? It could have been days or hours, maybe his whole life. He leant against a tree. *What is wrong with me?* He was sick because he needed something. Malombra? Yes, he needed her, but there was something else. His whole body was crying out for it. *Wine. Malombra's wine.* Maugris had given him food!

Dayraven took the bag off his shoulder and took out a bottle of drink. Not wine – beer. He tasted it, but that was not what he needed. He put it away, brought out some bread and chewed a chunk. *No. Not this, either.*

He thought back to when he had last seen Malombra. He wanted her but mustn't go back. Why? No, he must go on. But Malombra had the things he needed, and he remembered the bed under the white canopy. Malombra had given him drink. *Wine.* And herbs – he had eaten them out of her hand and would never forget their bitter taste. His body convulsed with shivering and he groaned, feeling he would die if he didn't get those things. He needed what only Malombra could give him. He needed *her*. She meant life to him.

Dayraven turned around and blundered back the way he had come, but he was lost. There was no way of finding Malombra's villa. *Better that way.* He had told Maugris that Malombra was evil and that she would kill him. *She will kill me as well; better to die out here than go back to her.*

There was something he had to do, a place he had to go, someone he had to find. *Sunniva.* Why was she

195

important? Could she give what Malombra could give him? But no – what Malombra gave meant death, while Sunniva meant life and he had to find her. Dayraven started walking again, brushing away the branches that slapped at his face.

He burst out of the trees and the ground fell away under his feet. Dayraven slid down an incline in a small avalanche of dirt and twigs, and tumbled over at the bottom. He sat up and the whole world spun around him. A road stretched away on both sides. *Road.* That would take him somewhere. *Back to Malombra!* But there was somewhere else he should go, he knew. *Liga.* He had to go to Liga and find someone near there, but no one could be more important than Malombra.

Dayraven sat back against the slope and faced the road with his eyes closed. He could hear voices somewhere and the sound of walking feet, horse's hooves and rolling wheels. Malombra's men must have found him. A chill ran through him. *No!* Malombra mustn't find him – she meant death. He had to get away from her and find Sunniva. Who was Sunniva? Someone near Liga. But he needed Malombra.

The voices and travelling sounds came closer and then passed in front of him. Dayraven opened his eyes and looked at the procession. *Pilgrims.* Hundreds of people on foot with walking staffs or riding on wagons. They looked thin and hungry, and their clothes were mostly rags. Dayraven lay back and closed his eyes.

He heard footsteps coming very close to him and then stopping. Male voices spoke above the sound of the passing pilgrims.

'Is this one of ours who got lost a couple of nights back?'

196

'I don't recognise him, but they come and go along the road as the Akhen commands.'

'Shall we take him with us? The more we have, the better.'

'Maybe he doesn't want to go with us.'

'Looks like he'll die out here if he doesn't.'

Dayraven felt a rough hand tilt his head back. A small flagon was put to his lips and he drank. *Wine. Malombra's wine.* He swigged it down, but this was not the wine he wanted.

'Hey, leave some for the rest of us,' one of the voices said.

Dayraven opened his eyes. He wouldn't share Malombra with anyone. He saw four men standing around him.

'Malombra,' he said and held out his hands for the flagon.

'Doesn't sound like one of ours,' one of the peasants said and the others laughed. 'But come along with us, brother.'

Dayraven tried to focus on the men but his head was spinning. 'Malombra –'

'Listen, brother – you can come along with us if you want, or you can sit here and wait until this Malombra visits you. If the wolves don't visit you first, that is.'

Dayraven tried to gather his thoughts. Liga was important somehow. He had to get there.

'Liga,' he said.

'Liga? You want to go there?'

'Liga.'

'We'll be going fairly close to Liga – you can leave us when we get there. Come on; give us a hand with him.'

Dayraven felt himself being lifted and the world turned over again. With the men steadying him, he walked towards the line of pilgrims that had almost passed by. He saw an empty space on a wagon, clambered aboard and then lay back. The world churned again, but he was going the right way: to Liga to find Malombra. Or was there someone else he had to find?

***

The sun was low in the sky and throwing deep orange light over the flat landscape. Sunniva rode around a turn and saw the tomb about a thousand paces ahead. Her heart froze and she stopped the horse. Everything was just as she remembered it from all those years before; the tall tomb of grey stone in the dawn light.

Sunniva looked all around her, but there was no one in sight and no sound. *The kingdom of the dead*. The cold wind whipped over the empty plain and cut through her cloak. Sunniva urged the horse on. Now was the time; she had the courage.

She trotted the horse forward and then walked him for the last hundred paces as the tomb grew and grew in size, just as it had when she came here with her father in a wagon. But her father must be dead now; he had written so himself. *Dead. And so is King Merech. There is nothing to be afraid of.* She had to find what she needed and leave quickly, but what was she looking for? The Fifth Planet and the First Planet? What did they have to do with this place?

Sunniva got down from her horse in front of the tomb and tied him to a bush. The horse blew with his lips and stamped his foot, so Sunniva stroked the stallion's forehead and murmured to calm him. *Even the horse doesn't like this place, but there's only the dead here and they can't hurt us unless we let them scare us.*

Sunniva brought out the spear that hung on the horse's side. Her father had not fully resealed the doors of the tomb after opening it, hoping to return, but he never had. Now it was up to her. The door might be hard to open after so many years, but it should be possible for her alone.

She walked up to the main entrance. There was no sound of any kind. She put her shoulder against the door and felt it give a little, then shoved again and the door opened a little. Sunniva used her spear to scrape away the sand and mud that had gathered at the bottom of the door, pushed again and the door slid open. The cold, musty air struck her face and her heart beat wildly.

Sunniva went back to the horse and brought out a flint and torch from the saddlebags, lit a flame and felt glad of the warmth. She stepped inside. The dawn light threw only a faint glow on the inside, so she raised the torch and the darkness lifted; everything was just as she remembered it. This upper room was almost bare, just cold, grey stone. She saw at the end of the room the gaping hole where the steps descended to the crypt and burial chamber. Her father had left everything as he had found it; this was a tomb built by the Clovians to honour their dead king, and he had said it would be wrong to take anything away.

Sunniva walked to the steps, holding the torch in one hand and her spear in the other. She could feel the sword hanging at her waist as well. She looked down into the blackness leading downwards. *There's nothing to be afraid of. Even without weapons, but it's good to have them.*

She brought the torch low to throw some light on the steps and walked down. Her feet crunched on the stone and she gripped her spear more tightly. At the bottom of the stairs stood the door to the crypt that Sunniva remembered so well. She lowered the torch to check the bottom of the door; there was dust, but not mud like upstairs. Sunniva leant her spear against the wall and pushed with her shoulder against the door, and it creaked open, scraping along the stone floor. The air was even colder and clammier now.

Sunniva took up her spear and stepped inside, feeling the blood pounding in her temples. She lifted the torch; the crypt was filled with chests, weapons and armour. She remembered all that, but there was nothing that helped her solve the mystery that had brought her there, so the answer must be in the tomb itself.

She took a deep breath of the cold air and walked to the back of the crypt, her heart hammering. She set her spear down again and pushed at the door, but it hardly moved. She took her spear and wedged the point into the door opening. It gave a little, so she twisted the spearpoint some more, and the door gave some more. She rested her spear against the wall, pushed with her shoulder and the door creaked open. Sunniva felt her heart turn to ice; just a few more seconds and she would be face to face with her greatest fear, but she had to face it. There was no other way.

Sunniva took up her spear and went into the tomb, holding up her torch. The torchlight lit up the centre of the room and left deep shadows at the edges. She stepped forward and the dead king leapt into the light.

Sunniva's throat locked with fear. This was her nightmare, still there after all these years: the king in his long white robe covered with gold bees, his long hair and beard, his long, curved fingernails, the crystal ball, the gold bull's head, the horse's skeleton, the piles of jewels and gold bees; King Merech sitting motionless on his throne but looking as if he could step down from it at any moment.

I must hurry and get out of here, but you're not going to get my soul. Last time she had been there, she had run out almost immediately, terrified, while now she had to stay and look around closely.

She saw something engraved on the back wall behind the king's throne and walked towards it. Sunniva stopped a few paces away, brought the torch closer and then jumped. *This must be it.* A kind of astronomical chart carved on the wall, with the names of the planets written on concentric circles. At the very centre was the earth, with the other planets surrounding it like spreading rings on a pool of water.

Sunniva looked for the Fifth Planet. There it was, written inside a square. She looked for the First Planet. It was also written inside a square. Sunniva ran her eyes over the diagram: all the other planets were written inside triangles, except for the Sun, which was written inside a square, just like the First and Fifth Planets. *Fifth Planet, First Planet, Sun: squares. Sun inside a square. Square Sun.* What did that mean? She would remember it, though. *Square Sun.*

Sunniva heard a sound behind her and spun around. The king was turning his head. A wash of cold swept over her. Her feet felt chained to the floor and she couldn't move.

The king stood up from his throne, keeping his dark eyes fixed on hers, and she could hear the clanking of the gold bees on his tunic as he moved. She could feel him tugging at her soul, wanting to drag it inside his head.

Sunniva screamed, making the room echo with her terror. The king reached towards her and she screamed again, then someone grabbed her from behind. She looked back and saw the tattooed face and half-shaved head of Death the Rider. Then the room was full of men who took her weapons and pinned her arms.

The king came closer and Sunniva felt as if her heart were going to burst. Her throat was too dry to scream again. The king held something out to her. A golden bee.

'Now give me your soul,' the king said.

***

Dayraven reached a trail that he knew very well. He was nearly there. Once he had left the pilgrimage on the outskirts of Liga, he had been sure of the way. Dayraven followed the narrow track over the hill and looked down. In the valley below stood his father's villa, just as he remembered it. A stream ran around three sides of the large house and disappeared into the forest. Dayraven sat down on the cold ground and watched the house. It looked very quiet. The grounds were quite overgrown, but the house was in good order. It was early morning and smoke was rising from the detached cooking room.

This is home. Home. No, it didn't sound right; he had been in exile for fifteen years and this place was just a memory, but there was nowhere else to go and he had to meet Sunniva here. He tried to think of her, but scenes of Malombra flashed through his mind. Dayraven shivered, but the feeling passed. All time he had been crashing through the forest and travelling with the pilgrims – he didn't know for how many days – his mind and body had been freeing themselves from Malombra and her potions,

202

but she was still inside him somewhere. *Maybe she will be forever.*

Dayraven stood up and brushed the mud off his trousers. He heard a metal clinking sound and crouched down again, looking to his left, away from the house. Two horsemen were waiting among the trees, watching the house. One of them rode off. Who were they? They must have seen him. After days of wandering half-mad with Malombra still inside his head, he had been careless in not checking more closely. Of course someone would be watching the house – it was the most likely place for him to go. But who were these horsemen? They were dressed in dark, simple clothes with no identifying marks and didn't look like Malombra's men or Clovians. They weren't trying to capture him. Or had one of them ridden away for reinforcements? In any event, he couldn't stay up here forever.

He moved off through the bushes on the hillside, crouching low to stay covered, and passed into a group of trees that led right down to the side of the house. About fifty paces from the house, Dayraven stopped to listen. There was silence and then a metallic clanging. Dayraven jumped and then calmed down as the noise continued. *Someone is shoeing a horse.* He heard footsteps, and an old man appeared from one of the back sheds and walked towards the house. Dayraven felt himself smiling. *Old Radoald.* He was still there; that shuffling walk, that bald head. It could only be him.

Dayraven felt a weight lift off him. Yes, this was home. He started forward and stepped into the open. Dogs barked and ran towards him, and Dayraven stopped. The old man came out, holding an axe.

'Who's there?' he said, staring at Dayraven. 'We don't want thieves around here.'

Do I look that bad? 'Radoald – it's me. Dayraven.'

Radoald calmed the dogs and looked at Dayraven's face. 'Lord Dayraven! But what's happened – how did you get here?'

'It's a long story.'

'But come in, my lord. This way. We heard you were back in the empire, but then we didn't know what had happened to you.'

The old man led the way into the house, which was also in good order. A few other servants appeared, and he recognised Gisela the old cook.

'Look who's here, everybody!' Radoald said. 'It's the young lord Dayraven come back to us.'

The young servants looked surprised and the old ones looked excited. Gisela burst into tears.

'Sit down here, my lord,' Radoald said. 'Bring food and drink for the master! Hurry up, woman! And a hot bath and fresh clothes!'

Dayraven smiled. His life had been some kind of dream for fifteen years and a nightmare for the last few days, but this was real. He realised that he was starving.

'The dogs don't know you anymore, my lord,' Radoald said. 'Remember Frey, the young black dog with the white patch on his chest?'

'Yes.'

'He would have remembered you and kept the other dogs from bothering you. He only died last year at a very great age – about the same time as my wife died. You remember her, don't you?'

'Yes, of course. I'm sorry.'

'Ah, she's better off without having to bother about me. My daughter looks after the house now. But I'd better go and see what's keeping them out there.' Radoald stood up. 'Bring ale for the young master! You're all going to have to be awake from now on.'

Shouts came from the kitchen and there was a bustle of noise. *This is home.*

***

Sunniva stopped in front of a tall double door, and two men kept hold of her arms while another pushed the door open. A low buzzing sound met her ears. She felt her arms released, and then someone shoved her from behind. She went into the room and saw Death the Rider leaning on a huge double-bladed axe, and the dead king standing by the window under an astrological chart. Fear lanced through Sunniva again and she fought to control it. The robe, the bees, the beard, hair and nails: all exactly like the mummified king she had seen as a child. *But he's just a man. Not a ghost or a phantom. Just a man.* The king had one hand on a golden bull's head and seemed to be talking to himself. Sunniva heard the door close behind her, glanced back and saw four armed men.

The king took his hand off the bull's head and looked at her. His dark eyes sought hers and she looked away. She could feel his mind probing hers, searching for a way to grip her soul and tear it out. Sunniva focused her thoughts on the river she had floated down with Dayraven: the sound of the water, the gentle movement. She could feel the king's thoughts prodding at this barrier, and she imagined the cool feel and taste of the water. His thoughts retreated and she sighed in relief.

The king stepped up to her. 'You have a strong soul – stronger than your father's.'

His voice was soothing, calming, inviting. Sunniva looked away and imagined the sunlight rippling on the water; if she thought of her father instead, it might give the king a way into her mind. She imagined the splash of oars in the river, and the buzzing of the bees merged into the gentle murmur of the countryside.

'I am Dagon, lord of the Clovians – soon I will be known as Emperor Dagon the Fourth. The ancestors have waited a long time for this moment. It was their idea that I temporarily took the place of my ancestor, King Merech, in his tomb.'

'You should stay in there forever.'

'Tradition is very important for us – respect for the past. Not like you people: Calvo's father stole our throne like a thief in the night, and your father defiled my ancestor's tomb. You risked going back there – why?'

Sunniva imagined floating on her back, looking up at the bright sky.

Dagon brought something out of his robe and the golden bees clattered softly. Sunniva looked; he held Halakh's bracelet among his thick, twisted fingernails. She shuddered.

'We know that there are two of these bracelets. This one we found on you – where is the other one? We know that Dayraven doesn't have it.'

Sunniva imagined her thoughts drifting off into the blue sky, where no one could reach them.

'We know how the Guardians worked – oh, yes, we know all about them. There must be a key to solving the bracelets as well: phrase, a word, a concept. You know what it is. The key.'

The square sun in the tomb flashed into Sunniva's mind, and she felt Dagon's mind snatch at it. Sunniva sent her thoughts plummeting back down, diving into the river, down, down out of the light to the very bottom.

'Bring her,' she heard Dagon say.

He led the way into another room. When the door was opened, Sunniva heard the buzzing sound grow much louder. She looked from Dagon to the big boxes standing in the room; the buzzing came from them. *There must be thousands of bees in there.*

Dagon stood by the window and Death moved to the other side of the hives. The guards closed the door and stood behind her.

Dagon put the bracelet on top of one of the hives. 'You have a very strong soul but a weak body – strong enough for fighting but not strong enough to eliminate fear completely. And fear kills.'

He stepped over to the big hive in the centre of the room and lifted the lid. The buzzing of the bees grew louder.

'Your father stood exactly where you are now. He wouldn't tell us anything either, so the ancestors decided to test his fear. Calvo's good friend Astolf was here as well, so we decided to show Astolf what fear could do. Since then, he's been useful to us. Your father failed the test – now it's your turn.'

Sunniva felt herself shaking with anger, with hate. It felt true; the Clovians must have captured her father, tortured him and then killed him. She could never be stronger than her father, so this was the end. But she would not tell them anything either.

Dagon took up a mass of bees in his hands. 'See how peaceful they are, calm. They don't smell fear, so they don't feel threatened. Take them.'

He passed the bees to Sunniva. She felt the hundreds of tiny legs crawling over her hands and arms and fought to control her breathing. *There's nothing to be afraid of.*

'Good.' Dagon took the bees back and poured them into the hive. 'Grab her arms – bring her forward!'

Sunniva felt herself grabbed from behind and thrust towards the hive. She looked down and saw the dark mass of bees swarming. She looked up and saw Death on the other side of the hive.

'Your father passed that simple test as well, but once his entire head was shoved in the hive, he must have got scared. Understandable, perhaps, but fatal.'

Sunniva felt her skin crawl, as if the bees were already covering her. She could feel panic rising up and clasping her throat and fought to push it back down. *Let them kill me, but I won't tell.*

'Imagine what it must be like with your head under the bees. You keep your mouth closed, of course, but you have to breathe through your nose eventually, and that sucks up bees inside your head, towards your brain. You keep your eyes closed, but you can feel them crawling all over your eyelids.'

Sunniva's throat was dry and choked. She wouldn't tell. Never.

'And they crawl into your ears, deeper, deeper in, hundreds of little legs scratching, scrabbling.'

A thought pushed at the back of Sunniva's mind: if she stayed silent but let the secrets show themselves inside her head, Dagon would find them and then she could tell herself that she hadn't betrayed the secret but that it had

208

been his power that had found them. She saw Dagon smiling; he knew what she was thinking. Sunniva shoved those treacherous thoughts back into the dark.

'Still nothing to say? No? All right – have a little taste of honey. Don't show fear.'

Dagon grabbed her head and shoved it down towards the buzzing heap of bees. Sunniva took a deep breath and closed her eyes and mouth. She could feel a million tiny touches on her face, her hair, and there was a sort of sweet smell everywhere around her. She could feel the blood throbbing in her temples. Dagon's previous words thrust themselves forward; soon, the bees would be crawling up her nose, in her ears. And then? Panic started to spread over her whole body. Surely, the bees would sense it, then that would be the end; let Dagon read the secrets from her mind. But no – there was no escape that way. She felt hundreds of tiny legs running over her eyes and stabbing at her nostrils. *No. Never.*

Then her head was lifted up and she breathed deep, her chest heaving.

'Very good. You've already lasted longer than anyone else, but next time, we won't bring you up again.' Dagon reached out and gently picked the bees off her face and hair. 'They mustn't get used to you. Now – the second bracelet, the key. You've already shown how brave you are, but this is your last chance.'

Sunniva could feel him probing at her mind again; it would be so easy just to let him read her thoughts and then it would be over. But Dagon had killed her father and he would kill everyone she knew if she gave him the power. She sent her thoughts flying back towards the deep, cool river.

209

'Enough,' Dagon said, grabbing her by the hair. 'Now you go back under forever.'

There came a crash from the window. Dagon and the men holding Sunniva's arms let go. She turned and saw Perin the Twister land on the floor and grab the bracelet from where Dagon had left it. Sunniva struck back with both her fists and heard the men behind her groan. She lashed out with her foot and knocked over the main hive; it fell towards Death, who was approaching with his axe, and the bees flew out towards him, buzzing furiously. Perin threw a throwing axe at Dagon, who ducked and ran for the far door. Sunniva covered her head with her cloak and ran towards the window, knocking over another hive. The buzzing of the bees had become a roar. She heard the whizz of two more throwing axes, the sickening impact of steel in flesh and the death groans of men.

'This way,' Perin said.

She felt Perin's hand on her arm, guiding her.

'Now jump.'

Sunniva let herself fall. She felt and heard Perin land just before her, taking most of the impact himself. She landed a little awkwardly on her ankle and pain shot up her leg. Sunniva uncovered her head and looked back; the bees were streaming out in an angry storm, and she could hear running feet somewhere.

'Take these,' Perin said, and held out the two bracelets. 'Take them and run – I'll hold them off.'

Sunniva took the two bracelets and felt their cold metallic touch. 'Thank you, Perin.'

She ran, hearing the roar of the bees and the sounds of battle behind her. Soon, she was hidden by the trees that covered the hill where the villa stood. She tripped over fallen trunks and branches but kept heading downwards.

At the bottom of the hill, Sunniva found more cover in the forest. Horns sounded from the villa; the pursuers were on their way. She had to hope that the dense trees would hide her.

Sunniva staggered on for what seemed like hours until she emerged from the trees. Her ankle was sore and she was very tired. She didn't know how long she had been walking, but night was closing in. There had been no signs of pursuit for a long time now, and she was sure that this was the right direction. Urland's estate near Liga was her goal, as agreed with Dayraven; she might not be that far away, but there was no chance of finding the place tonight, so she would have to find shelter somewhere and go on tomorrow. Would Dayraven even be there? She told herself not to think like that; all she could do was try to reach the meeting place. She felt the bracelets inside her tunic. With Dayraven, she could solve their mystery.

Sunniva stopped to catch her breath and looked around. The landscape was flat but covered with trees, and there was no farm or other habitation. At least, the lack of hills meant that she couldn't be spotted from far off as long as she kept to the trees. She hated being alone in this country, so close to the old Clovian burial place and to Dagon's castle. And she was very thirsty and hungry.

She reached the edge of the small wood she had been skirting. The light was getting dim, but Sunniva thought she saw an abandoned town off to the right, covered with plants. There were many abandoned towns in this area, she knew; wars and plagues long before had driven the people away. This was an area for the dead and for ghosts and near-ghosts like Dagon. She shivered and tried not to think of him. She was exhausted, but it was time to make a decision. Without food, water, weapons or extra clothing,

211

it would be very cold and dangerous to try and sleep outdoors tonight; there would probably be wolves and maybe bears. The empty town might be full of those animals as well, and maybe human thieves and outlaws, but it might also still have a useable freshwater well, and perhaps she might even find some tools or be able to make some. So, there was not much choice, really; Sunniva looked around one last time and then set off as fast as she could for the crumbling walls of the town.

The stone arch of the main gateway was fairly intact. The wooden gates themselves were long gone, but there were some rusted bits of metal on the ground that might have been fittings to the large doors. *Even now I'm still thinking like my father, the scholar. I have to think about food and drink.*

Twenty paces away from the gate, Sunniva stopped. Tiredness was making her see things, surely; it looked like there was an old-style amphora, unbroken and intact, standing upright under the arch. Sunniva tried to swallow. Her throat was very dry, but she was not that thirsty that she should be imagining things to drink. She listened carefully; there was no sound. The town was dead, but the amphora was there. Sunniva walked up to it and touched the curved surface of rough orange ceramic. It was real. She looked around; night was closing in. She grabbed one of the handles, tilted the amphora and heard a sloshing sound of liquid. Sunniva caught her breath; could there really be something to drink in there? She pulled out the stopper and lifted the amphora to her mouth. *Water. Fresh water.* She drank again and her throat sang with pleasure. Not all water was safe to drink, but that was a risk she had to take.

Sunniva lowered the amphora. She had water, and now she needed shelter for the night. Something hot dripped on her hand, and Sunniva jumped and looked around. No rain in sight and why would rain be hot, anyway? She lifted her hand and tried to see what had fallen on it, but the light was too weak, so she sniffed. *Blood.*

She looked up at the archway and the stone buildings connected to it. There was nothing moving up there.

'Perin! Is that you?'

'Perin is dead,' came a voice from somewhere over her head. 'I am the Twister.'

'It *is* you! But you're bleeding – you're hurt.'

'That does not matter. You have the bracelets now – I realised they were no use to me.'

'You saved me from Dagon. Thank you. And thank you for this water.'

'The water is safe. The animals here drink it – they know. But now you need food.'

'Where are you?'

She heard feet scrabbling on the stones above, heading into the town. Sunniva slung the amphora over her shoulder and walked down the main street, following the sound. Plants grew between the paving slabs under her feet, and there were fresh animal droppings that were difficult to avoid in the fading light. *Goats and other creatures must crop the grass, or else the street would be completely overgrown.* She tried not to think of the wolves that hunted the grass-eaters. Stone buildings overhung the street all the way along. She tried to check the rooftops for movement, but the street was often blocked by fallen stones and she had to watch where her feet fell in the fading

213

light. The clammy air of the dead town gripped her and she shivered.

There was no more sound from above, so Sunniva continued down the street. Something was sitting on a big block of stone in the middle of the street. She went up to it. It was a white cloth that shone a little in the near-darkness. She opened the cloth and put her hand on what was inside. *Bread.* Sunniva tore off a piece and ate it. The bread was not particularly fresh, but it tasted wonderful.

Sunniva found herself laughing out loud. 'How do you do it, Perin?'

'You give me the strength,' the voice said from above.

'But you are bleeding – come down and let me help you.'

'I must help myself.'

'At least eat some of this bread.'

She heard the feet moving off again, away from her. Sunniva placed the bread inside her tunic and carried the amphora over her shoulder down the main street. Up ahead she could see the archway of the other town gate; soon, she would be outside the town walls again. A noise reached her ears. Despite her tiredness, Sunniva could feel herself smiling. It couldn't be, could it? The sound came again. *A horse! No, two horses!* She walked forward more quickly and laughed. Just outside the town gate stood a wagon with two horses hitched to it. How had he done it? But here was the wagon.

Sunniva placed the amphora in the back of the wagon. By touch she could make out other things in there. Warm clothes, more food, a small cask of wine.

She turned back towards the gate.

'Thank you, Perin! I'll never forget you!'

214

***

The Twister shivered in his tree. The night was cold, and even the extra-thick cloak wrapped around him was not enough. His breath flowed out in a white stream. Night birds made their usual sounds in the forest that sprawled away in every direction. His hump always kept some warmth in reserve, and now it glowed and then let a little of that heat flood through his body. His poor hump! He reached back to scratch it with the hilt of his knife and sighed. His hump had saved them both after he had rescued the water spirit from the master of the bees. In the confusion caused by his sudden entrance and the swarm of angry insects, he had fought well against the bee master's soldiers, but the bees stung him many times. When he was running away afterwards, an arrow had struck him in the hump. The Twister smiled. His enemies didn't know that that was his least vulnerable point. His hump had blocked the arrow for him, but he still had to cure the wound and the bee stings. In the hermitage, he had learnt about herbs and other plants as remedies. He had found the plants in the forest and crushed them up into pastes, one for his wounded hump and one for the stings. Once the pastes were applied, the bleeding and swelling had stopped. There was just this terrible itch in his hump. He scratched it again.

He looked down at the ground. The water spirit lay under a pile of clothes close by the fire she had made earlier that evening, and the wagon stood nearby. The horses that had drawn the wagon were hobbled a little farther off. The spirit had driven quite slowly away from the deserted town. She had had to get used to driving the wagon, so it had been easy for him to follow her on his own horse. She had been so tired that she slept immediately after eating, seeing to

215

the horses and setting the fire. It was important to have the fire going all night in the forest to keep wild animals away. With the light from the fire and with him watching over her from above, she was perfectly safe, but the fire was getting low now and sending up a lot of smoke that stung his eyes. Normally, the spirit would have woken up more than once during the night to add fuel to the fire, but her exhaustion meant that she slept on while the fire got lower.

The Twister fidgeted. He wanted to descend to the ground and tend the fire, but he knew that he should not get so close to the spirit unless she wanted him to. He wanted more than anything to be near her beauty, but it was wrong. *I must only watch from this tree*, he told himself. *It is your duty to look after her*, his hump replied. *She would be angry if I went near while she was sleeping*, the Twister thought. *She will be angry when she knows you did not do everything you could for her,* his hump replied.

His hump was right once again, the Twister decided. A thrill ran through him at the thought of getting so close to the water spirit. He took off the cloak and hung it on a branch, and scrambled down the tree to the ground. The horses stirred a little. The Twister stayed motionless for a few seconds to let the animals get used to him, and they settled down again. He looked at the sleeping spirit. She lay on her back with layers of clothes up to her neck, and others on the ground underneath to provide a softer bed to lie on. More clothes were bunched under her head for a pillow. Her blond hair shone in the firelight, and he could see the gentle rise and fall of her breathing.

He walked softly to the fire and shuffled the ends of the branches with his shoe until the smoke lessened. The fire gave a sudden *pop* and he glanced around. The water spirit moved a little in her sleep but then lay still again. He

216

added some more wood from the pile next to the fire, and the flames rose and illuminated the spirit's face. *So beautiful.* The Twister looked around at his shadow flickering on the trees. She was beautiful, but he was not. That was the fault of the evil creature. Once he had destroyed it, the water spirit would be his.

You have done your duty now, his hump whispered. *Go back up into the tree. I must check the horses and the wagon,* he responded. *You are just making excuses to stay near her,* his hump said. *You are just jealous, hump,* he replied. *Ha-ha! What could be more ridiculous than a jealous hump?*

His hump went cold. The Twister had never argued like this with his hump before. It shocked him, but he had his duty to perform. He went quietly to the wagon and tested the wheels. They seemed sound and the supplies in the back should be enough for her journey. The Twister approached the horses. They shied away at first but then stood calmly as he ran his hand over their muzzles and flanks. They were still in reasonable condition and well fed. The way they stood showed that neither had any problems with their hooves that he needed to fix. Everything was in order. He looked over at the sleeping water spirit.

So, go back to your tree now, his hump said. *What are you waiting for?* The Twister ignored the voice. The spirit's beauty was calling him. And why not? She was his. The Twister moved towards her. He could hear his hump laughing sarcastically, but pretended not to hear.

The Twister stood over the spirit. She slept on. To do his duty properly, he should check that she was healthy. He knelt down beside her and put his hand on her forehead. The skin felt smooth and cool. No fever. Just soft white skin touched red by the fire. He placed his hand on her cheek. No fever there, either. His hump was saying something, but his thumping heart shut out the sound.

He placed a hand, palm up, just above her slightly parted lips and felt the gentle, regular breath. The Twister stared at her full, ripe lips and gulped. He had checked that she was breathing well. It was time to go, but still he stood there, his own breathing racing on. *Breathing. Must check her breathing.* His eyes slid down to where her chest rose and fell under the layers of clothes. *Must check her breathing. My duty. Must do my duty.* He lifted the clothes that covered her. Underneath, she was wearing only a thin tunic. Her chest rose and fell in the firelight. *Duty. She would be angry if I did not do my duty. Must check her breathing. Must check everything.* He slowly ran a finger down her neck. *Must do everything. Everything.*

One of the horses stamped its hoof. The Twister looked up with a start; everything was as before. The water spirit was safe. He covered her again up to her neck, bent down and kissed her lips, and then raced back up his tree and huddled under his cloak. His hump kept silent and throbbed icy cold.

***

Dayraven knelt in front of a heavy oak chest, lifted the lid and felt towards the bottom. He found the object he was looking for and brought it out: a sword wrapped in oiled cloth. His sword Bloodraven, which he had had to leave behind when he went to Magia as a hostage. Durendal, his father's sword, had been lost when Malombra captured him, but Bloodraven was waiting here, where Radoald had cared for it, oiled it and kept it safe all these years.

Dayraven stood up and swung the sword a few times. *Perfect.* When he was fifteen years old, Bloodraven had felt too heavy for him, but now it was just right. He had grown into this sword, but all the rest of the world had changed so much as well.

He had only arrived home the day before yesterday, but it felt much longer than that. There was a lot to do to get the estate running well again, but it could be done; it would even be a pleasure, but that was just a dream for now. Malombra and her potions still had a grip on him, weaker than before, but she still flashed into his mind now and then, and there could be no rest and no normal life until the mystery of the Hidden Face was solved. And where was Sunniva? She should have been there by now. He had decided to go to the Clovian tomb and try to pick up her trail. Dayraven realised how much he missed her and needed her to help rebuild his life, but was that even fair on her when Malombra still haunted his mind and body?

Dayraven put the sword back in its scabbard and strapped it around his waist. It was dawn now and he had to finish preparing for the journey to find Sunniva. Weapons and clothes he had, so he had to find a horse. He went out the back door and turned towards the stables. The pink sunlight was filtering through the trees, and the air was full of country smells. He turned and looked back at the house. Smoke was puffing through the roof vents, and Dayraven could imagine exactly what everyone was doing inside at this moment, as if he had lived this life every day for the last fifteen years. *But I haven't; I'm just imagining that I've lived this life all those years. I was far away in Magia, living a life that was planned for me, and before that, a life without parents.* Dayraven turned away from the stables and walked towards the trees at the edge of his land, hearing the cows and sheep in their pens.

I've lived a life of learning many things that other people have wanted me to know: the Jaelite language and mysteries from Halakh; Magian language and shatranj *from Al-Suli; fighting from the weapons masters of Theodorica, all to prepare me for my destiny that Halakh claimed he had seen long ago. But who am I really? Just a blank sheet of parchment on which all these things have been written like an illuminated manuscript? The manuscript might contain a lot of useful information, but it is still just a sheet of parchment.*

Am I really a good enough person to carry all the responsibility that Halakh and others gave me? I enjoyed hurting Astolf on my first day in Theodorica all those years ago, like I enjoyed beating others in fighting practice and in shatranj. *Like I enjoyed what happened with Malombra; I was drugged at the time, but I would have enjoyed it anyway. Maybe Halakh and others put too much trust in me.*

Dayraven turned back towards the house. Darkness was starting to fall, and the smoke showed white above the roof. He shivered from the rising cold and thought of the enemies who were probably watching him at this very moment. *I shouldn't walk so far from the house like this.* The unknown soldiers had not made any threat so far, but he was sure that Dagon's men and Malombra's were also nearby. *As if they are all waiting for something. If they wait for me to figure out who I really am, they'll get pretty cold. This house and land are a starting point. And Sunniva, perhaps – if I ever see her again.* Dayraven stood a moment, taking in the smoke, the cooking smells and the sounds of home, and then headed for the stables. His eye

220

fell straight away on the tall brown stallion. He was perfect: fast but with a lot of endurance.

Dayraven stepped towards the practice block he had set up in the yard, an old tree stump with the branches and roots hacked off. His sword was sharpened; a few trial swings and he would be ready to go and search for Sunniva. The horse he had chosen looked in good condition, and his supplies were ready. The early-morning light glinted on the sword blade as Dayraven swung it through the air a few times to loosen his arm.

'Lord Dayraven!'

He turned. Radoald was running towards him, red in the face.

'My lord! Someone to see you!'

Dayraven felt a weight shift from his heart; it had to be Sunniva. He passed the sword to Radoald, who took it with a surprised expression. Dayraven ran back towards the house, and the old man followed him, puffing.

'Who is it, Radoald?' Dayraven asked over his shoulder.

'A young soldier just arrived in a wagon, my lord. Wouldn't give his name.'

Dayraven ran faster and the dogs barked in excitement. He almost ran down old Gisela carrying a pot.

Dayraven reached the large front room. Sunniva was standing there, looking tired and pale. He leapt forward and held her tight. Sunniva held him just as tightly. Dayraven drew back a little and bent to kiss her and Sunniva kissed him back. Everything was so simple in that moment. Nothing else existed except the two of them.

'I was going to start looking for you,' Dayraven said. 'I would never have given up till I found you.'

'But now I've found you.'

Dayraven turned back towards the door. 'Radoald, bring some beer.'

The old man rushed off.

'I think you've got some explaining to do to your old servant,' Sunniva said. 'I bet they didn't greet soldiers this way when he was in the army.'

'What? Oh, yes – he probably thinks it's some custom I picked up in Magia. But we've got plenty of time to tell everyone you're a woman. Sit down – here.'

Sunniva sat in the chair he indicated, took off her helmet and shook out her hair. Dayraven felt a spasm of longing for Malombra. *No. That's all over. It's part of the past. The future is sitting in front of me.*

'Dayraven – my father's dead.'

He jumped. 'How can you be sure?'

'Dagon told me – and it feels true. I know it's true.'

'I'm sorry. But wait – Dagon told you? You've seen him?'

'Yes. But first – how did you escape from Malombra?'

'Later – what happened at the tomb? You did go there, didn't you?'

'Yes. Dagon was waiting inside, with Death the bounty hunter.'

Dayraven gulped. 'How did you get away?'

'I didn't. They took me to Dagon's villa. Perin the hunchback rescued me.'

'Perin? He stole the bracelet from us.'

'He gave it back.'

'So, you've got both of them now?'

'Yes – look.'

Dayraven looked at the two bracelets. 'Perin killed Halakh – why would he help you?'

Sunniva put the bracelets away. 'The Clovians and Malombra were using him. He didn't know who he was really working for back then, but now he must have realised what was going on. Perin's not evil, Dayraven – life has made him like that. He helped me with food and horses along the way, as well.'

Radoald brought in a pitcher of beer and two mugs. Dayraven couldn't help smiling at the old man's confused expression as he looked at Sunniva and went out again.

'Poor old Radoald,' Dayraven said. 'He'll have to get used to it, though – that's my mother's chair you're sitting in.'

'And is that your father's?'

'Yes.'

Their eyes met. He saw a lot of trust in Sunniva's but also a little doubt.

'You still haven't told me how you got away from Malombra.'

'One of her men helped me to escape. Maugris – remember him?'

'Maugris! Is that what happened to him?'

'Yes, he's practically a slave to Malombra.'

'Did you find out who she is?'

'No – she was always hidden behind a curtain. All I saw was her hand.'

'And what are all those scratches on your face and hands?'

'It was dark. I had to run through the forest to escape.'

'You look different somehow. Your eyes –'

'I'm still tired. It was a long journey back here.'

Dayraven saw the fire of doubt almost go out in Sunniva's eyes, and sighed in relief. It was cruel to lie to her like this, but telling the truth would have been much worse, and all that had happened with Malombra was just a phantom of the past. *Isn't it?*

'About the bracelets, Dayraven – Dagon tried to make me tell him where the second one was. But he also wanted to know the key – a phrase or word that would show the way to interpret the bracelets.'

'The Guardians built in an extra element for safety, like the twenty-four kings in the Octagonal Temple at Axo. I would need the key to be able to decipher the bracelets.'

'I didn't tell Dagon what the key was, but I think I know what it is.'

'What?'

'"Square Sun."'

'What does that mean?'

'I was hoping you could tell me.'

'I don't see how that's going to help us solve two Jaelite bracelets. But how did you find that phrase?'

'On the way to King Merech's tomb, I guessed that your father's hunting horn must have something hidden inside. So, I broke it open – sorry.'

'It doesn't matter – this is much more important.'

'Inside there were just two symbols inscribed – those of the First and Fifth Planets. In Merech's tomb, before Dagon captured me, I saw an astronomical diagram. All the planets' names were written inside triangles except for the Fifth Planet, the First Planet and the Sun, which were written inside squares. So, the key must be "Sun" or "Square Sun".'

'It still doesn't mean anything to me, but let's think about that later. Right now, it's more important to get you some food, a bath and some female clothes – there should still be some of my sister's here somewhere. She married

224

and moved far away years ago but left some things behind. Then we'll try and solve the bracelets together.'

'I agree with everything, except for one small detail.'

'What's that?'

'We'll solve the bracelets together later. For now, I just want to be with you.'

Dayraven felt himself smiling. The future had become the present and the past was gone.

The Twister shifted position until he got comfortable with his hump wedged between two branches of the tree. From there, he had a good view of Dayraven's house. There were soldiers around the house, but his hump did not think they were dangerous. The soldiers were waiting, so he and his hump would wait as well. His hump had forgiven him for the scene with the sleeping water spirit. They were brothers, the Twister and his hump. Brothers often argued, but they stayed brothers.

He checked the rear entrance of the house. There was no movement; Dayraven and the water spirit would not be going anywhere tonight. A spasm of worry shot through him. Dayraven and the spirit were together in that house! She was his, but Dayraven wanted the spirit for himself; he had even tried to kiss her by the river once. There was nothing to worry about, the Twister told his hump, and felt it calm down. The spirit was his; she loved him. He had saved her from the bees and brought her food, a horse, a wagon. Dayraven would not possess the spirit in that house this night or any other night, as long as she belonged to the Twister. His hump glowed with contentment.

The Twister shifted position again. All he had to do was wait. He had a horse, food, water and weapons hidden in the forest nearby; when the spirit left this house, he would follow her. Somewhere, he would find the evil creature that had ruined his life and kill it. The creature's true form was a bee, but not the thousands of bees that had attacked him before. He had to find the one single evil creature and destroy it. Then he would have his life back and the water spirit would be his.

He scratched his hump again. *Patience, patience.*

***

Sunniva walked around her room. All the servants knew who she was by now and seemed pleased. Radoald's daughter, the housekeeper, had brought out chests of things belonging to Dayraven's sister, all well preserved. Sunniva had chosen some day clothes and this nightgown. After a hot bath and some good food and wine, she felt wonderful. Being without Dayraven for a few days had made her realise how empty a future without him would be. Soon, they would have to go back to the world of the Hidden Face and the Clovians, but for now, their world would be just the two of them. There was something different about Dayraven, though; his eyes seemed far away and he often looked worried. She would watch and find out, but at least they were together.

Still wearing the nightgown, she climbed into bed and stretched out; the lamps, the sheets, everything was just right. Her heart raced as she imagined Dayraven walking through that door. And he would soon, she sensed. The thought was delightful but a little frightening. Sunniva glanced at the chalice and wine goblets standing on a small

226

table on the other side of the bed. Drinking a little more wine would help calm her, but it would be much nicer sharing it.

The door was pushed open and Dayraven stepped into the room. Sunniva felt a warm glow rush over her body. He closed the door.

Dayraven stood looking at Sunniva lying in the bed. Her hair was spread out over the pillow. *So beautiful.* Malombra flashed across his mind like a shooting star. *But that's all over. She can't hurt me now.*

'Are you pretending to be surprised to see me here?' Sunniva said, and laughed.

Dayraven felt himself blushing. He undressed and slipped naked into the bed. Sunniva shifted a little towards him and he put an arm around her neck and kissed her. What if he kept thinking of Malombra while he was with Sunniva? That was some kind of betrayal, wasn't it?

'What's the matter?' Sunniva said. 'You're supposed to be happy.'

'I am.'

'Well, I'm nervous as well. Let's drink some wine.'

Dayraven felt a shock of panic. He saw Malombra offering him a goblet of wine and him trying to refuse. And failing.

'No wine for me,' he said.

'Well, get me some, anyway. It's on your side.'

Dayraven pulled back the sheets and swung his legs out of the bed. It was too soon for this with Sunniva. He needed time to get over Malombra and her potions. But what could he do? He couldn't tell Sunniva the truth. He stood up and poured some wine into a goblet.

'What's that?' Sunniva said.

'What's what?'

'On your backside – some kind of mark. Like a tattoo.'

Dayraven put the goblet down and twisted around, trying to see. 'A tattoo? I've never had one of those in my life.'

'Well, there's something there. Let me see – it's a black square. Oh, no!'

Icy guilt and shame ran through Dayraven and he spun around. Sunniva was cringing on the far side of the bed with the sheets up to her neck, her eyes wide with fear and horror.

'Sunniva –'

'You've had her, haven't you? Malombra.'

'I didn't want it.'

'With the most beautiful woman in the world? I'm sure she really had to force you to do it.'

'Yes – I couldn't help it.'

'Malombra probably had Halakh killed and you went to bed with her. And to think that I was about to – ugh!'

'It wasn't like that.'

Dayraven saw the hate in her eyes turn to anger and fear.

'She's made you a slave, too, hasn't she? Like Maugris. She wants you to get the bracelets for her, doesn't she?'

He saw Sunniva looking around the room, searching for a weapon.

'Sunniva – I wanted to tell you, but how could I? If I were working for Malombra, do you think I would have

228

waited until now to try and get the bracelets? You have to trust me.'

He saw the fear subside in her face, but the anger and loathing remained.

'Trust you? You're pathetic. Why can't you just admit it? You wanted Malombra and you've had her. And put your clothes back on – you disgust me.'

Dayraven pulled on his underpants and trousers. 'You have to believe me, Sunniva. I didn't want it.'

'I suppose she had to drug you.'

'Yes. And I was tied up.'

'Is this what you learned in Magia all those years?' She started to cry. 'Malombra killed Halakh. How could you?'

Dayraven felt as if a giant hand were wrenching out his heart.

'I don't know what I can say.' He moved towards her.

'Keep away from me! Don't you ever touch me again! Get dressed and get out of here. No, it's your house – I'll leave.' Sunniva jumped out of bed and started putting her clothes on over her nightdress.

'Sunniva, please – at least stay to help me find the Hidden Face. Remember what your father and the other Guardians wanted. We have to work together till the end.'

Sunniva stared at him. Her face was deathly white and her tear-filled eyes stood out like flames.

'All right,' she said. 'For my father and Halakh. We follow the mystery till the end because that's how they wanted it. Then I never want to see you again.'

Dayraven gulped. The mix of feelings inside was tearing him apart. But Sunniva was right – he was still partly a slave of Malombra. She was in his head and in his body, although less every day that passed. How could he have a real life with someone like Sunniva until he was completely free of Malombra? It had all been an empty hope, a dream. He put on his shirt and shoes and went to the door. He turned back. Sunniva was fully dressed, staring at the floor. Her face was so sad that he wanted to hold her and chase everything away, but he didn't dare move.

She looked up. 'I need some time alone. Wait for me in the big room and light all the lamps. I'll be there in half an hour. I'll bring the bracelets and we'll work on them.'

Dayraven nodded and opened the door. He stepped outside and closed it behind him. A little window of the future had opened, but now it was shut, maybe forever.

* * *

Dagon stepped down from his ox-drawn wagon, motioned to his guards to stay behind and walked towards the white canopy set up on the grass. Astolf and Death followed him. The evening light turned half of the canopy red and put the rest in shadow. Malombra's guards stood well back from the canopy, and Dagon's ancestors sensed no danger. *Be careful, though – until the empire is ours again, everyone is an enemy.*

Dagon stopped in front of the canopy. He could see a shape seated behind the white veil and felt his blood quicken; Malombra would be his when he was emperor.

You must wait for that pleasure, the ancestors said. *The throne must be won first.*

'You called this meeting, Malombra. We are here.'

'It is you – really you. You have hardly changed. Except for your name.'

'How can you say that? You have never seen me.'

230

'Oh, but I have. And you have seen me. In another kingdom.'

She knows of our shameful exile.

'I don't remember, Malombra, but if so, I must be the only man to have got away so easily.'

'So far.'

We are wasting time. What is the point of all this?

'You still have not told me why you wanted this meeting, Malombra.'

'Very well, I will get to the point. I propose that we combine our forces.'

Dagon's head filled with the angry murmurings of the ancestors.

'An alliance? Our forces are bigger than yours already and getting bigger all the time.' Dagon indicated Astolf and Death.

'Yes, your sweet promises and money can win over some but not all.'

'You sometimes make use of sweet promises and money yourself. But you've been working against us – why should we ally ourselves with you now?'

'Because we have both failed so far, Dagon – I hear that the woman Sunniva escaped from your very hands.'

'And we hear that Dayraven escaped from your bed.'

She laughed. 'Yes, but if we work together, they will not escape again – and neither will the Hidden Face.'

The ancestors muttered. 'That is what we cannot understand about your proposal of an alliance, Malombra – we want the same thing as you. How can we share it?'

'We both want to find the Hidden Face and, through it, the Face of the Akhen. The Fifth Unmasking is near – you know this as well as I do. But you want the Face in order to control him and make the Clovians masters again.'

'And what do you want?'

'I want to be the Face's mother.'

'So, you want to make yourself more powerful than us.'

'We can share power – I as wife and mother, you as emperor and husband.'

The ancestors all spoke at once.

'Marry you? I already have many wives, as you must know – that is our tradition.'

'But you could have one wife above all the others. I promise you – you would forget the others immediately.'

We do not trust this woman or your desire for her.

'Up until now, you have acted to block our plans, Malombra.'

'I wanted revenge. On you – for what you did to me as a child.'

'Revenge?'

'My father's house in Seanor – a little girl in bed. A man goes into her room with a gift for her.... You know the rest.'

The ancestors all spoke at once as the scene flashed into Dagon's mind. The bribe for the servant at the door, the beautiful face of the girl. Seanor, under another name, towards the end of generations of exile. So long ago and it seemed even longer, given how much had changed. Dagon had thought to leave everything behind when he returned to Faustia, but the past was right there in front of him.

'You were that girl! But haven't you already got revenge on enough men over the years?'

'Not on you. I hated you so much, although it was only recently that I learned who you really were. All those years, I waited and waited for my revenge and put my hate on other men.'

'And you expect me to believe that now you can simply forget?'

'I have realised that you are the only man great enough for me, and only you can help me get what I really want. There's a much bigger prize at stake, so let's work together. Otherwise, we risk losing it.'

Dagon thought of how beautiful they said Malombra was now; he might be able to possess her again very soon and regain the empire. The ancestors' voices buzzed and then fell quiet.

'Very well,' Dagon said. 'We agree, but you will obey me. We have little time, so we can arrange our marriage later.'

'Good. As husband and wife, we will have time for each other later. As allies, let's exchange information. Dayraven is at his father's estate near Liga, but he doesn't have the bracelets.'

'Sunniva has them. She probably knows the key to interpreting them, but she wouldn't tell us what it was.'

'I hear that Sunniva has just joined Dayraven. I know that your men are waiting at Dayraven's estate, just as mine are, but there are other soldiers as well – do you know who they are?'

'No. We are not sure whether they are protecting Dayraven and Sunniva, or whether someone else is chasing the same prize as us. Those soldiers stayed near Sunniva all the way back to Dayraven's estate; we have not risked an attack so as not to draw attention to ourselves.'

'That was right – if we wait a little, Dayraven and Sunniva will probably lead us to the Hidden Face. If we combine our forces, we can deal with this third hunter as well.'

'Agreed. Let us proceed.'

The ancestors approved and Dagon filled with pride; he would be greater than any of them.

***

Sunniva entered the big room. The fire was burning and there were many lamps shining on the long table and lit torches hanging in brackets on the walls; she felt warm and safe. There was wine, beer and a small stack of wax tablets and writing materials, but no Dayraven.

She sat down at the table and brought out the bracelets. They gleamed in the torchlight. Sunniva put them down in front of her with a soft *clunk. So much death and danger because of the secret these bracelets lead to. But that secret also led me to Dayraven, and then it took him away. Forever?* She wanted to believe so, but something inside her wouldn't give him up.

Sunniva poured some wine and drank. She hoped a little of it would get her mind working to solve the puzzle of the bracelets. *Very different from why I wanted to drink wine before. Dayraven ruined that.* But was that really true? She knew how Malombra could control men, like she controlled Maugris. She used them for a while, even blinding them, and then killed them and she would have killed Dayraven as well in the end. *Good. No, that's not fair. It was Malombra's fault, not his. The impossibly beautiful Malombra that no man can resist – she ruined everything with Dayraven.* Sunniva felt cold hate of Malombra rising inside her. As that hate grew stronger, she felt herself growing less angry with Dayraven. *Still, he must have enjoyed it – let him suffer a bit longer.*

234

Sunniva heard a shuffling kind of sound approaching and looked around. Dayraven limped into the room; his face showed he was in pain.

'Not that I care,' Sunniva said, 'but what happened to you?'

'I've been in the baths, trying to scrub that mark off. I've nearly rubbed my backside raw, but it won't come off.'

Sunniva felt herself smiling. *I hope it hurt.*

Dayraven sat opposite her, leaning over to one side and wincing. He looked so miserable that Sunniva almost laughed, but she fought to control herself.

'I just have to hope that the colour will fade over time.' He squirmed around on his chair, gasping in pain.

Sunniva felt sorry for him. *He's still a pig, though.*

'If you are very, very well behaved,' she said, 'one day, I might check if the mark is completely gone.'

His face lit up. 'Really?'

'I'll think about it – very slowly. Before we start work, you might as well tell me, just to completely ruin things. Is she really as beautiful as everyone says?'

'Malombra? I don't know – I didn't see her face.'

'What?'

'She wore a mask the whole time.'

'I should have known – more of your Magian games.'

'Sunniva, you know that's not fair.'

'I'm not in the mood to be fair.'

'There's something else I forgot to tell you about Malombra.'

'I think I've heard too much already.'

'This is important. She told me why she wants to find the Hidden Face.'

'Go on.'

235

'Malombra wants to have a child with the Face.'

'What!'

'She thinks she can start a dynasty.'

'Have all your lovers been so crazy?'

He looked stung and sad, as if she had slapped him in the face. 'I thought you were going to forgive me.'

'I don't remember saying that. We'd better start work on these bracelets, so get comfortable – if you can.'

She watched him shift on his chair. *He's a nice kind of pig, really – but still a pig.*

Dayraven changed position, and then again. No matter what he did, it hurt; his entire rear end felt like one large burn. *I'll have to put some ointment on it later. But look at her – I've scrubbed half my backside off and she doesn't even care. She's even laughing at me.* He thought of standing up, but that would make Sunniva laugh even more. *No, I won't show I'm in pain – I'll sit here and grit my teeth. The best thing to do is to keep busy with the bracelets.* Malombra had receded further in his mind and was hardly there at all now.

He picked up the two bracelets and set them side by side. Each contained six rows of six Jael letters: thirty-six letters on each bracelet, and seventy-two letters between the two bracelets put together.

'Well?' Sunniva said.

'I don't know what to make of them. I thought the letters would make one of the seventy-two-letter names of the Akhen used as the basis for a code, but these just seem to be blocks of letters with no order or sense.'

'What about "Square Sun" – does that help?'

'No. I don't understand what that means, so we just have to work with the letters on the bracelets. I'm trying to make words from them, but it all comes out as nonsense.'

'"Square Sun" must mean something. Urland's horn contained the symbols for the First and Fifth Planets, and in Merech's tomb, the names of those planets were written inside a square, just like the Sun was. That must be the solution, but wait – an idea's just come to me. Would it help if the solution in the tomb were "Sun Square" instead of "Square Sun"?'

Dayraven looked at the bracelets again. 'Well, the letters on each bracelet are written in the form of a square, but I don't see how it helps us.'

'"Fifth Planet", "Sun" and "First Planet" are the names of magic number squares. I used to have fun with those when I was a child – my father taught me about them.'

'I don't remember them that well.'

'I do. The Fifth Planet square is made up of four rows of four letters – sixteen letters in all. The First Planet square has eight rows of eight letters – sixty-four letters in all. The Sun Square has six rows of six letters – thirty-six letters.'

Dayraven jumped in his chair and felt a jolt of pain, but he didn't care anymore. 'So, each bracelet is based on a magic number square – thirty-six letters each! Show me the Sun Square, if you can.'

Sunniva grabbed a wax tablet and scratched out a grid pattern with the stylus. Dayraven watched her long blond hair flouncing about and wanted to reach out and stroke it, but the pain in his backside reminded him that this was not the time; he would have to be patient.

'I'm writing out a basic Sun Square as well as I can remember it. This must be the starting point for solving the bracelets – here.' She turned the tablet around and pushed it in front of Dayraven:

31	32	33	34	35	36
25	26	27	28	29	30
19	20	21	22	23	24
13	14	15	16	17	18
7	8	9	10	11	12
1	2	3	4	5	6

Dayraven looked from the bracelets to the magic square Sunniva had drawn. 'That's the same shape as the letters on the bracelets, but tell me more about the Sun Square.'

'As children, we played at substituting numbers along the diagonals – my father would remember that. From bottom left to top right, the diagonal reads 1-8-15-22-29-36. You could reverse that to make 36-29-22-15-8-1. And the same with all the other diagonals, even the small ones.'

'So, in the top left-hand corner, where there's a small diagonal 19-26-33, you could make that read instead 33-26-19?'

'Yes, and so on for all the others.'

238

'So, every number on every diagonal is interchangeable with another number on the same diagonal. Let's try applying that to the bracelets. Once I get used to making the substitutions, it shouldn't take that long to try out the various possibilities.'

Dayraven took up a piece of parchment, pen and ink, and put one of the bracelets in front of him and the diagram next to it. Halakh was dead, but it was almost like hearing his voice again.

Sunniva drank some more wine and watched Dayraven working; there was nothing she could do now except wait. She watched Dayraven shift in his chair. *He needs some ointment rubbed on his rear end. But no – he has to behave himself for a while yet.*

She saw Dayraven make a face and cross out some letters from his diagram. 'These letters aren't producing any proper Jael words.'

'Is it possible to use the Jael letters to make words in Faustian? Maybe the final words are meant to be comprehensible to me – the Guardians have always expected us to be working together on this.'

'I'll try it.'

Sunniva watched him go back to work, looking from the bracelet to the diagram on the wax tablet and then writing a letter on the parchment. *Bracelet – wax – parchment. Bracelet – wax – parchment.*

Dayraven looked up and his eyes were shining. 'It's working.'

Sunniva poured him some beer. He nodded but didn't touch it. *Bracelet – wax – parchment. Bracelet – wax – parchment.*

Dayraven stopped and read over what he had written on the parchment, then smiled and pushed the sheet of parchment towards her. Sunniva took it up.

'That's one of the bracelets done,' he said. 'Our system works, but I don't know what it means yet. I'll start working on the other one.'

Sunniva was vaguely aware of him swapping bracelets and taking up another sheet of parchment. She moved a lamp closer and looked at what Dayraven had written:

TEMPLE
WITHBI
WINDOW
ESSALL
GNSTOG
NDERTH

Sunniva squinted at the letters. The first and third rows made perfect words: "temple" and "window", so the system Dayraven was using must work, but what about the rest of it? All the letters were jammed together without spaces, just like the Jael letters on the bracelets. She tried to think where the spaces could go to make sense of the letters. In the second row, a space after the "H" would make the word "with". But that left the two letters "BI" – after them came the word "window" in the third row. In the fourth row, a space after the second "S" would make the word "all", but that left the three letters "ESS".

Sunniva put the parchment down. Something was not quite right, but the system was producing genuine words, and the way they had arrived at that system by following the clues from the horn and the tomb had to be right. Or was that a trick built into the code? They had no other clues to follow, though, so this must be the right path; it just had to be.

She picked up the bracelet that Dayraven wasn't using. The Jael letters looked back at her like frowning masks guarding a doorway – or were they laughing at her because she couldn't find the way in? The Guardians would have made the solution difficult out of caution; that was how they had worked so far. To solve the mystery, it would be necessary to have all the clues – Fifth Planet and First Planet – and the key – Sun Square – and both bracelets. No clue was meant to be comprehensible on its own. *So, of course this single bracelet doesn't make sense – it's only supposed to be read together with the other one!*

'I've finished,' Dayraven said. 'Here. It's got to be right according to our system, but I can't make any sense of it.'

'I think I can.' Sunniva carried her parchment around to Dayraven's side of the table.

She looked at the second sheet:

INWALL
GSMALL
ARCHPR
FOURSI
ETHERU
ETUNIC

241

'If we put in spaces, there are some real words,' Dayraven said. 'IN and WALL in the first line, SMALL in the second, ARCH in the third, FOUR in the fourth, ETHER in the fifth and TUNIC in the sixth. But that leaves a lot of extra letters unused – do we leave those out, or is there another level of code to use?'

'I don't think so. The six rows of six letters on one bracelet have to be put next to the six rows of letters on the other bracelet, making six rows of twelve letters. Let's put the bracelet you've just done on the left and add the other one on the right – what does that give us?'

Sunniva reached forward and lined up the two sheets of parchment, and her hair fell on Dayraven's shoulder. She felt him jump a little, but she let her hair rest there. She brought a lamp closer and looked at the result:

INWALLTEMPLE
GSMALLWITHBI
ARCHPRWINDOW
FOURSIESSALL
ETHERUGNSTOG
ETUNICNDERTH

Dayraven squeezed her hand in his excitement, and she let it stay there.

'The first line says "In wall temple",' Dayraven said. 'I think we've got it!'

Sunniva was shocked. *In wall temple.* That could only mean one thing.

'Then what's next?' she said. '"G small with bi". What does that mean?'

'Like I said, perhaps we have to leave out the extra letters. Let's go on.'

242

'"Arch pr window." Then "four siess all".'

'Then "ether".'

'Then it's just nonsense: "rugnstog".'

'So let's trying leaving out the nonsense letters and look at the rest. IN-WALL-TEMPLE-SMALL-WITH-ARCH-WINDOW-ETHER. Then there's TUNIC in the last line. Maybe we can make sense out of that somehow.'

Sunniva reached back into the past. If her father had been involved in creating this message, then "in wall temple" was meant for her. They were very close to solving the entire message, but if that phrase was so clear, then the rest of it should be as well. The answer was somewhere in front of her in the dark. She just had to reach out for it; and then she knew how.

'We have to reverse the order of the bracelets,' she said. 'I'll move the parchment on the right over to the left and then we'll see what happens.'

She took her hand out of Dayraven's and tried to look angry at him for touching her. She picked up the parchment on the right and lined it up on the left:

TEMPLEINWALL
WITHBIGSMALL
WINDOWARCHPR
ESSALLFOURSI
GNSTOGETHERU
NDERTHETUNIC

Sunniva's heart jumped. The first line now read TEMPLE IN WALL, so the meaning was the same. This had to be it.

'TEMPLE IN WALL, Dayraven said, writing quickly on another sheet of parchment. 'The next line says WITH BIG SMALL.'

'Then WINDOW ARCH. Then "PR".'

'That joins on to the next line. "PR-ESS makes PRESS.'

'ALL FOUR –'

'SIGNS TOGETHER –'

'UNDER THE TUNIC.'

'I think it makes a complete message of perfect words!'

'Read it back.'

'TEMPLE IN WALL WITH BIG SMALL WINDOW ARCH PRESS ALL FOUR SIGNS TOGETHER UNDER THE TUNIC.'

Sunniva felt a beautiful but sad glow spread over her. This was her father talking to her, even after his death.

Dayraven turned to look at Sunniva. *She's so beautiful with the torchlight shining like that on her face and her hair, but she looks so sad.*

'I know exactly the place this is describing,' she said. 'My father knew that I would recognise it. Remember how I told you about a game we used to play when I was a child – the "seeing game"? My father used to test how well I observed things, and this message is describing an actual place that he had me observe closely.'

'The "temple in the wall"?'

'Yes. I grew up in Trevi. "The Wall Temple" is what we used to call the temple built into the old gateway – the gate tower now contains the altar of the temple.'

244

'What does "big small window arch" mean?'

'The arch was the old city gate – it was filled in with different-coloured stone to convert the gate into a temple. The windows facing out of the town are small because the gate was originally meant for defence, while the windows facing into the town are bigger because they were added for the temple. There might be other temples somewhere built into city walls, but these extra details leave no doubt. The Hidden Face is in Trevi, close by the house I grew up in. I even know a secret passage we can enter by – if the passage is still there.'

'But then the second half of the message says "press all four signs together under the tunic." That must mean the tunic of the Face – the tunic he was wearing on the day of the Fourth Unmasking. It's still kept in Trevi, isn't it?'

'Yes – in the tower of the Wall Temple, in a reliquary on the altar. The Tunic is only brought out once every fifty years or so – never in my lifetime.'

'So, "under the tunic" must mean the altar.'

'Yes.'

'And the four signs we have to press?'

'They must be the signs of the Four Unmaskings on the altar.'

Dayraven stood up, his heart thumping. 'So, we've nearly reached the end. We know where the Hidden Face is – now we just have to go and get it.'

He saw Sunniva's eyes shining. There was some sadness in them but also a lot of excitement; was there something in there for him as well?

'Don't forget who else is looking for the Hidden Face,' she said.

They stood looking at each other. Dayraven knew they were thinking the same thing; one or both of them might not get out of this alive. His insides were being torn up with the thought of losing Sunniva forever, and with her still angry at him.

'Sunniva, we may never get another chance. So, I want to say –'

'Don't say it. If we both make it, we'll have plenty of time to talk.'

'Let me at least say I'm sorry –'

'I know, and you're forgiven.'

Dayraven felt himself glowing all over. 'You mean you're not angry with me?'

'Angry? I'm furious. But you're forgiven just the same.'

'So, you mean we –'

'I mean that we're close comrades again. It will still take me a while to get over things. Afterwards – well, I'll think about it.'

Dayraven felt a heavy weight lift from his shoulders. 'Well, we'd better get to sleep – just as comrades, I mean. We've got a long journey to prepare for.'

'If you're going to ride all the way to Trevi, as a good comrade, I advise you to put plenty of ointment on your rear end. For now, you've got to do it yourself.'

***

The Twister woke with a start. He gripped the trunk of the tree he had slept in, and looked around. It was dawn, he could tell by the light, and there was a lot of movement in Dayraven's house. He found the best place to view the house and watched; something was definitely happening. Servants were leading out two horses and saddling them, while others brought out weapons, clothes and food from the house, and Dayraven was checking the fittings of one of the horses. The Twister felt his hump itching with excitement so that he jumped up and down and the leaves shook all around him. *Patience*, he told his hump.

The water spirit came out of the house. In these days of watching, he had not been worried about her, but he knew that sooner or later, she would have to go back to the water that was her natural home. Now she was going, and he would follow. *The servants of the bee master will follow as well – they will lead me to the bee creature and I will destroy it. There are other soldiers watching the house as well*, his hump said, and *they will also follow the water spirit. Yes, but it doesn't matter*, the Twister replied. *What matters are the water spirit and the evil creature. The creature thinks I don't know its true form, but I do – a bee.*

The Twister shifted to see what was happening in front of the house. Dayraven and the water spirit were about to mount the horses: a white horse for her, a brown one for Dayraven. They were leaving! So must he.

The Twister jumped into the next tree and then the next one, the leaves and branches whizzing and hissing around his head. His hump was sizzling. He had a horse of his own ready and hidden, along with a supply of food he had scavenged during the cold nights of waiting. Wherever Dayraven and the spirit went, he and his hump would go.

***

It was near sunset when Dayraven and Sunniva decided to camp near the river. They had ridden all day and Dayraven was tired; he could still feel some soreness in his backside, but it was almost gone. He and Sunniva knew they were being followed, but no one had attacked them or

247

even shown themselves, so they had just ridden on. They could only resolve everything by reaching Trevi.

Sunniva knew the way and the distances perfectly. Their plan was to camp tonight, then start early tomorrow morning and camp overnight again along the river. That meant that they should be able to enter Trevi at dawn on the third day. And then? There was no way of knowing.

Dayraven was afraid not for himself but for Sunniva. They had travelled so far – both together and separately – to reach this point. If something happened to her, he couldn't imagine what he would do. Malombra was mostly out of his head by now and Sunniva had forgiven him; that mattered most of all.

They walked the horses into a small clearing and dismounted. The river rippled somewhere up ahead, and the reddish sun gleamed through the thick leaves above their heads. Dayraven lifted the load off his horse's back and saw Sunniva doing the same. They had brought a lot of things; there had been spares of everything at Dayraven's estate, and Sunniva had managed to find good replacements there for what Dagon had taken from her.

While he rubbed his horse down and gave it some feed, Dayraven thought yet again about what would happen at Trevi, but there was no way of knowing until they got there. During the journey, he and Sunniva had discussed the mystery over and over. Their solution to the Sun Square puzzle was definitely correct, but they couldn't do any more until they reached the Wall Temple in Trevi.

Dayraven arched his back, wiped the sweat from his brow and drank some water. 'I'll take my horse to the river to let him drink. What about yours?'

'I'll check her hoof first – I think she might have a stone stuck in there.'

248

'All right. I'll be back soon.'

He took his horse by the bridle and turned towards the river. After about thirty paces, Dayraven was out of the clearing and saw the water. The setting sun shone in his eyes and licked the river red. He looked both ways; there were no boats, and no one in sight at all. Dayraven led his horse to the riverbank and let him drink. The water looked very fresh and cool. He looked around again – no one. Dayraven stripped off and piled his clothes on a rock, walked into the river and felt the water soothe his feet and ankles. *This is going to be good.*

The Twister tied his horse to a tree trunk. He reached above his head for a strong branch and swung himself up into the tree, jumped into the next tree and then the next, heading for the river. His hump was tingling, and the branches and leaves raced past him in a green-and-brown blur. Dayraven and the spirit had travelled quickly and it had been difficult to keep up with them without being seen, but now the river was very close, and that meant that the water spirit would soon show herself as she really was. He moved even faster between the trees, his hump burning now with excitement. The Twister could hear the murmur of the river over the swish of the branches, so he slowed down and then stopped, catching his breath as he clutched a thick branch.

He peered between the leaves of the tree, his breath rasping and his hump searing hot. There was the river. He moved a little and saw a pile of clothes to the right. The spirit's clothes, but he needed to change trees in order to see the spirit herself. He launched himself at the next tree, but the branch he grabbed snapped and the Twister swung down towards the thick trunk of the tree. He turned in the air and took the impact on his hump. The branch broke and he slid down to the base of the tree; he was unhurt, but his hump had gone quiet and cool.

The Twister looked around the trunk towards the river. There were too many bushes for clear viewing, so he crawled forward to find a gap to look through; now he would see the water spirit as she really was. He peeped through the leaves of the bushes and his hump went icy cold. Instead of the white curves of the spirit, there was a naked male figure in the river, bronzed, tall and straight. The Twister choked and whacked his hump in frustration. The water spirit must be angry with him: that was why she had taken on this male form to hide herself. She was no longer his and this was her way of telling him. But why? Then he knew: the spirit was angry because he had not understood the true nature of the evil creature. It was not really a bee at all, but now he knew what it was.

The figure in the river turned around to face him. Panic ran through the Twister and his hump screamed. He turned and ran through the trees towards his horse. His breath nearly gave out and branches cut at his face, but his hump drove him on.

He found his horse, untied it and rode off. He knew where the spirit was going. *Trevi.* That was where the road led. *Trevi.* And where the spirit went, the evil creature would go. And he and his hump would go. *Trevi.* He would protect her, but that was all; she did not belong to him anymore.

The Twister rode on. *Faster, faster,* his hump said. *Trevi.* He would wait along the road until the spirit arrived, then she would lead him to the evil creature. He would never spy on her again. *Faster, faster. Trevi. Trevi.*

Dayraven stood in the river, looking back at the thick forest. The crashing sound that had made him turn around was receding. *Probably a wild pig.* He glanced at his horse; its ears had stood up at the sound, but now the horse was drinking again. *There's nothing to worry about.*

He lowered himself until the water was up to his neck; it was cold at first, but he got used to it. Dayraven floated on his back, looking up at the darkening sky. A big wading bird flew over on its way home for the evening, and he could hear ducks and other birds somewhere nearby preparing for the night. Dayraven felt the tiredness of the day's travel slide off him. He searched his mind for traces of the madness that Malombra had put there. *Nothing. All gone.*

The sun was now hidden below the tops of the trees. His horse had drunk enough and was looking restless, so Dayraven decided that he had better get dressed and get back to camp. He stood up, sending a shower of droplets into the river, and waded through the water towards the rock where he had left his clothes. There was the rock, but his clothes looked a different colour. *It must be a trick of the light.* Dayraven heard a splash in the river behind him and spun around. There was Sunniva's face above the water, with her hair splayed out on the surface, tinged red by the sunlight. Dayraven caught his breath – she was gorgeous. He covered himself with both hands.

'You don't need to hide from me,' Sunniva said. 'I've seen it all more than once, remember?'

Dayraven felt himself blushing. He took away his hands and watched as Sunniva's face turned redder than the setting sun. She ducked under the water and reappeared straight away, shaking the water out of her hair. Dayraven rushed back in, sending up splashes of water, and grabbed her by the hips. Sunniva dug her nails into his backside.

'Aah!'

'Now you've got my mark on you,' she said.

Dayraven kissed her. Her lips were wet but hot and her eyes shone. He kissed her face, her eyes, her neck. For a moment, a scene from somewhere long before and far away flashed into Dayraven's mind, a dark-haired woman in an ancient-style bath covered with steam, then that was gone and he was back here and now with Sunniva.

'I love you, Sunniva,' he said, and kissed her lips again.

He felt her tight nipples pressing against his chest. He stood up and lifted her with him, still kissing her. Dayraven carried her out of the water and laid her down on his clothes about ten paces from the rock. Her skin gleamed in the sunlight.

'I love you, Dayraven,' she said, pulling him down on top of her.

Dayraven felt her curves under him. Her body was strong and delicate at the same time. Now there was no sun, no river, only Sunniva. The burning heat that flowed through Dayraven was made by them together. The long, winding river they travelled now was the flow of their bodies. Every turn that Dayraven took, she was already taking it with him; every time she surged ahead, he was already there waiting for her. Together they raced down the rapids and drifted through the calm stretches until they

252

landed on the far shore at the same moment, both gasping for breath.

Dayraven smiled down at her and she smiled back. Their chests heaved up and down in the same rhythm. It felt as if he had just sailed around the world and arrived back at the same point. He stroked a strand of hair off Sunniva's face and kissed her; it was time to set sail again.

***

The Twister stood up in his tree to look back down the road. Two horses approaching, he could hear. This must be the water spirit and Dayraven; his hump was sure of it.

It was early morning, and already some wagons and groups of riders had passed his tree on the way to Trevi. He and his hump had been sure that the spirit would pass this way, so he had only needed to wait and now here she was. The Twister could see her white horse clearly now, with Dayraven riding next to her.

The Twister shivered when he remembered how angry the spirit had been with him yesterday evening when she had changed herself into a man. He had been punished for spying on her, and he would not do it again. *Mustn't do it again*, his hump whispered.

He watched as the spirit rode closer. His tree was well back from the road and his horse was well hidden, so he would let the spirit and Dayraven go by and then follow them to Trevi. They would probably camp again by the river tonight and he would stay far away. *Mustn't see anything. See nothing*, his hump said.

Early next morning, the spirit would probably travel again, so as to reach Trevi at dawn. He and his hump would follow and he would kill the evil creature. His hump glowed with satisfaction. *Kill, yes,* it said. *In Trevi. Tomorrow.*

Sunniva knew this part of the road well, even before the sun was fully up; Trevi was just around this next turn of the road. She turned to look at Dayraven riding next to her in the semi-darkness. She couldn't see his face, but she remembered well how he had looked at her for the last two days, ever since the river. During the long ride to Trevi, she had seen Dayraven suffering a bit from sitting on his raw backside, but he seemed to be over that now, and the cloudy look in his eyes that Malombra had put there was gone completely. Their time together by the river had been wonderful and their life together would be even better, but now they had work to do.

She rode around the corner. This was far enough; Sunniva stopped her horse in a gap in the trees, dismounted and heard Dayraven do the same behind her. She led her horse to a tree and tied it up. The first dawn light was breaking through away to the left, and the city of Trevi was quiet and dark; up ahead, the Wall Temple rose like a giant shadow.

Sunniva checked her gear yet again: helmet, mail coat, sword, knife, spear, shield, torches, flints, lamps, wax tablets, parchment. There was just a glimmer of moonlight, and she could see Dayraven making the same checks.

The horses were a little restless, so Sunniva stroked them and whispered to calm them. Dayraven walked over to her, and the weak light showed the love in his face. *Just like there must be in mine – please let us both live through this.*

254

'The secret passage starts over here,' Sunniva said softly.

She led the way over to a mound of earth sloping up to the city wall, pushed aside a large rock and wrenched away some plants that covered the entrance.

'It's not very wide, is it?' Dayraven whispered.

'We'll have to crouch at the beginning, then it opens out. I was a lot smaller last time I used it – and I wasn't wearing armour then, either.'

'This is the tunnel that should bring us out in the tower near the altar?'

'Yes, if I remember the turning my father showed me – it's also possible to reach the crypt from here. There are other passages into the Wall Temple, like I told you, but this is the easiest.'

'The easiest? After you, then.'

Dayraven lit a torch and handed it to her. Sunniva ducked her head and stepped in. She slipped a little on the loose dirt and propped her spear against the wall to steady herself. The torch showed only a low roof and it smelt like a grave in there. *The smell will be even worse if we end up in the crypt.* She heard Dayraven slide in behind her, his torch throwing her shadow on the roof of the tunnel up ahead.

Sunniva walked on, bent almost double. There were only blackness and that tomb smell. She prodded at the roof with her spear; it was still low. She went on, feeling the blood beating in her head. Last time she had used these tunnels around the Wall Temple, she had been a child and it had just been a game. She could never have imagined returning like this. Sunniva prodded at the roof again; now she could almost straighten her arm out before her spear met the earth above.

255

She stood up straight and sighed in relief. 'You can stand up now.'

'Good.'

Sunniva went on, holding her torch up higher. The tunnel was much taller than she was now.

She saw a passage branching off to the left. 'We must go straight on.'

A solid wall appeared ahead. *That should be the end of the tunnel and the entrance to the tower.* Her heart was thumping. She went on, gripping her spear tightly. They had been through so much to get this far, and now they were nearly there; she had to keep her courage up.

Sunniva reached the entrance, stopped and moved her torch around, looking for the opening mechanism. The smell of earth and damp was very strong; she wanted to get out of there as quickly as possible. She reached out for where the lock should be and felt around, but it was all smooth and slimy.

'The lock is overgrown,' she whispered. 'Probably badly rusted as well.'

Dayraven edged past and gave her his torch. Sunniva held both torches in one hand and pointed with her other hand, the flames hot on her face. Dayraven took out his knife and scratched away some of the dirt and lichen, then wedged the knife in and pushed down on it. Sunniva heard a dull *click*. Dayraven took back one of the torches and drew his sword, shoved at the wall with his sword hand, and it gave way with a groan. A little patch of dawn light appeared; Sunniva had never been so pleased to see it. Dayraven pushed again and the wall creaked open. He ducked and passed through, and Sunniva followed, realising that her breath was racing. She stepped through and saw that they were in the tower of the Wall Temple.

Their footsteps echoed under the high stone ceiling. Just ahead and to the right stood the rectangular altar; they were alone. *But for how long?* She left the door open and rested her spear against the wall.

'There are brackets for the torches here,' Sunniva said softly.

'Good – light some more, if you can. I'll set up the lamps on the altar.'

Sunniva used the torches to light others that were hanging on the wall, and placed the ones they had brought into two empty brackets, and the space around the altar glowed orange-red. She heard the clinking of Dayraven's flint as he lit the lamps, and went over and picked one up. She saw a big metal box with many locks resting on the altar.

'This is the reliquary containing the tunic of the Face,' she said.

Dayraven lowered his lamp to light up the rear of the altar carved with scenes from the Book of the Fourth Unmasking.

'These must be the signs the bracelets were talking about,' Dayraven said. 'Look for the signs of the four Unmaskings.'

Sunniva passed around to the front of the altar and held her lamp up close. There were rows of carved figures. She ran her eyes over them and an eagle jumped out at her.

'Here's an eagle. The sign of the Second Unmasking.'

'There's an ox here – that's the First Unmasking.'

Sunniva passed her eyes back and forth all the way to the bottom.

'I can't find any others,' Dayraven said.

'Neither can I. Try the short sides.'

Sunniva moved around to her right and checked the short side of the altar, while Dayraven did the same at the other end.

'Here's a wolf,' Dayraven said. 'The Third Unmasking.'

Sunniva kept looking, feeling her throat locked up. She needed to find the lion, the symbol of the Fourth Unmasking. *Lion. Lion. No. No. No. There!*

'Found it!'

'Good. It will be difficult for us to reach all four of them at once, though.'

'That has to be deliberate, but it must be possible. Let's try.'

Sunniva kept her right hand on the Lion, feeling its cold outline under her fingers. She put her lamp on the altar and stretched around with her left hand to the front of the altar, and twisted her neck back and around, searching for the eagle. *There.* Her back was aching and her arms felt like they were about to fall off, but she could do it. She glanced up and saw Dayraven doing a similar thing at the other end of the altar; his arms were longer, so he seemed in less trouble. Sunniva felt her right hand slipping off the lion and strained to reach back to it again. Her back, arms and neck were burning.

'Ready,' she said, gasping.

'Ready. Now!'

Sunniva pushed with both hands. From somewhere below there came a *clunk*, and the heavy stone altar shifted a little. She looked up; Dayraven's eyes were shining in the torchlight.

'We've done it!' he said.

Sunniva let go and stood up straight again. Her arms relaxed and the burning feeling faded.

Dayraven came around to the front of the altar. 'I think it swings backward.'

He pushed and the altar moved back with a scraping sound. Sunniva grabbed two torches and handed one to Dayraven, and they pushed together with their free hands. The altar swung farther back, the screeching echoing loudly. Sunniva lowered her torch and looked down. A hole had opened underneath where the altar had stood, and in it sat a large gold box. She caught her breath. *This must be it.*

Dayraven handed her his torch and knelt down. He picked up the gold box and lifted it onto the altar. Sunniva leant forward to see; there were Jael letters engraved on the top of the box. She glanced at Dayraven and their eyes met. She could see he was as excited as she was. Dayraven took a lamp, brought it close and the box glowed a fiery red-yellow.

Dayraven looked at the letters, his lips moving. 'These are ancient Jael letters, but I learned to read them with Halakh. It says, "Here is contained the Hidden Face of the Akhen."'

He looked back up at her and Sunniva felt stuck to the spot; this was what they had searched so long for, and now they had found it.

Dayraven checked the sides of the box. There was a small raised square on one side just below the level of the lid. He pressed it and the top sprang open. Sunniva felt her throat go dry. Dayraven opened the lid and Sunniva saw a pile of gold plates. The top one was engraved with letters like the lid of the box.

Dayraven picked up the first plate. 'It says, "The long-awaited one, the Face, will Unmask for the fifth time in the land between the lakes and the cold northern sea, at the edge of the world, where the sun sets.'

'That must be Seanor.'

This was a kingdom in the north-west, allied to Faustia. If the prophecy was correct, the Akhen had chosen it to become the next great power when the Face Unmasked again. *Unless the Clovians find him or her first.*

'Yes, Seanor,' Dayraven said. 'I have relatives there, although I've never visited. The Akhen always seems to extend its power northwards with each Unmasking.'

'But when will the Fifth Unmasking be?'

'It says, "In the time of the great northern king known as the Great Man, grandson of the Man."'

'The king must be Emperor Calvo – his name means "man" in Faustian, and we call him "Calvo the Great". His grandfather's name was Calvo as well.'

'Then it says, "The Face will Unmask in the fifty-first year of the reign this great king."'

'This is the thirty-sixth year of Calvo's reign, so fifteen years from now! The emperor will be very old by then – that would make sense for the end of one era and the start of a new one. So, the Face must be about fifteen years old at the moment. But go on – go on! Who is it? And where?'

'The first plate finishes there.' Dayraven put it on the altar and took up the next one. 'This is a genealogical list of all the Face's ancestors going back centuries. It looks like it starts back at the time of prophecy.'

'Forget the old lists – get to the most recent one!'

'I'm trying.' Dayraven put the plate aside and took up the next one. 'More of the same. And the next one, but getting closer to our time.'

'Just jump to the last one, before I burst!'

Dayraven lifted up all of the gold plates except for the bottom one, put the pile on the altar and reached back into the box to bring out the last plate. Sunniva realised that her free hand was clenched hard and relaxed her fingers. She watched Dayraven reading the plate, his lips moving.

'It says "The Face will be the daughter of a shadow king and a shadow woman."'

'So – a woman this time. But where? Who is it exactly?'

'She's the daughter of Malombra,' said a voice.

Sunniva spun around, drawing her sword. A young man stepped out of the shadows towards the main entrance of the temple, wearing a cloth wrapped around his eyes.

'Maugris!' Dayraven said.

Sunniva realised how light it had become inside the temple; she had been too absorbed to notice before then.

'Yes. Me, Maugris. Put your sword away, Sunniva – I can hear that it's you there. I've been listening to everything you said. I came in after you through the same tunnel.'

Sunniva slid her sword back in its scabbard but kept her hand on it. She remembered Maugris from years before, but he was so different now; apart from his blindness, he was thinner and looked hunted, possessed even.

'But what did you mean, Maugris?' Dayraven said.

'The Face is the daughter of Malombra. She was raped by Dagon, head of the Clovian Dynasty, when she was very young and had a child by him. That child was given away as soon as it was born, and Malombra has never seen her. That's why the prophecy says "the daughter of a shadow king and a shadow woman". The shadow king is Dagon, leader of a deposed dynasty. The

261

shadow woman is Malombra – her name means "evil shadow".'

'But –' Dayraven began.

'Don't argue – there isn't time. Malombra and the Clovians will soon be here. I slipped away and came here because I knew what you were going to find. They are working together now – Malombra is going to marry Dagon. She tried to keep it from me, but I overheard. I forgave everything else but not this. She always promised there would only ever really be me. Now I know that I must stop her.'

'How do you know about this child?'

'She was adopted by my family – that was how I first heard of Malombra. The girl is hidden in a place no one knows about except the two old servants who look after her. She is fifteen years old now, as you said.'

'All this just might be –'

'Crazy ideas in my head caused by Malombra's potions? No, I'm not mad, but she will always control me. You can understand that, Dayraven, even though you were with her for just one day. I've lived with her for much longer, so there's no escape for me.'

'But the prophecy? How can you be so sure?'

Sunniva kept her eyes fixed on Maugris and her hand steady on her sword hilt, with the attached thong looped around her wrist. Maugris said himself that he was Malombra's slave; was this just a trick to delay them until Malombra arrived?

Sunniva heard shouts and the clash of weapons from outside, and drew her sword.

'They're here,' Maugris said, 'but they have to fight their way through the enemy to get here.'

Dayraven drew his own sword. 'Enemy?'

'Soldiers who followed us all the way here.'

'What is the name of this child? Where is she?'

'I won't tell you that. That's what I came here for, but now I realise that I must forget – I must. I haven't told Malombra because she didn't realise how important it is, but now she will force me to tell her, and I won't be able to resist.'

'We still can't be completely sure, Maugris.'

'But we can. You've forgotten the other tablets in the box – they are part of the Hidden Face as well.'

Sunniva swung around to look at the altar. Maugris was right; in their shock and excitement, she and Dayraven had looked at only the first and last tablets.

'We haven't had time to look at them,' Dayraven said.

'I know what they say already – the other tablets give the ancestry of the Face, starting from the time of the prophecy. Once I understood about this child from things she did and said, I had a servant read me Dagon's family's genealogy for generations in the past over and over until I memorised it. Do you have the most recent gold tablet in front of you, Dayraven?'

'Yes.'

'I'll tell you what it says: "The father of the shadow king shall be Ferumbrad married to Radegund, son of Florsmard married to Ortruda, son of Rinald married to Bertha, son of Chilrith married to Cunegund, son of – is that enough for you?'

'Every word of it's written here. It's true, Maugris – it's really true!'

Sunniva's head was whirling and she heard the sounds of fighting getting closer. 'Maugris is the only one who knows who and where the Face is, so we have to get him out of here safely. We'll go out the way we came in.'

263

'You think I can just leave like that?' She saw Maugris's face twisted by distress. 'I'm Malombra's slave – now and forever. As soon as I'm with Malombra again, I'll tell her everything.'

'No, Maugris! We will keep you away from her. Let's pack up the tablets and leave before anyone comes.'

'There's no point in running – I belong to Malombra.'

'Maugris is right,' a female voice said. 'He belongs to me.'

Dayraven spun round, his sword ready. Malombra was standing near the main entrance of the temple, dressed in white, with a veil over her face. On one side of her stood Death, on the other Astolf. Behind her was a group of her guards and some other armed men dressed in the old Clovian style.

'No old door in Faustia is closed to my Clovian allies,' Malombra said.

Maugris turned and ran to the wall, feeling with his hands for a way out. He found the stairs leading to the upper floor and ran upwards, slipping as he went.

'Leave Maugris to me,' Malombra said. 'Death – you wanted to kill Dayraven. There he is. The rest of you kill the woman.'

Dayraven grabbed his shield and covered himself with it, and saw Sunniva do the same with hers.

A Clovian soldier came running in. 'Malombra – they're breaking through. We need more men.'

'Two men are enough to kill the woman. Take the rest with you.'

264

Two of Malombra's guards stayed behind while the rest of the men ran out. The sounds of fighting grew even louder outside. Dayraven felt calm and ready. He looked at Death's head, with the long hair on one side and the shaven skin on the other, the tattoos. Death sniffed the air and Dayraven felt a ripple of fear. *That's just nerves before battle – it will make me fight better.*

Malombra crossed to the stairs. 'I'll get Maugris. You two men leave Dayraven to Death – it's part of his payment.'

'Maugris will break free of you, Malombra,' Dayraven said.

'No man breaks free of me, Dayraven – you know that very well.'

Dayraven to his right, holding his sword and shield ready. He kept his eyes on Death but sensed Sunniva moving to her left, drawing the two guards with her. Now they had a smaller space to fight in, which was better as they were outnumbered.

Malombra's two guards rushed at Sunniva with their spears lowered, and Dayraven couldn't help glancing across. Out of the corner of his eye he saw a blur of movement in front of him as Death drew two small throwing axes and launched them. Dayraven ducked and felt one of the axes thud into his shield, while the other one whizzed overhead and clattered somewhere behind him.

He chopped at the axe embedded in his shield and dislodged it as Death brought out the huge double-bladed axe hanging on his back in both hands and charged, his mouth open in a soundless roar. Dayraven moved forward and blocked with his shield. The blow from the axe knocked him sideways and hacked a big chunk of wood out of his shield. Dayraven staggered back towards the

265

altar. He could hear Death's breathing, but his own shield blocked his vision for a moment. Dayraven made to move to his left and then jumped right, slashing with his sword. The giant axe clanged on the stone steps of the altar, sending up chips of marble. At the same time, Dayraven's sword sliced partly through the weapon harness around Death's body and drew blood. Death jumped back and Dayraven pressed forward.

Sunniva shoved forward with her shield to meet both spears together. The force knocked her backwards as the spear points bit into the wood. Both men tried to wrench their spears free at the same moment. Sunniva sliced at the man closest to her. Blood spurted and he groaned and fell, while the other man backed away and drew his sword. Sunniva chopped at the wooden spear shafts to free her shield of the weight, and both spears clattered on the floor.

The man moved forward, covering himself with his shield, and Sunniva edged backwards. She could hear the hacking of steel on wood as Dayraven fought Death on the other side of the temple. Her opponent swung his sword, and Sunniva blocked and stepped back a little again. Her spear was resting against the wall somewhere there, she knew. *There.* She let her sword hang by the thong tied around her wrist, grabbed the spear and threw to the right of her enemy. He blocked with his shield but overbalanced and left his body open. Sunniva grabbed her sword and swung into the unprotected space. Blood spurted and the man screamed.

She looked over at Dayraven; his shield had taken some heavy blows, but Death was bleeding.

'Don't worry about me!' Dayraven shouted. 'Go after Malombra!'

Sunniva knew he was right – finding Maugris was too important. She stepped over the dead bodies and the blood and ran up the stairs.

***

Astolf took a spear from the Clovians' supply near the main door of the temple and headed back inside. There was no escape outside that way; the sounds of fighting were too close. He followed a corridor into the cold centre of the temple and heard fighting inside as well. *That must be Dayraven and Sunniva.*

Astolf rested his spear against the wall to light a torch hanging in a bracket. The battle outside sounded farther away, but he knew that the enemy soldiers were very close now. They might win, and he needed a plan in case they did. He had to hide until the battle was over; then, whoever won this battle, he could find a way of ending up on the winning side. *The crypt!* No one would look for him down there. They said there were underground passages leading out of the crypt, and if he could find one of those, he could hide outside the temple until the battle was over.

He followed the corridor until he reached a set of stairs heading downwards. Astolf shivered a little as he saw the black hole gaping, but the noises of battle pushed him on. Astolf went down the stairs. The air was close and damp. No, he couldn't wait all that time down there; he had to find a passage to get out.

Astolf reached the bottom of the stairs, and his torch lit up most of the crypt, showing stone coffins, shrines and piles of bones. There had been a fever that had killed many in Trevi a few years before, and it looked as though there had not been time to bury them all, so a lot of bodies had just been dumped there. It was too late for them but not for him. He found more torches hanging on the walls and used his to light them. The sound of battle was dull and distant and the crypt was now fairly brightly lit; if there were a passage out of there, he should be able to find it. He prodded with his spear behind a shrine. *Nothing.* Behind another one. *Nothing.*

Astolf heard a noise behind him and swung around. There was no one there, but he could feel sweat running down his forehead. The noise came again – a sort of banging, shoving sound. Astolf started to run up the stairs holding the torch, but halfway to the top, he heard the sounds of fighting inside the temple and stopped, feeling panic grab hold of him. He went back down the stairs and checked behind every shrine and every coffin; there was no one hiding there.

The noise came again from the other side of the crypt near the wall, where stood a pile of bones, the wide-open mouths of the skulls laughing at him. The pile of bones jumped, and Astolf's heart stopped for a moment and then started racing. He couldn't move. The bones jumped again and a few rattled down the pile and onto the floor. Astolf trembled, unable to stop it and unable to move away; all he could do was watch the bones come alive. The pile started heaving and shaking. Astolf wanted to scream, but his throat was too dry. A shower of bones flew out and the pile slid forward. A low door opened behind the pile and a small, dirty figure climbed out onto the heap of bones and looked up at him.

'Twister!'

The Twister crunched over the bones and stood on the floor. Astolf could see that he was wounded and limping, and his face showed he was in pain. Astolf felt his courage returning. He hung his torch in an empty bracket and gripped his spear in both hands.

'Are you still looking for the evil creature, Twister?'

'I've found it – it's you!'

'Me? I got you out of the hermitage.'

'It was you who put me in there. You've poisoned my father's mind for years – against me, against himself, against the empire. You're the evil creature I have to destroy. I realise that now.'

'Don't worry – there will be no more monasteries. A crypt like this is the best place for you!'

Astolf lunged with his spear, but the Twister dodged out of the way, cackling. Astolf moved forward with his spear lowered, and the Twister picked up a skull and threw it, and then another. Astolf ducked and edged around towards the stairs. He mustn't let the Twister escape – he would never have a better chance to finish him off. The Twister moved back to the big pile of bones. Astolf waited for his chance; if the Twister tried to get out through the tunnel, his back would be exposed to a spear thrust. Astolf reached the stairs and waited. The Twister picked up two thigh bones and came forward.

***

Sunniva ran up the stairs, holding her sword and shield ready. She reached the first level, an open gallery broken by stone columns, but there was no one there. Sunniva heard the sounds of fighting below, stopped and looked down. Dagon's wagon was standing in a patch of open ground and he sat motionless in it, with a white cloak draped over his head, leaving his face in shadow. The wagon was surrounded by Clovian guards fighting against the unknown soldiers.

She ran up the stairs again and reached the top level. At the far end she saw Maugris, tears running down his face, being led away by Malombra.

'Malombra!' she called. 'Leave him!'

Malombra spun round. 'Wait for me here, Maugris.'

Sunniva went forward and Malombra advanced as well. About twenty paces away, Malombra stopped and drew two long, thin swords from the folds of her loose white clothes.

'Swords, Malombra? I thought you only fought in bed.'

'Did Dayraven tell you that?'

Sunniva felt her cold hate of Malombra boil over. She ran forward, slashing with her sword at that beautiful, hidden face. Malombra moved to one side, blocking with one sword and attacking with the other. Sunniva blocked with her shield and chopped again, but Malombra skipped out of the way and out of range.

'See, Malombra? You can't control me like you control men.'

'I couldn't control Dayraven – he went for me like a hungry wolf.'

Sunniva felt an angry red mist filling her whole body. 'Liar! You made him do it.'

'Is that what he told you? And you believed him.'

Sunniva roared in anger and hacked with her sword. Malombra blocked with one sword and counterattacked with the other, and Sunniva blocked with her shield. Malombra was very fast and Sunniva could feel her own breath getting heavier; she was much slower in her armour. She had to keep her defence up, though – knowing Malombra, her sword blades were almost certainly poisoned. Sunniva stood still to catch her breath. She had to stay calm; Malombra was trying to make her angry, make her lose her fighting discipline and leave an opening in her defence. Sunniva fought to get hold of herself.

Malombra edged forward and then launched an attack with both swords at the same time. Sunniva blocked with sword and shield and shoved Malombra away.

'You're strong,' said Malombra. 'And pretty. Dayraven must have enjoyed it much more with me, though.'

'If you're really as beautiful as they say, you shouldn't need to drug men.'

'Every man wants me.'

'No one will want you after I've killed you.'

'Even when Dayraven was with you, he would have been thinking of me.'

Sunniva screamed and swung her sword at Malombra's neck. Malombra jumped to one side, and Sunniva felt a sword blade slice through the tunic on her sword arm but miss her skin. She stepped back, fighting to hold herself steady – the next time she lost control like that might be fatal. Sunniva searched inside herself for that icy cold hate she used to have for Malombra. She needed it now: freezing, deadly hate.

***

Death rushed forward, heaving the big axe left and right, left and right. He wanted to see Dayraven's blood flow. The heavy blade met Dayraven's shield, smashing off chunks of wood. Dayraven backed around the altar.

This was the part of killing that Death loved the most: the time when he usually saw the fear grow on their faces, the sweat, the panic in the eyes when they realised there was no escape. Dayraven had already lasted as long as anyone ever had in single combat against him and had drawn blood, but that would only make it better when the end came. Death's strapped ankle gave him no trouble, but he still had the memory of his shame in Axo – no one drove him away limping like that and lived. He was ready to kill, but he couldn't smell Dayraven's fear. There had been a whiff of it at the start, but now it was gone; it should have been very strong by now, but there was nothing.

Dayraven kept the altar between them. Death moved to the left and heaved the axe back to the right at Dayraven's head. Dayraven blocked hard with his shield, forcing the axe down onto the altar with a clang. Dayraven's sword was slicing down to cut his hands off at the wrists, so Death let go and sprang back, drawing two throwing axes as the big axe slid off the altar. No one had ever disarmed Death like that before, no one. He felt a new choking sensation in his throat – was this fear? No, it couldn't be. The others had that, never him. He launched one of the axes and Dayraven blocked. That left an opening and Death threw the second axe. It whirled into the gap and slashed into Dayraven's shoulder as it passed. He saw the blood and heard Dayraven gasp in pain. Now it would soon be over – Death drew two medium-sized axes from his harness and leapt forward.

***

272

The Twister thrust at Astolf with the two thigh bones, first one and then the other. *Left leg, right leg. Left, right.* Astolf tried to block with his spear, but the Twister landed a blow on his collarbone. Astolf yelled and thrashed with his spear, knocking one thigh bone out of the Twister's hand. The Twister jumped forward and hit him on the head with the other thigh bone. There was a crunching sound and the bone shattered. Astolf staggered and groaned but then thrust with the spear, and the Twister jumped aside.

He felt his hump glowing. He was tired and hurt, but his hump never let him down. It had led him to the secret passage, it had warned him of danger and now it was guiding him in this fight. It told him to stay near the pile of bones; that was his supply of weapons. Astolf come closer, his head bleeding, and the Twister scooped up a skull in each hand and threw them. The first one flew past Astolf's shoulder and crunched against the wall, but the second one hit him in the chest, driving him back.

The Twister's hump glowed more strongly.

***

Malombra jumped forward, swinging both swords one after the other, and Sunniva blocked.

Malombra spun away and caught her breath. Taunting Sunniva about Dayraven had almost given her an opening to finish off the battle. She had only been guessing that Sunniva felt something for Dayraven, but she had been right. Malombra couldn't understand that kind of feeling, but it was a weakness to be exploited.

Sunniva pressed forward; that shield, helmet and mail coat were like a protective wall. Sunniva was calm and determined now; Malombra needed a new way to stir her up.

'Have you found your father yet?' she said. 'Look in the crypt.'

Sunniva just narrowed her eyes. 'You'll have to do better than that.'

Sunniva swung her sword. Malombra blocked with her left-hand sword, swung with her right, felt the dull thud against the shield and stepped away. Sunniva came on again. *She's tough. And pretty – how good it would be to slash that pretty face and ruin it for Dayraven.*

Malombra thrust both swords at Sunniva's face. She met them with her shield and slashed back with her sword, and Malombra felt the blade cut through her loose clothes. She edged away and glanced back at Maugris. He was cringing against the open terrace; he was still hers. She just had to kill this woman. *If Sunniva were a man, I wouldn't have even had to fight.*

***

The Twister stood on the pile of bones, feeling them crack under his feet. Up there, he was taller than Astolf, could launch himself in different directions and had plenty of weapons. He grabbed a complete ribcage by its knobbly spine – that would be his shield. And his sword? He picked up a jagged piece of shinbone.

Astolf lunged at him with the spear. The Twister blocked with the ribcage and jumped off the pile, yelling. The spear went through a gap in the bones and got caught, dragging Astolf sideways. Astolf thrashed the spear around, trying to free it, and sharp pieces of bone flew. The Twister shoved his shinbone sword into Astolf's neck.

274

Astolf gurgled and slumped down as blood poured down the bone and onto the Twister's hand.

Astolf clattered down among the bones and lay still. The Twister slumped to the floor, exhausted. It was over; the evil creature was dead. Now he had to go and find the spirit and help her, but his hump told him to rest first. *Rest.*

***

Sunniva knew the time was right; she was calm and ready. Dayraven, Maugris, all the other things could wait – now it was just her and Malombra. It was time to finish this.

She advanced and Malombra came to meet her, slashing with a sword. Sunniva thrust out with her shield and heard Malombra stumble. Sunniva rushed forward, raising her sword, but Malombra dodged to one side and tripped her up. Sunniva fell forward, propped herself up on her shield and looked around. Malombra was gone, but Sunniva could hear her quick, light footsteps somewhere. Maugris was still there in the corner. Sunniva lifted herself up, gasping for breath.

***

Dayraven gritted his teeth against the pain in his shoulder; his sword arm was weakening. He had to end this quickly, before his arm became useless, even if it meant taking a risk. He guessed that Death would attack first on his sword side; Dayraven was wounded there, and it was more open without the cover of his shield. If he was wrong, he was dead.

Death rushed forward with both medium axes raised, his mouth wide in a silent war scream. Dayraven saw the shield-side axe start to swing forward. *That's just a trick – the real attack will come on the sword side.* Dayraven shifted his shield to the right, anticipating the axe swing on his sword side, felt the crash against the wood and stepped to his right. Death lashed out with the other axe, but there was nothing there to hit now. As he flashed past, Dayraven chopped at his exposed neck, felt the sword bite and the hot blood spatter.

Death crashed to the floor. Dayraven transferred his sword to his other arm and flexed the wounded one; strength was draining out of it. *Sunniva!* He ran to the stairs and rushed upwards.

Dayraven heard the sounds of battle outside. On the first level, he looked out as he ran and saw Dagon's wagon surrounded by dead Clovians and a few live ones who fought on. They were now hopelessly outnumbered by the unknown soldiers. Dagon sat immobile in the wagon; he would soon be captured, but who were these other soldiers?

Dayraven ran up the stairs to the second level. The pain in his shoulder was increasing and he was out of breath. He reached the top level and saw Maugris in the far corner and Sunniva walking towards him.

'Sunniva!'

She turned. She was unhurt, but tired like him. He saw joy on her face and then concern.

'You're wounded!'

'Only slightly. I won – and Malombra?'

'Gone.'

Sunniva sheathed her sword, realising how harsh her breathing was. She looked at Dayraven's shoulder; it needed dressing. She wanted to get this armour off and cuddle up to Dayraven forever, but there was something they had to do first.

She turned back and looked at Maugris in the corner; behind him, the open sky was bright and cloudless. Dayraven stepped up beside her. Sunniva could hear battle sounds off to the right near Dagon's wagon, and it sounded like there was fighting in the temple as well, right below them.

She took a step forward. 'Maugris – it's Sunniva. Dayraven's here with me. Malombra's gone. She can't hurt you anymore.'

'You don't understand. She will want the knowledge that I have – where to find her daughter, the Face. I can't resist her. I would have gone with her – I was leaving with her when you got here. I didn't want to, but I couldn't stop myself.'

'That's all over now, Maugris.'

'You don't know the terrible things she wants to do with her daughter's power. Malombra needs me to tell her where she is and what name she is hidden under, but I won't!'

Sunniva glanced at Dayraven, who took a step forward.

'Stop where you are!' Maugris said. 'I can hear your feet.'

'All right, Maugris,' Dayraven said. 'We won't move – you come to us.'

'To you? I want to go to her.'

'To Malombra? You just said she would do terrible things.'

'But I want her, I need her! She's inside me – it's as if she's calling me.'

Sunniva shivered. She had seen a little of Malombra's effect on Dayraven, and Maugris had been her slave for a very long time.

'Maugris,' she said. 'That's the effect of her potions that you feel. We'll keep her away from you, and it will pass.'

'Too late – I can feel her hold on me growing again. I will do whatever she wants. She wants the world, and I want what she wants.'

'I understand, Maugris,' Dayraven said, 'I really do, but the effects of Malombra's power wear off. I know you've been under her influence much longer than I was, but it will pass – I promise.'

'How do I know that you don't want to control the Face for your own reasons? I came here to tell you about the Face, but maybe no one should know.'

'Don't tell us, then. Not until you really want to. But come with us now – we will protect you from Malombra.'

Maugris' face was torn by conflict, then it cleared and he took a step forward. He looked taller now and more confident. She held her breath. Maugris came closer and then smiled; it was the first time she had ever seen him smile. Sunniva heard a fast whistling sound. Maugris staggered and blood trickled from his mouth. Sunniva wanted to rush forward, but her feet were frozen solid. Maugris fell face down and lay still; she saw an arrow sticking out of his back. Sunniva ducked and looked around; she saw Dayraven staying low as well, but no sign of the archer. No more arrows were shot.

Keeping below the level of the outside wall, Sunniva ran up to Maugris, and heard Dayraven running as well. Sunniva knelt down next to Maugris; he was dead but still smiling. She looked at the arrow shaft. There was a tiny bee etched into the wood.

'Dagon,' Dayraven said. 'The symbol of the Clovians.'

Sunniva felt Dayraven's arm around her. She turned and clung to him and the tears came. They stung, but she needed them.

'Maugris was walking towards his death smiling,' she said between sobs.

'Dagon knew that he had lost, so he didn't want Maugris to live to tell us what he knew.'

Sunniva heard lots of heavy feet running up the stairs. She sprang away from Dayraven and drew her sword.

Dayraven gritted his teeth and lifted his sword; his arm was almost useless, and he struggled to hold the weight. His chest was heaving. This might be the end, but he would make them pay heavily for himself and Sunniva, whoever they were.

A group of soldiers reached the top level and stopped just after the stairs. Dayraven tensed; he and Sunniva had the best defensive position, deep in the corner, so they just had to wait. More soldiers appeared and stopped. They were all dressed in plain dark colours, just like those he had seen near his estate. Dayraven stood waiting. He glanced at Sunniva and saw her eyes shining. She was thinking the same as him: they would die together, just like they had followed the trail together all the way from the Octagonal Temple.

The soldiers parted and their leader stepped forward. Dayraven fought to stay calm. The leader took off his helmet and Dayraven's heart jumped.

'Emperor Calvo! My lord!'

Calvo came closer. Dayraven relaxed; this was not the tired, confused old man he had seen in the baths at Axo.

'I finally woke up from my long bath, Dayraven,' Calvo said. 'Meeting you again in Axo helped me.'

'So, it was you who were following me, my lord?' Sunniva said. 'I saw your soldiers outside Metos.'

'And I saw some of your men near my father's estate at Liga,' said Dayraven.

'I was following and watching, Dayraven,' the emperor said. 'I did not intervene earlier because I realised there was a lot at stake and I might have influenced the outcome in a bad way. I haven't deserved your loyalty, Dayraven – or yours, Sunniva. I let others control me for too long, but that's all over now. After the defeat at Ronca and the loss of Urland, I – couldn't recover. I forgot about you all those years you were in Magia, Dayraven. Forgive me – I will do whatever I can to make up for it. I was cruel to my eldest son, Perin, as well; he was illegitimate, but it was wrong to treat him the way I did. I have a lot to make up for. You were right back in Axo, Dayraven, when you mentioned the Fifth Unmasking: our era must nearly be over, and we have to prepare. The Akhen has decided that my fate is to be emperor at the end of an era, not at the beginning, or at its height.'

Two soldiers approached.

'My lord,' one of them said. 'We found high priest Astolf dead in the crypt.'

280

'Astolf was a traitor, my lord,' Dayraven said.

'I know, but who killed him?'

'We don't know, my lord,' the soldier said. 'Someone had got into the crypt through a hidden passage that came out behind a pile of bones. They must have got out the same way.'

Dayraven heard Sunniva gasp and looked at her. *She knows who killed Astolf.* Was it Perin the hunchback again? There would be time to talk about it later.

The emperor turned back to Dayraven. 'But you are wounded, Dayraven – here, take this.'

The emperor took off his short cloak, tore it in two and held one piece out to Dayraven. Sunniva took the torn cloth and tied it tight around Dayraven's wound. He sucked in his breath at the pain, but it passed.

'But this dead man here – it's Maugris!'

'It will take a long time to explain, my lord,' Dayraven said.

A soldier came running up. 'My lord – the Clovian guards are all dead. As you ordered, we have surrounded their leader but not approached him.'

'Come with me, both of you.'

Calvo walked down the stairs, and Dayraven and Sunniva followed.

Sunniva's head was whirling. It had all been too much, too quickly: the Hidden Face, Maugris, her fight with Malombra, Calvo. *The Face of the Akhen is alive somewhere! The Faustian Era is nearly over.* And Perin – she was sure that he must have killed Astolf in the crypt. But later, there would be time to take it all in. Time for explanations, apologies; for tears and laughter. She glanced at Dayraven, and his face showed the same mix of feelings. The look he gave her promised that there would be time for themselves as well. *Lots of time.*

Sunniva glanced towards the altar as they passed. Men were shifting the bodies and cleaning up the blood. They went towards the main entrance to the temple. The bodies were so thick on the ground that they had just been shoved aside to make a path. She saw the emperor's dead soldiers mixed with Malombra's guards and Clovians. Malombra had vanished and the emperor had come back to himself. And Dagon? She would soon find out.

The ground outside the temple was covered with dead bodies and blood. Sunniva followed the emperor to where a wide circle of soldiers stood with Dagon's wagon standing in the middle. He was still sitting under the white cloak, motionless. *Is he talking with his ancestors? What can he tell them now? What can they tell him?*

A soldier approached the emperor. 'Dagon has not moved or said a word, my lord. We have not tried to approach him, as you ordered.'

'Good. He will only surrender to me. Dayraven, Sunniva – come with me.'

Calvo stepped through the circle of soldiers and approached the wagon. Dead Clovians were piled up to the wheels. The long-horned oxen, the heavy wooden wheels – it all seemed so solid, so real. Dagon had been like a dream, a nightmare, but there he was, waiting silently.

The emperor stopped about twenty paces from the wagon. Dagon didn't move.

'Dagon!' the emperor called. 'Dagon of the Clovians! This is Calvo, emperor of the Faustians!'

Sunniva kept her eyes on the wagon. Dagon didn't move or make a sound.

'Dagon!' the emperor called again. 'Give yourself up – you know I won't harm you. My father did not spill Clovian royal blood, and neither will I.'

Calvo's father deposed the last Clovian king, a relative of Dagon, shaved his hair and put him in a hermitage. Will Dagon allow them to do that to him? She remembered his piercing eyes and shuddered. *No – he would rather die.*

'I will bring him to you, my lord,' Dayraven said.

'I'll go as well,' Sunniva said.

'Very well, but be careful – both of you.'

'I've faced Dagon before,' Sunniva said.

She went forward with Dayraven beside her. Now she could see Dagon's long black hair and beard under the thin white cloak, and his long white robe covered with bees. Sunniva drew her sword and climbed up onto the driver's seat. Dagon didn't move. What was he saying to the ancestors? That their long dream of power was over?

Sunniva pulled back the cover and gasped. There sat the mummy of king Merech the First. The long-dead king's dry mouth was stretched out in a mocking smile.

She looked around but knew that Dagon would be far away by now. There was a movement in the trees behind the wagon. Sunniva started and then relaxed; it was Perin. He waved at her and then he was gone.

Dayraven shivered as he stared at the mummy. *This was what Sunniva faced alone!* He spun around, searching,

283

but knew that Dagon was long gone. He was out there somewhere, waiting for another chance.

'Dayraven!' the emperor called out. 'What is it?'

'Dagon is not here – he left one of his ancestors instead.'

Sunniva slid her sword back into its sheath. He looked at her pale face and knew what she was thinking: one day, she might find herself face to face with Dagon again. *But next time, I'll be with her. Next time, every time, always.*

He turned and walked back to the emperor. The soldiers crowded forward, chattering.

'There's a lot you'll have to explain to me, Dayraven,' the emperor said. 'But we'll have time – from now on, I will keep you near me.'

'And I will keep Sunniva near me, my lord.'

'I am pleased to hear it. One last thing – we just found Malombra's canopy.'

Dayraven jumped. 'You've caught her?'

'No, but my men found these inside the canopy. We are searching for her.'

He held up the long white robe and the veil that Malombra had been wearing. Dayraven gulped; they would not find her, and soon she could be anywhere. And no one knew where to find her daughter the Face, or even what her name was, but they had to find her before Malombra, Dagon or anyone else did.

He glanced at Sunniva, and she squeezed his hand and met his eyes.

LIST OF CHARACTERS

Dayraven, son of the late hero Urland. A Faustian hostage just returned from Theodorica

Sunniva, Faustian warrior woman and daughter of the scholar Ado of Metos

Calvo, emperor of Faustia

The Twister, formerly Perin

Dagon, head of the Clovian Dynasty

Astolf, high priest of Axo

Death, bounty hunter; one of the Riders

Malombra, mysterious woman and *shatranj* master

Maugris, her lover

Halakh, Jaelite scholar and Dayraven's teacher

Al-Suli, Magian scholar

Ado of Metos, Faustian scholar and father of Sunniva

Urland, Faustian duke and hero; late father of Dayraven

CHRONOLOGY

The story takes place in the year 575 of the Faustian Era.

The Faustian Era was preceded by:

Apollinian Era – 507 years

Periclean Era (Damo and Quintus's time) – 459 years

Magian Era – 579 years

Sisan Era (Akhnan's time) – 481 years

Irisan Era – 505 years

Urohan Era – 631 years

Archaic Era – 414 years

There is no precise chronology any earlier than this.

Acknowledgements

My wife Claudia, Richard Shealy, John di Giovanni, Shawn King, Paul Weimer, Paul Walsh, Tim Marquitz, Mieneke van der Salm, Lynn Williams, Bob Milne, Tyson Mauermann, Maddalena Tarallo, Dave Flynn, Bruno Oniboni, Doretta Bologna.

Apologies to anyone I have forgotten—you know who you are!

About the Author

S. C. Flynn was born in a small town in South West Western Australia. He has lived in Europe for a long time; first the United Kingdom, then Italy and currently Ireland, the home of his ancestors. He still speaks English with an Australian accent, and fluent Italian.

He reads everything, revises his writing obsessively and plays jazz. His wife Claudia shares his passions and always encourages him.

S. C. Flynn has written for as long as he can remember and has worked seriously towards becoming a writer for many years.

THE HIDDEN FACE is his second novel and the first book in the Fifth Unmasking series.

S. C. Flynn blogs at www.scflynn.com.

www.ingramcontent.com/pod-product-compliance
Lightning Source LLC
Chambersburg PA
CBHW060852250626
47159CB00008B/2702